The Ghosts of Tullybrae House

VERONICA BALE

For my Christopher

ONE

T HE MORNING WAS warm. It was a languid, lazy sort of warm, the kind that was perfect for hammocks and cloud watching. It was August, but in the Highlands of Scotland, where weather rarely conformed to the conventions of seasonal rhythm (unless it was winter), warmth and summer did not always go hand in hand.

Larks chirped from their perches on the stone windowsills of Tullybrae House, a seventeenth-century manor, the estate of which stretched to the horizon in vast, empty swells of emerald hills.

Inside, sleepy yellow sunlight filtered through the diamond lattice glass of the manor's oriel windows, creating ribbons of dust motes. Clunie, Tullybrae's resident house cat, luxuriated in a particularly thick mote-filled ribbon in the study. His rich purring filled the otherwise silent room. Occasionally his ragged tail twitched against the worn Oriental rug beneath his fat, orange body.

In the drawing room, old Harold Lamb whisked his Swiffer duster over Tullybrae's antique mahogany and oak furniture, a collection which had been amassed through centuries of continual occupation by the same family. He was fighting a losing battle; if Lamb had not been so set in his ways it might occur to him to wonder why he bothered.

But Lamb was set in his ways. At eighty four, he was too old to change the majority of his routine—the simple act of switching to a Swiffer from a traditional feather duster ten years ago had been a big enough step. Since the passing of Lamb's employer last month, the vacuuming had been scaled back to once a week (the only other change to his routine). Lamb had been loyal to Lord Cranbury for more than forty years. Yet the old codger would never pony up the cash to buy a second vacuum so that his butler-slash-housekeeper-slash-cook would not have to drag the only one Tullybrae had up and down three storeys on a daily basis.

Not that Harold Lamb ever complained.

Much... or, at least, aloud.

The crunch of car tires on the gravel drive announced the arrival of a visitor.

"She's here, she's here," squealed Mrs. Lamb, who hovered at the drawing room window. Her starched black wool dress rustled as she bounced in place.

"Yes, Mother," Lamb sighed.

A persistent tugging on his sleeve stilled the Swiffer's methodical strokes. "Come to the window. Come see."

"I'm no' done my dusting yet, Mother."

"You old fool, nobody cares about your bloody dusting. Come see the girl. Oh, she is a lovely wee thing, isn't she?"

"I'll see her when I let her in."

Mrs. Lamb harrumphed. "Suit yourself. Stubborn goat." She went back to the window to watch the girl, who was climbing out of a powder blue Fiat Panda.

Less than a minute later, the grand chime of the front doorbell echoed through the manor. Clunie did not trouble himself to lift his head.

Lamb placed his Swiffer duster on the ledge of a cherry wood bookshelf and shuffled out into the corridor. Out of habit, he closed the door of the drawing room behind him. It had been a requirement of the late Lord Cranbury: Doors to unoccupied rooms *must* remain closed at all times. Under the earl's orders, the house was sparingly heated, so where the radiators were going, the heat must *not* be lost to empty spaces.

Frugal was too charitable a description for the man.

In the foyer, from within heavy gilt frames mounted on the wall above the grand staircase, the oil-painted likenesses of generations of lords and ladies stared out at him. Their eyes were always eerily alive, even in the dead of night. Especially in the dead of night. Lamb felt the weight of their collective gaze every time he came through here.

Being somewhat less spry in recent decades than he once was, it took him a long while to reach the front entrance. When eventually his stiff legs made it, he opened the massive paneled door to the young woman standing on the step.

She smiled eagerly at him, her fresh, pink face raised upwards. Sunny curls were twisted at the nape of her neck and secured in a tortoiseshell clip. Her slight torso was clad in a stylish tweed jacket with three-quarter-length sleeves, and underneath it was a white blouse of gauzy satin. She wore snug, black pants with brown, knee-high riding boots overtop. A silver charm bracelet dangled from a delicate wrist.

"Are you the new Lord Cranberry?"

"It is Cranbury, madam. No' Cran*berry*."

The woman's glossed lips opened slightly, and her hazel eyes widened. "Oh, geez. I'm so sorry, sir. Your Lordship, I mean. I thought your wife was saying 'Cranberry' when I spoke to her on the phone." She laughed nervously. "I thought to myself, 'Am I hearing that right? That's a funny name,' and—"

Her eyes widened further, and her cheeks flushed scarlet. "Oh, crud. Now I've gone and made fun of you. I'm so sorry, sir. Your Lordship, I mean ... Well aren't I off to a great start?"

Lamb waited for the young lady's flustered self-admonishments to fade into an embarrassed silence.

"No need to fret, madam. I am no' his Lordship. The late Lord Cranbury passed nigh on a month ago, and it's his eldest daughter, Lady Rotherham, who arranged to bring you here. I am the butler at Tullybrae House."

A whoosh of air left the young lady's lips and a manicured hand pressed to her breast. "Ah, okay. That clears up a lot. I was confused about the whole thing. I thought Rotherham was the family name, and Lady Rotherham was his wife. But she was talking about 'Daddy' and 'Oliver' and 'Anne-Marie'—she kept throwing out names like I knew these people. And I didn't want to ask and risk looking ignorant in case I *was* supposed to know them." She giggled. "Thank God. That would have been awkward, wouldn't it? You must be Mr. Lamb, then."

"Just Lamb, madam."

"Sorry. Lamb. I should know that. I'm no less of a Downton Abbey fan than anyone else in Corner Brook." She stuck her hand out rather forcefully, her wide smile revealing a uniform row of white teeth. "I'm Emmie. Emmie Tunstall."

Lamb assessed her hand quickly before submitting to a brief, energetic pump.

"Let the lass in, for pity's sake," barked Mrs. Lamb from behind. She jabbed her son in the back with a bony forefinger.

Lamb moved back, holding the door for the young lady to pass. She stepped gingerly through, hugging her leather tote—which, he noticed, matched her boots—to her side. Her eyes immediately lifted to the carved wooden bannisters of the second-floor gallery as he closed the door.

"Wow. Talk about grand, huh?"

"Aye, it is a grand house. No' as grand as it once was, mind."

"No, it's gorgeous. We don't have anything like this back home, and the only manor houses I've seen on my year abroad in London were museums."

"And 'back home' is Corner Brook?"

"Yeah. Corner Brook, Newfoundland."

Lamb furrowed his brow, the paper-thin skin wrinkling even more than it already was. "*Newfin*-land? Where is that, if you don't mind me asking?"

"Canada. Atlantic coast. A world of its own."

"I see," Lamb said. He didn't, but there was no point in telling her. "Well then, let me show you to your room. I'm sure you must want to freshen up after your drive."

"Thanks, that would be great. It's so nice of her ladyship to let me stay here. Saved me the hassle of finding a place in town."

"I think you'll find her ladyship is exceedingly generous. And besides, you'll probably want to be close to the work since there is so much of it to do."

"No kidding." Emmie laughed lightly. It was an infectious laugh. Lamb decided he liked the young woman. His mother certainly liked her; she was practically bouncing with glee.

He led the way, taking Emmie up two flights of the main staircase to the second floor of the house. He walked slowly. Though it was not for her benefit—his old stiff bones being what they were—it did give her time to absorb her surroundings.

"Watch there." He pointed to a section of carpet which had ripped four years ago. Too late. With her eyes fixed above her on the paisley papered walls and the crumbling crown moulding, the toe of her boot caught, and she stumbled.

"Clumsy me," she muttered.

"No' at all, madam."

"I really wish you'd call me Emmie. We're colleagues."

He thought about it, weighing the word "colleague" carefully. "I suppose you're right. Emmie then."

"Good." She nodded, pleased. Which pleased Lamb—not that he made any hint of it.

At the end of the corridor, he pressed on a section of wall that was a concealed door. Up until the last century, servants had come and gone through these doors like ghosts. Unseen, unheard. The paper peeled away from the edge, revealing a layer of paint in a muted robin's-egg blue—the second floor's last iteration of décor.

With a groan, the door swung inward, revealing a narrow, uneven staircase. Sunlight streamed through a tall, plain window. The natural light revealed the dust in the corners of the stairs where Lamb had missed when he went over them the night before.

"Oh, now look," his mother clucked. "Her first impression of the house and she's got to trudge her way through a mountain of dust on each step."

Lamb let the jab pass without comment. "I hope you don't mind being quartered in the servants' wing," he said to Emmie, "but the rest of the rooms are no' in any fit state to be inhabited at the moment. There haven't been servants enough to fill this wing for decades, I'm afraid, so the rooms are all empty."

"That's just fine." Emmie stepped through into the stairwell. "Is your room up here, too?"

"It is, madam."

"And are you the only one here, or are there others?"

"I am by myself, ever since his lordship passed."

"I'm sorry."

They climbed up the stairs in silence. Emmie went slow, acting as though it were a normal speed for her, but Lamb knew she was just being courteous. She glanced around her, interested.

"Are these stairs original to the manor?"

"They are, madam. Emmie. Roger Pratt himself worked on the layout. He was a friend of the sixth Lord Cranbury."

"Ah, yes. Sir Roger Pratt, famous for rebuilding Coleshill House in Berkshire and effectively removing servants from communal life by popularizing the concept of a separate servants' quarters."

Lamb's white brows rose a fraction. "That's an impressive recollection."

Her answer was a shrug and a sheepish grin. "I looked it up before I came here. I was hoping I might get the opportunity to pull out that little nugget."

A hint of a smile cracked on the old man's pale lips.

"This staircase was wired with an electric light in the late nineteen-twenties." He pointed to the bare lightbulb suspended from the peeling ceiling. "The light switches are at the top and bottom of the stairs."

There was no door at the top. There had been once, and the frame and rusted hinges still remained, but the door itself had been removed when Lamb was a boy. He didn't recall the reason, and made a mental note to ask his mother about it.

Their footsteps echoed down the empty, unfurnished corridor of the servants' wing. Lamb led her to the last door on the left, which stood ajar.

"It's the largest one up here," he offered, pausing at the threshold. "It's unfortunate there is no true window, or else you would be able to see down to the gardens. But this room gets the most natural light. And it's the warmest. Just don't touch that radiator in the winter. It gets fiercely hot when the furnace is going."

Emmy entered the room, inspecting her new home. Her hand ran unconsciously over the utilitarian brass frame of the single bed he'd made up for her that morning. A plain chest of drawers stood against the far wall, and a night table stood beside the bed. A wooden chair was placed in the corner, beside which was a timeworn armoire a little more than six feet tall.

The natural light of which he spoke was owing to an antique skylight that looked down onto the bed.

"I'm afraid it's nothing fancy," he apologized. "You are of course free to liven it up as much as you see fit."

"I wouldn't dream of it. It's perfect. Thank you, Lamb."

"I'll fetch your baggage, then, while you get used to the place."

"Really, it's no bother. I can do it myself."

He hesitated. "If you wish."

"I insist. I'll come down in a bit." Her hazel eyes fixed on his with earnest appreciation. "Thanks so much. I can see the trouble you've gone to."

If Lamb still had colour to blush with, he would have. He gave a curt nod, and excused himself, shuffling back down the corridor to the stairs.

"Why did you say that?" His mother was at his side, nudging him annoyingly.

"Say what, Mother?"

"You said you're alone here."

"What did you wish me to say, Mother? I *am* alone, as alone as she needs to know."

Mrs. Lamb snorted. "Well, isn't she going to be surprised when she finds out how untrue that is?"

Lamb huffed, irritated. "Oh, shoo, you old ghost!"

Mrs. Lamb's chuckling laughter echoed down the hall, and then it was gone.

Lamb shook his head. Fifty years dead, and the wretched woman was still hovering at his shoulder like she did when he was a boy.

TWO

ALONE IN HER new lodgings and surrounded by a house full of antiques, Emmie sat gently on the edge of the bed. Even it was old. The serviceable brass frame was reminiscent of the Victorian, or perhaps the Edwardian era. Curious, she inspected the visible parts of the frame for a manufacturer, and when she couldn't find one, she got down on her hands and knees and tugged apart the bedding. There it was, on the support rail for the mattress: R. W. Winfield & Co.

Indeed an antique. Circa 1900 she recalled, thanks to a third-year paper on the boom of mass manufacturing in industrial England.

She re-tucked the bedding and, still on the floor, sank back on her heels. Chafing her hands on her thighs, she breathed in the intoxicating scent of old wood, old house and old dust. To Emmie, there was nothing like the smell of the past—and it did have a smell, history. It was the mellow, earthy and not unpleasant scent of decay.

Tullybrae House. So far it was everything she'd hoped it would be. A three hundred and fifty-year-old mansion in the northern reaches of the district of Argyll, it had undergone few structural renovations since its construction, and contained a seemingly unending collection of originally purchased antiques. Furniture, paintings, documents, ornaments, books, fabrics. Even clothing was piled in steamer trunks—themselves antiques— and stashed heedlessly in Tullybrae's rambling attics.

Emmie had seen the photos which Lady Rotherham had emailed her, of course. But photos could never do the real thing justice. Even in sore need of repair as it was, the house was stunning. Breathtaking. Everything a Scottish manor house should be. It was such a shame Lord Cranbury let it go the way he had.

She supposed she should be grateful, though. If the old man hadn't let it go, then she wouldn't have this wonderful opportunity. She should be thrilled the old miser had been too much of a penny pincher to maintain the place, and hadn't held any aspiration towards modernization.

She *was* thrilled. More than thrilled.

Her new room was perfect. There were no windows at eye level, but the one yellowing skylight above the bed was large enough that it let in sufficient light. Beyond the glass, in the rare, cerulean blue sky, drifted traces of the powderpuff clouds she'd admired on the drive up from Glasgow.

There wasn't much in the way of furniture in this room, but Emmie didn't need much. The armoire, scarred and nicked from what looked to be more than two centuries of use, was big enough to hold the clothes which she needed to hang. The single chest of drawers, equally scarred and nicked, gave her plenty of room to store the rest. The bedside table could hold her makeup and toiletries, and it had a shelf at the base that she could store her books on.

The walls were unadorned. They had once been white, but the years had turned the paint to buttercream yellow. In the corner where the armoire was, the plaster had crumbled, revealing horizontal slats of wood that made up the frame of the wall. The oak floor was slightly warped, the widths of the individual planks non-uniform.

How many pairs of feet had stumbled across these planks on cold mornings? Instinctively, she traced a forefinger over the rough, dented grain. A wistful half-smile tugged at her lips.

With a quick, satisfied breath and a glance to where the plastered ceiling met the wall, Emmie left the room, walked briskly along the corridor of the servants' quarters, and pattered lightly down the stairs. She took care to mind their uneven heights. From her time as a history major in university, she knew that the long, heavy skirts of the Victorian maid were not the only reason so many of them fell to their deaths. It was the stairs themselves. High and narrow, there was no thought to uniformity, and some stairs were shallower than others. That, added to a platform that wasn't even half the length of a typical foot, and long hours of physical labour, it was no wonder stairs had been so fatal back then.

She'd been worried about Lamb when they'd come up here. She liked the stoic old butler on sight. And besides, no matter how enamoured with all things history she might have been, witnessing one of those historic fatalities was one experience Emmie was happy to forego.

Outside in the sunshine, she pulled open the rear hatch of the boxy, ugly blue car she'd picked up three days ago. She'd spent a week in Glasgow after her flight out of Newfoundland (from which she'd had to make a maddeningly delayed connecting flight in Toronto), and had taken the opportunity to peruse used car lots for something that was both sturdy and budget-friendly.

Unfortunately *sturdy* was too pricey. She'd had to settle for a demure, rinky-dink 'city' car.

Fiat Panda. And powder blue at that. The GMC Sierra pickup truck her brother drove would steam roll right over it without so much as a hiccup.

Emmie struggled to dislodge her bags, which she'd packed into the back with the precision of an engineer. She'd paid a mint to have all this stuff flown over, but it was an expense she was willing to bear. Scotland would be her home now for the next few years at least, assuming she didn't do anything to displease Lord and Lady Rotherham... like calling Lady Rotherham's late lamented father Lord Cranberry to her face. Three enormous suitcases were stashed in the back, and another one was squeezed into the passenger seat. An oversized and overstuffed gym bag was wedged under the dashboard on the passenger side, on top of which sat her purse.

Her most valued books were being shipped directly to Tullybrae from Corner Brook. She was glad she'd made that snap decision. She never would have been able to find room for them in the Panda.

It took Emmie three trips to lug her baggage up to her room on the third floor. Once they were carefully ordered beside the lone wooden chair, she went to work unpacking. Removing items one by one, with the care of someone who had saved her money to buy every precious piece, she began assigning them to their appropriate places. Jackets and blazers that had been neatly folded for the flight were put to one side of the bed; they would likely need dry cleaning to remove the wrinkles. Her silk and satin blouses, too. Knit and cashmere sweaters were stacked snugly in the drawers, and her cotton dress pants and skirts were slipped onto wooden hangers and hung in the armoire.

Each article of her wardrobe had been chosen deliberately, with thought to how it might complement existing pieces. Emmie was, by self-imposed rule, mindful of her appearance and the impression she made on people. Her hair was always groomed and immaculately highlighted, her nails always filed so that they extended only slightly past her fingertips, and flawlessly painted in demure colours. In her sleepwear, her active-wear, and even her frump-around-the-apartment wear, there was an air of careful composition.

It was not that she was vain, though. Far from it. Structure, order. They were the code by which Emmie lived her life. They were ingrained into her psyche.

She knew all too well what happened when one lost sight of structure in one's life.

The last item at the bottom of the duffle bag was wrapped in white tissue paper and a bath towel for extra security. Taking it in both hands, she tenderly unwrapped the soft, protective layers to reveal the framed photograph within. The frame, a hand-buffed wood with gilded decorative scrolls, had been a high school graduation present from her adoptive mother. It had been meant to hold a photo of her family, and to sit on her desk in her dorm room at college so that she wouldn't feel homesick.

Photos of her family were packed neatly beside her wallet in her purse: her adoptive parents, Grace and Ron Tunstall, and her adopted brother Chase. But they weren't the ones she put in the frame. She would never tell Grace whom she did put there, because it would hurt the kind, loving woman's feelings. The photo she chose for the coveted spot smiled out at her from behind the glass. The bright, hazel eyes of her real mother were full of light, and love, and the optimism of youth.

Emmie positioned the photo on top of the dresser, angled towards the bed where she could see it before she fell asleep each night. As she did every morning and every night, she kissed her forefinger and touched the glass.

"Here we are, Mom," she said into the stillness of the room. "Are you proud of me? Your little girl did it. Her first, real job as a full-fledged curator."

AT SEVEN THAT evening, Lamb tapped an arthritic knuckle on Emmie's partially opened door. It creaked inwards an inch, revealing a sleeping Emmie. She was on top of her quilt, with the bedside lamp on and her finger wedged into a paperback novel. Not wishing to disturb her, Lamb scuttled back a step. The faint sound woke her; she opened a sleepy eye and squinted towards the door.

"Beg pardon, madam— er, Emmie. I didn't mean to wake you," he said in his raspy voice.

Emmie grunted and sat up. She scanned the room for her alarm clock, which she'd set up on the dresser beside the photo of her mother.

"No, please, wake me. I shouldn't have been sleeping." She rubbed her eyes with a balled fist. "Oh—is that the time? I didn't realize how tired I was. I just meant to close my eyes for a bit."

"It has been quite a day, I imagine. I came to tell you that supper is ready, but I can always keep some warm for you, if you'd prefer to eat later."

"Don't be silly. It's not your job to wait on me."

He shrugged. "A habit. I've waited on Lord Cranbury and his family for most of my adult life. I am no' accustomed to having no one to look after."

"You're too good. Did anyone ever tell you that?"

Emmie stretched her arms over her head and yawned delicately. Then, swinging her legs over the side of the bed, she slipped her feet into her riding boots, which stood at military attention on the vintage braided rug below.

"I'll show you the way to the kitchen." Lamb turned and tottered away.

She trailed behind, following him down the narrow stairs to the main part of the house. Instead of turning right to the grand staircase, as they had that morning, he went straight and down another corridor that led around the back of the house. Here, yet another camouflaged servants' door stood open a crack.

"Kitchen's this way."

The steps down this rear staircase were no less narrow and treacherous. Lamb had to switch on the light, since there was no window like in the stairwell to the third floor. Emmie clutched the railing with her left hand as she descended behind him, and prepared to make a grab at the collar of his sweater vest with her right, if he were to take a tumble. Once both sets of feet were firmly on the tiled floor at the bottom, she breathed a silent prayer.

The riven-surfaced grey slate was uneven; it felt like the floor of a cave. Her boots made a charming echo with each step, and she imagined what this underground world must have been like in its heyday. If she closed her eyes, she could picture servants in their black dresses and elegant livery rushing to and fro. An army of Victorian ants.

"Mmmm, I can smell dinner." She sniffed appreciatively. "It smells delicious. I totally forgot about lunch. I'm starved."

"We're having venison stew. His lordship always did like his venison. I'm sorry it is no' fresh, it's been in vacuum packs in the freezer since the fall."

"I've never had venison before."

"I hope it suits your palate, then. It is leaner than beef, and has a distinct flavour to it. I cannot place it, exactly, but you'll know it to taste it."

"Freedom?" Emmie suggested, somewhat tongue-in-cheek.

Lamb cocked his head to one side; a low, airy chuckle bubbled up from his sunken chest. "Aye, freedom. I suppose that's what it is."

The corridor at the bottom of the stairway led to a main, central hallway, with several closed doors down the length. Some had windows looking into the hall, but those windows were unlit. Peering through, Emmie could see that one or two had windows to the outside as well, but the dust on them was so thick that not much of the fading evening light made it through.

"There's plenty of old items in there," Lamb noted when she paused and leaned close to the glass. "Mostly just pantry rubbish, cooking pots and skillets, jugs, crates, flatware—those kinds of things. But if you're interested in researching them, too, I'll fetch the keys. Just say the words."

"Yep. I'll be knee deep in all this stuff eventually."

"I've no doubt."

The last door on the right led into the kitchen. It was the only lit room, besides the corridor itself. A cozy glow warmed the windows that looked into the central hallway. The unpainted plaster walls were tiled to about waist height, with old-fashioned orange tiles arranged in a subway pattern. The wooden countertops were easily a century old, and an authentic Victorian range stood unused in the corner farthest from the door. Copper pots and pans hung from hooks on the walls, and from a suspended pot rack over the counter beside the romantic black range.

A solid work table dominated the centre of the room, at which sat two wooden stools painted a cheery sea green. Two placemats had been set out, with empty drinking glasses, forks, spoons and knives. Each placemat also had a small plate with a slice of whole-wheat bread. A crock of butter waited in the middle of the table, along with a utilitarian, but still antique-looking set of porcelain salt and pepper shakers, and a ceramic water pitcher.

"You didn't have to go to all this trouble." She pulled out the stool that faced the back wall of the kitchen, and sat down.

"It was no trouble. I would have been doing this for myself anyway, if you hadn't been here."

Lamb hobbled over to a modern stove where a pot of venison stew was simmering, and began ladling the thick, brown liquid into bowls which had been laid out on the sideboard next to it.

Emmie watched his hunched shoulders thoughtfully. "You know, I sometimes forget that this is a way of life for people."

"What is?"

"Eating dinner at the table."

"You don't eat at the table?"

She shrugged one shoulder. "Well, I mean, we used to when I was a kid. Grace—my mom, that is—would always have dinner ready for us, and we'd sit down and eat as a family. But then, when I went away to university, I got into the habit of eating on the go, or eating in front of the TV. I don't ever really bother with the formality of dinner anymore."

"I'm sorry," Lamb offered. "I didn't mean to assume." He shuffled back to the table with two steaming bowls of stew.

"Oh, no, don't get me wrong. I'm happy to be doing it again." She paused, and added shyly, "I'm happy to *have* someone to eat dinner with again. It gets kind of lonely eating in front of the TV all the time."

Lamb sat carefully on his stool, and once he'd set the bowls down, he placed his palms on top of the table. He stared intently at his spotted hands.

"I'm... happy to have someone to eat dinner with again, too."

His awkward honesty warmed her heart. Grinning to herself, Emmie tucked her spoon into the rich stew, pulling up a mound of chucky potatoes, carrots, celery and venison. Leaving the conversation at that, she popped the spoon into her mouth.

"My God, Lamb, this is amazing," she moaned once she'd chewed. "My compliments to the chef."

He nodded, and brought his own spoon to his mouth with a shaky hand. "Is there anything in particular you like to eat for breakfast?"

"I hope you don't think it's your job to cook for me."

"I don't mind."

"Maybe not, but I do. I'd prefer to pull my weight around here— although if the rest of your cooking is anything like this, it'll be hard to resist." She shook her head decisively. "No, we'll take turns. How 'bout this: for this week, why don't you take breakfasts and I'll take dinners? Next week we'll switch."

He considered her proposition. "If you're sure. What about lunch?"

"Actually, I often forget about lunch," Emmie admitted. "I get so involved in what I'm doing when I'm working that sometimes I go all day without even a snack. It'll probably be best if we just fend for ourselves for lunch. I can't be relied on for that."

Lamb frowned. "I don't like the idea of you no' eating lunch. You're thin as a rail as it is."

"That's kind of you to say." She laughed lightly. "Tell you what: I promise to try to remember to eat lunch, if it makes you happy." When he agreed and went back to his bowl, she changed the subject. "So… I meet Lady Rotherham tomorrow."

"Oh, aye?"

She hesitated, pushing a chunk of soft carrot around with the edge of her spoon. "Any words of advice? I've only talked to her a few times over the phone."

Lamb finished chewing a piece of venison. "I imagine she's much the same in person as she is on the phone."

Then, oddly, he jerked his shoulder and scowled.

"You okay?" Emmie ventured.

"Oh, quite. Just a *nagging* ache," he responded rather forcefully. "I'm sure you have nothing to concern yourself with, where her ladyship is concerned. She's personable enough. It was her particular instruction that you be well looked after in your time here."

"That's nice of her." She popped the disintegrating carrot into her mouth. "It's just that this is my first real job in the field. I want to make the right impression."

"You'll do fine." Lamb jerked his shoulder again, but said nothing.

Emmie watched him briefly, wondering about the strange mannerism. Was it a tick?

Or perhaps it was a ghost, begging for a bite of supper.

She laughed to herself at the notion, picturing the late Lord Cranbury himself standing over the old butler's shoulder.

THREE

EMMIE PASSED A rough night in her new bed at Tullybrae House. From an unknown location somewhere near the stairs, the wind was finding its way in. It whistled through the empty rooms, a hollow sound that prevented her from drifting off. At times, she wondered if Lamb was having the same trouble sleeping, or if the male quarters were more insulated.

When she did manage to sleep, she would periodically wake to find herself shivering. Every time she got up to search for her blankets, there they'd be, in a rumpled heap below the footboard.

Five bloody times this happened.

If those things alone hadn't been enough to make any night unbearable, her dreams had been plagued by a strange, high-pitched giggling. Like that of a child. By the time her alarm clock went off at seven thirty, she could have sworn she'd only just nodded off.

The bed made a metallic creak when she stumbled out of it. Emmie yawned heavily, then pulled open the bedside drawer for her toiletries.

With the pearl-pink, faux silk bag tucked beneath the crook of her arm, she yanked her fleece robe from its hook on the back of the door, and stuffed her arms inside the plush sleeves. Last, she slipped her manicured toes into a pair of terrycloth slippers, before she trundled off to the remodeled bathroom.

Having made a scouting tour of the servants' quarters last night before turning in, Emmie had confirmed that, like most houses of this period, the servants' quarters were divided into male and female wings. A long time ago there would have been a door separating the two which (she imagined fondly) a dour-faced head housekeeper had once kept firmly bolted and the key secured in a starched pocket. Neither the door nor its lock remained, though.

The male wing, too, had its own washroom, which suited her fine. Emmie liked Lamb immensely, but something about the idea of sharing a shower with the octogenarian Scot butler she'd just met seemed a little queer. Both his bedroom and his washroom were separate from hers, and on the other side of the house.

When she reached the bathroom, she shut the door and twisted the brass cabin latch above the handle to lock it. The shower in her bathroom was a repurposed clawfoot tub. It had probably been at Tullybrae for the last century… like everything else around here, including Lamb. Giving in to her historian's curiosity, she searched the tub for a manufacturer. None could be found, but she did find a model identification number beneath the nickel-plated faucet.

The rolled lip of the tub indicated it, too, had been mass-produced. She clucked her tongue sadly. A less coveted antique, probably. But still worth a check. She made a mental note of the location of the model number for later research.

An oval-shaped metal curtain rod had been bolted to the ceiling in a more recent decade. To keep the water in, Emmie had to pull a series of mismatched curtains, three of them, around the circumference of the tub. To her relief, the strong odour of new plastic suggested that *they* were not antiques.

She fiddled with the handles at the head of the tub. One final twist, and water gushed loudly from the mounted shower head. It, too, was new by the looks of it. A small lever on the underside would adjust the flow. Emmie tested out the four different positions, deciding on a powerful, steady stream. She needed the water drumming into her head to wake her up.

The water was hot. It felt good biting into her shoulders and the back of her scalp. With her hands dangling loose at her sides, she stood for a while, letting the water pound into her tired bones. When she'd loosened up enough, she shampooed and conditioned her hair, scrubbed her body vigorously with a loofah and her favourite watermelon bath gel, and washed her face with a cleansing milk. The familiar scents swirled inside the shower's vortex of steam, providing a measure of comfort.

Once she was done, Emmie turned the knobs smartly, and stepped onto the cheap bathmat at the base of the tub. She reached for her towel which she'd hung on a peg beside the door, and rubbed herself dry. The mirror over the worn marble sink was steamed up when she approached it, so she made a swipe with her hand. The glass made a satisfying squeak beneath her palm.

She then set up her personal care products and plugged in her flat iron and blow dryer. Today, she decided, she would straighten her hair so that it hung like corn silk to the bottom of her shoulder blades. She made quick work of getting ready, slapping on her skin care products, applying a restrained amount of makeup, and styling her golden hair. When she was done, she padded back to her room in her bathrobe and slippers, pajamas draped over her forearm. Her makeup, toiletries and appliances she left in the bathroom. Now that she knew the space was hers alone, there was no need to carry her personal effects to and fro each time.

By eight thirty she was dressed and bounding down the servants' stairs by the rear corridor to the kitchen. She felt much more alert, and excitement about her first day on the job had put a spring in her step. The heavenly aroma of a home-cooked breakfast quickened her pace.

"Baaaacon," she drawled when she entered.

Lamb stood over the stove with a spatula in one hand. A full-length apron with green and white stripes protected his brown sweater vest and slacks.

"Good morning, Emmie. Did you sleep well?"

"Yes, thanks," she lied. "Here, let me help you."

The plates, cups and saucers were visible within the glass-front cupboards, which were painted a creamy yellow. Before Lamb could protest, she got to work setting the bare table. He tossed her an appreciative nod before flipping the frying meat.

"Forks and knives are in there," he offered, pointing, when Emmie started opening drawers.

"Is there anything else I can help with?"

"No, no. You just sit down. Bacon's the last thing."

Turning the contents of the skillet onto a square of paper towel, Lamb patted the grease before sliding the ten russet strips onto a platter waiting on the sideboard. He flipped a switch on the stove to turn off the element, picked up the platter, and brought it to the table.

"What's this?" Emmie asked, inspecting the other items on the platter.

"Black pudding and haggis."

Lamb fetched a china cake plate stacked with brown toast. Balancing it in the crook of his elbow, he grasped a waiting tea pot with one hand, and a coffee pot with the other. Emmie rose to help him, but he shook his head.

"I can manage. You stay put."

"I've never had black pudding and haggis before," she said hesitantly, sitting back down.

"They have a bad reputation across the water, I'm given to understand. But many people like them when they try it."

Gingerly, Emmie helped herself to a portion, and took a test bite of the haggis first. It was... different. Not quite what she was expecting, but not terrible, either. The black pudding was next. It too was unusual, but far from inedible.

"Well?"

She licked her lips, considering. "If I can separate what it *tastes* like from what it *is*, I don't mind it at all."

The old man chuckled. "You mean the offal? If you can eat steak and kidney pie, this is no' much different. But instead of steak, it's oats."

"What about sheep's stomach?"

"There's no stomach in it. Haggis is simply cooked in a sheep's stomach." When she searched the sideboard behind him for the offending item, he smiled. "You won't find it. This here comes out of a can. Best haggis I've had that wasn't homemade."

"What about the black pudding? That's blood, isn't it?"

He shrugged. "Aye, it is. Would you like something else, then?"

"No, I didn't say that. I'm just getting used to it, that's all. You know, it really is kind of tasty. Thanks for making it." She took another bite to demonstrate. It actually was quite good. Salty and rich, with no hint of the metal tang one might expect from something made with blood.

"Would you like coffee or tea?" he inquired. "I made both."

"Coffee, thanks." Emmie reached for the pot, and poured. She held the pot up and raised her eyebrows in question.

"Tea for me, please."

"I had the Starbucks every day on my stopover in Glasgow. It was okay. Not the same as home, though. I knew I'd miss Tims, but I didn't expect to miss it this much."

"Tims?"

"Tim Hortons. Our beloved national coffee emporium."

"The name—does it mean anything?"

"It does, actually. He was a hockey player for our Toronto team, the Maple Leafs, through the fifties and sixties." She paused, adding sadly, "He was killed in a car accident, in the end."

"That's a shame," Lamb said earnestly.

"It is. Sad story of drinking and driving and not wearing a seatbelt. A sorry way to end for a national treasure."

"I'm sorry."

She shrugged. "It was before my time."

"Things needn't happen in our lifetime for them to affect us," he answered sagely.

"I suppose you're right. I should know, being a history nerd and all, shouldn't I?"

They ate in silence for a time before Lamb picked up the conversation again.

"I expect you're looking forward to meeting her ladyship. When does she arrive?" He bit firmly into a triangle of buttered toast.

"About ten." Emmie's voice crackled, her nerves jangling at the mention of her employer.

"You have nothing to worry about," he assured her.

"I hope not. Do I look all right?" She chafed her hands against her wool skirt. It was an above-the-knee piece which she'd matched to a pair of black tights and her black peep-toe booties. A black knit top with three-quarter-length sleeves brought out the chunky necklace of turquoise stones she'd chosen to complete the outfit.

"Oh, aye, fetching," he answered vaguely. Only the telltale warming of his pale cheeks gave him away.

When they were done, Emmie helped Lamb with the dishes—the "washing up," as he called it. It was a literal thing. There was no dishwasher at Tullybrae House. They completed the chore in amiable chatter. Once they were done, he noted a few of the chores that awaited him, and suggested that Emmie retreat to the library to wait for Lady Rotherham.

The library was a beautiful room, stately yet modest. It wasn't half the size of some of the libraries she'd seen in the mansions and castles of Europe, yet the dark wood shelving and the marbled fireplace gave it a quiet grandeur that made her feel very comfortable. A quaint bay window gave her a view of the manicured lawn and hedged gardens at the rear of the house. Beyond them, the Highland hills nudged a slate grey sky.

"Not a soul out there for miles," she whispered.

Once she'd had her fill of the scenery, she left the window to browse some of the titles on the lower shelves. All of the books were hard-cover, and the majority of them were leather-bound. They were probably centuries old. Books were a particular weakness for Emmie. There was something about the smell of old books, and the feel of their weight in her hands. It was euphoric. Words put to paper by writers who'd lived and died long ago. Hopes and dreams recorded in ink for future generations to read.

Carefully, she tilted one book off its shelf and gripped its leather cover in her hands.

"The Works of the English Poets with Prefaces," she read, "Biographical and Critical, by Samuel Johnson. Volume the Twenty-Seventh. London: Printed by A. Strathan, seventeen ninety."

She sat down on the green velvet settee in front of the hearth. Victorian era, she noted for future reference, carved walnut or maybe alder, cameo back. Delicately, she turned the pages of the book, with no more than a fingertip to the edge of each frail sheet. Her eyes scanned words upon words that had been written more than two hundred years ago. She was so absorbed in the book that she jumped when Clunie leaped his fat body up onto the cushion beside her.

"Oh, hello. What have you been up to this morning, handsome fellow?"

She scratched behind his ears and under his chin. Clunie responded with a rich, warm purr and a sideways flop into her thigh.

With the contented house cat settled beside her, and the thrill of history in her hands, Emmie spent nearly half an hour reading. The chime of the doorbell brought her back to the present.

Her stomach churned as she reshelved the book and walked swiftly to the front door. She arrived at the same time as Lamb, who had a can of furniture polish tucked into the crook of his arm and a dirty rag in his hand. Deftly, Emmie plucked the workaday items from his grasp and slipped them into a nearby vase.

Lamb opened the door to Lady Rotherham, who stood on the stoop outside with a file folder full of papers clasped to her chest.

"Hello Lamb," she greeted affectionately, stepping through to the entryway. She allowed the old butler to take her shawl and wide-brim floppy hat, then ran her fingers through her chin-length hair, which was dyed a rich shade of red.

"And you must be Emmeline." The lady swept towards her in a larger-than-life manner. Grasping her firmly by the shoulders, she air-kissed Emmie's cheeks.

Before Emmie could get out a hello, Lady Rotherham was off, striding down the hall towards the library. "Do be a dear, Lamb, and make us a spot of tea." Her cultured English accent held only a hint of Scots.

Emmie raised her eyebrows to Lamb, then trotted after the trim, small figure of Lady Rotherham. Reaching the library, she closed the door, and joined the lady who had seated herself on the settee that Emmie had just vacated.

"Oh, shoo, Clunie," the lady chided, scooting the cat off the seat.

Emmie took the spoon back armchair opposite, and folded her hands expectantly in her lap.

"Well, my dear, I'm happy to have you here."

"I'm happy to be here. Thank you, your ladyship, for the opportunity." Feeling a need to make the first overture, she added, "May I ask: Why do you ring the doorbell to your own home?"

The lady laughed, tossing her small head back. "I like you already." She looked around the library, thinking. "Well, I suppose it's habit. It's something Daddy insisted on as soon as Anne-Marie and I got married and moved away. We no longer lived here, you see—if one does not live here, one must ring the doorbell to be let in."

"Maybe he wanted to give you the guest treatment," Emmie said charitably.

"Hardly. Putting us in our place, more like. Not that I resent the old darling for it. In the end, the house became mine."

Sighing elegantly, Lady Rotherham placed the file folder in her hands onto the rosewood end table at her right. She tisked, tracing a centuries-old scar in the surface. "Everything's an antique, here. This table, for instance. A Victorian reproduction; Louis the Fifteenth; Ormolu mounted."

"You're a bit of a historian yourself, I see."

"I Googled it," Lady Rotherham deadpanned. "Apparently, there's another one at La Maison Mont Du Lac. It's a vineyard outside of Bordeaux, in a town called Pauillac."

"How... prestigious." It was all Emmie could think to say. But it seemed to please her new employer.

They were briefly interrupted when Lamb brought in a silver tea service with china cups and saucers.

"How you manage to make tea so quickly, I'll never know, Lamb." Lady Rotherham waited for him to place the tray on the low table between them.

Emmie, too, wondered about that. He must have had everything ready in anticipation of her arrival.

"Oh, and Mrs. Lamb's shortbread cookies. These are legendary around here." The lady poured herself a cup of tea and helped herself to a buttery white biscuit.

"Your ladyship," he said, then left the library quietly.

Before she poured her own tea, Emmie sneaked a peak at the bottom of the cup. The mark read "Fine Bone China; Crown Staffordshire; Est. 1801; England." Lady Rotherham noticed, and winked.

"You're not on duty just now," she jested, then took a sip of her tea. "So. Emmeline. How are you liking Tullybrae?"

"It's just Emmie," she corrected politely. "Tullybrae is beautiful. Exactly as you described it."

"You haven't decided to turn tail and run then, after seeing how much work is ahead of you?"

Emmie smiled knowingly. "It's not like you didn't warn me your ladyship."

"Camille." Lady Rotherham's face grew serious. "All kidding aside, I would like to be frank about why I hired you. You know you're not being paid a salary appropriate to your title."

Emmie had known. She nodded.

"The fact is, my dear, that I simply cannot afford to hire an experienced curator for the amount of work that needs to be done. No one would take the post if I tried." She gestured grandly to the air as if all of the potential candidates for curator were hovering in the background.

"I know." Emmie put her tea cup down; she winced when the delicate china clicked against the equally delicate saucer. "Professor McCall went over all this with me. I know what I'm getting into. It is a lot of work, and the pay is not comparable to what I would expect if I were to be offered the curator position at, say, the Museo Del Prado. But then again I would never be *offered* the curator position at the Museo Del Prado or anywhere like it." She knew she was being handed an opportunity to gain experience, and she appreciated it for what it was.

Lady Rotherham beamed. "Oh, good. I was worried old Boomer hadn't given you much to go on."

Emmie stared. "Who?"

"Oh, Boomer is Ethan McCall's nickname from way back at UCL. He spoke so highly of you when he put your name forward for the position. He thought it was right up your alley."

"Boomer." Emmie snickered. "Professor McCall is always so serious, I can't imagine him as a 'Boomer'."

"Yes, well, he can be a bit stuffy when he's working, can't he? But put a scotch in his hand and he can let loose with the best of them." Leaning forward, she lowered her voice. "When you see him next, you will have to ask him about how he got that name. I won't tell you, but it involves a sheep, purple dye, and a value pack of glow-in-the-dark condoms."

Emmie choked on her tea.

"Right then," Lady Rotherham continued, "as far as the work goes, I'm sure you don't need me to go into detail with that. But I will say that I do want everything catalogued. *Everything*, no matter how small or insignificant it may seem. Do you have any idea where you might start?"

"Um—" Emmie eased her teacup back onto the saucer with exaggerated delicacy. "I think it will be to take valuable antiques like these out of rotation for everyday use."

"These aren't the most valuable ones we have, dear. For Lamb, these *are* the everyday alternatives. Now, I believe Boomer mentioned, I'm thinking of turning Tullybrae into a museum now that Daddy's gone. Maybe a hotel, too. I haven't decided yet."

"He did mention."

"Oliver—that's Lord Rotherham—wants me to sell it. But I just can't bring myself to do it, not even to the National Trust. It was my childhood home, you see. My younger sister and I spent our youth here."

"I understand. It's hard to let go when you love something so much."

Lady Rotherham smiled sadly. "That's why Lamb is still here, you know. I love him too much to let him go. Oliver tried to get him to retire, but he wouldn't hear of it. And I didn't have the heart to support Oliver—which, believe me, I heard about once we were home." She took another bite of her biscuit. "I do worry about him having a fall when he's here alone. You wouldn't mind terribly keeping an eye on him, would you?"

"Not at all."

"Good. Well then, perhaps I should tell you what you can expect these next few months." The lady flipped open the top cover of her file folder.

Within were what looked like contracts, which she fanned out for closer inspection. "I've been a very busy woman, contacting the networks."

"The networks?" Emmie leaned in to take a look.

"Yes. I heard back from two. Stannisfield Films is picking us up for an episode of Digging Scotland with Dr. Iain Northcott—and you'd best be prepared for that one; they want to start digging by the end of the week so they don't get snowed out."

"Digging?"

"Didn't Boomer tell you? There's a legend of a burial on the property— a grave, murder victim from God knows when. The team came out a few weeks ago and did a scan with ground penetrating radar. They found a disturbance out in the east field that might corroborate a burial, so they're coming to film an episode. I've already had my interview with Iain." She primped her unnaturally red hair.

"So they'll be filming here?" Emmie felt a little faint. Professor McCall hadn't mentioned anything about filming.

"Yes, but it shouldn't affect you at all. They won't need you for the camera. The most you'll have to do is help Lamb see them off each night, and make sure they're not damaging the property at all. You probably won't have anything to worry about there, though. They are archaeologists, after all."

Emmie nodded vaguely. "And the second network?"

"Yes," Lady Rotherham nodded. "Well… you see… how to say this? Perhaps I should be totally honest. Tullybrae is haunted." When Emmie's eyebrows shot up, Lady Rotherham explained. "It's nothing to worry about. They're nice ghosts. I grew up with them, and they've never done anything to me. One is the sixth Countess of Cranbury, who died in sixteen ninety-one. She won't bother you much. The most you'll catch is a glimpse of her, or perhaps a whiff of her perfume. Rose—you'll smell it. And the second, we think, is the ghost of a little girl named Clara. She's the only child's death we have registered at Tullybrae. In seventeen eighty-three. Tuberculosis. She's not harmful, but she likes to play. You may hear giggling, or things might fall off shelves. That kind of thing."

Emmie recalled the strange giggling she'd dreamed of last night, and shivered.

"I hope I haven't frightened you," Lady Rotherham put in.

She met the lady's concerned gaze, and tried so smile. "No, not frightened, exactly. I can't say I was expecting that, but I'm sure it will be fine. As long as nothing jumps out at me."

"Oh, no. Nothing like that. Anyway, BBC Two is coming out for an episode of Haunted Britain. That's happening mid-September. You won't need to be on camera for that, either, but they will be staying overnight at the house to shoot."

Emmie breathed, absorbing the news she'd just been blindsided with. "I think I can handle that."

"I'm sure you can," Lady Rotherham agreed airily. "For now, I just need you to work on the items in the house. You're free to come and go as you please. I'm not a stickler for in-office hours… or in-house hours, in this case. As long as you're making progress, that's all I care about."

"Understood."

Lady Rotherham gave Emmie an appraising look. "I have a feeling we're going to get along famously."

She hoped the lady was right. Because after everything she'd just been told, be in over her head.

FOUR

THE FIRST WEEK on the job was slow-going. Emmie began her first real day of work with enthusiasm. Perhaps also a touch of idealism. She was a soldier of history. Her mission: To return to the present those lives which had been lost to the past. She would be the voice that spoke for those who could no longer speak.

Lamb must have anticipated her eagerness. When she came downstairs that morning, he had a full Scottish breakfast waiting for her. She ploughed through it, enjoying—truly *enjoying*, imagine!—the haggis and blood pudding, and washed the lot down with three cups of coffee. When she got up to help with the washing up, he wouldn't hear of it.

"You go on. You've a long day of… whatever it is you do, ahead of you."

"Lamb, you're a doll." She gave him a one-armed, sideways squeeze. He hadn't been expecting the familiar gesture. Sputtering, he patted her hand awkwardly.

"Yes, well… you go on then."

Taking the stairs two at a time, Emmie barrelled into her career as an official curator.

By noon, she was ready to give up.

When she'd thought about how she would start the night before, she had decided the sitting room would be a good place to ease herself into the job. Old Cranberry (or so she'd taken to calling the curmudgeony earl in her head) had used this room until his death. It was one of the few rooms at Tullybrae which hadn't fallen prey to consolidation and storage; the general cramming of too many items into too-small spaces.

At her side were her four favourite items, highly specialized equipment for historical cataloguing: a yellow notepad, an easy-glide ballpoint pen, a digital camera, and a box of pre-threaded manila tags. Cataloguing was one thing she knew how to do inside and out, since it was what she did most often under the tutelage of Professor McCall. Each item would need to be meticulously described, with as many distinctive marks and identifiers as she could locate. The item's condition would also be recorded. It would then be photographed from multiple angles, assigned a number for future identification, and tagged.

But even the study quickly proved to be an overwhelming room. Everything, *everything*, was antique. The furnishings, the paintings, the rugs, the window treatments. Even the wallpaper. And although the room had the outward appearance of livability, there were mounds upon mounds of items stacked haphazardly within the hutch, the credenza, under the window seating, and inside a large ornamental chest in the far corner.

By lunchtime, Emmie hadn't evaluated even half the room, much less catalogue her finds and determine their historical significance and value.

At twelve-thirty, Lamb brought a tray into the sitting room. Hearing his short-stepped gait, Emmie looked up from where she sat, cross-legged, on the floor in front of the credenza. Arranged neatly on the tray, which the butler clutched with a death grip, was a watercress sandwich, four homemade shortbread cookies, a Granny Smith apple cut into slices, cubes of sharp cheddar cheese, and a tall, frosty glass of milk.

"Lamb, you sweet man. I said I usually skip lunch. You didn't need to do this."

Lamb bent, his knees creaking, and handed her the tray when she rose to meet him half-way. "I couldn't bear the thought of you going from dawn to dusk without eating. I hope I haven't included anything you don't like."

"I'm grateful, thank you. It all looks delicious. I love watercress."

"Do you? 'Tis an old-fashioned taste, I think. No' what the young people like to eat nowadays."

"In case you hadn't noticed by my line of work, old-fashioned is kinda my thing."

Lamb let out a huff that was almost a chuckle. "Fair enough."

That first day tired her more than she thought it would. Emmie was asleep less than a minute after her head touched the pillow. If the strange giggling and the tugging at the covers happened again, she was too far gone to notice. Every night thereafter she slept soundly as well. Whatever had disrupted her that first night must have been an anomaly. A product of her over-active imagination, stimulated by the atmosphere of the house.

Or so she tried to convince herself. But her historian's imagination, its fascination with the past, wouldn't be subdued for long. No sooner would she chastise herself than her mind would drift back to the idea that there were beings in the house whom she couldn't see. There were times, too, when she was alone that a spider web sensation would tickle along her spine. And though she knew she was being a little absurd, Emmie would find herself slowing down around corners, steeling herself against the possibility of coming face to face with a lurking spectre.

Nothing like that happened.

She asked Lamb about the ghosts one night at dinner. He wasn't much help.

"Old houses like this have had many lives come and go through its doors," he evaded. "It would no' be a far stretch to imagine that they've all left their mark on the place in one way or another."

"True enough. That's why I do what I do, I suppose." She forked a green bean and crunched it thoughtfully.

It was hardly the answer she'd been looking for, and he knew it. Emmie stared at Lamb. There was something he wasn't saying. He studied his plate like he would be tested on its contents, and chose his next pan-fried mushroom with deliberate care. She let the matter drop.

That night, before she crawled under the covers, she stood in front of the dresser, kissed her forefinger, and planted it on the glass over her mother's photo.

"Ghosts, Mom," she whispered to the smiling face. "I'm not sure if I'm frightened or not. You'll protect me, right?"

The face smiled back at her. That silent smile, frozen in time, meant different things at different times to Emmie. This time, she took it for reassurance.

As she became accustomed to life at Tullybrae, Emmie found that she was able to put the thoughts of spirits out of her mind most of the time. Her work kept her busy, and she enjoyed slipping into the routine of research.

There were three stages to the process of cataloguing. Once she'd written down as much as she could about an object by sight, and had taken photos, she then retreated to her laptop to see if she could identify her finds through reputable websites. Those items to which she could not assign a manufacturer and year, she tagged with the frustratingly simple, moniker *TU*: Temporarily Unidentified. Originally, Professor McCall had instructed her to use just a "U," but Emmie was never comfortable with the permanence it conveyed. Thus, she began adding the "T" early on in her career.

For these "TU" items, she could forward what details she had to the university archives at Edinburgh or Cambridge, which would do a trace on them—for a fee. But as yet, she had not taken this step. Emmie had not discussed it with Lady Rotherham. She had no doubt the lady would approve. But, as Lady Rotherham openly admitted, it was her husband who would be paying the fee, and he might not consider a positive identification worth the cost.

So, Emmie's "TU" pile grew.

Mid-week found her moving from the sitting room to the library. By then, her days had fallen into a comfortable rhythm. Mornings she would spend doing the grunt work of cataloguing, and afternoons she would spend researching. For this part of the job, she'd set up an office of sorts in a room which had once been the nursery.

Emmie liked this room the best. Being at the east corner of the house, its hexagonal shape was a result of the manor's turreted architecture. High, bright windows which faced both east and west flooded the room with light through most of the day. The children's items had been moved out and stored in the attic over a quarter of a century ago, Lamb informed her when she asked. In their place, the late earl's personal documents and records had been moved in. Brown, crumbling banker's boxes were stacked willy-nilly around the room. Some were so old that they threatened to collapse, which would send almost fifty years' worth of yellowing paper spilling out onto the threadbare carpet.

It was a simple matter to restack the boxes against a wall, only an hour's heavy lifting. Emmie wasn't too pleased that it had to be a window wall, but the walls on the inside of the house were unsuitable. One had a small, old-fashioned radiator which, like the one in her room, was still operational in the winter months. Beside that was the wall with the door, and the wall beside that was the fireplace wall.

By the time the weekend limped in, she was satisfied with the amount of work she'd accomplished, and was looking forward to a break.

Saturday morning dawned dim and foggy, but her mood was light enough to drive away the shadows.

"You look like you have some plans for the day," Lamb noted at the breakfast table.

Emmie nodded as she dunked a narrow strip of toast—a "soldier"—into her soft-boiled egg. "I'm thinking of driving into Aviemore today to do some errands. This is really good, by the way."

"Nothing I can help with?"

"Just dry-cleaning and some groceries. Nothing I can't take care of, myself. And I have a few things I want to pick up that I've run out of. Why—you wanna come?"

"Nay, you're all right," he answered. "But thank you all the same."

"Do you need anything while I'm out?"

He thought for a moment. "Well, as long as you're asking, I wouldn't mind a nice bottle of red wine. His lordship has a fine reserve in the cellar, but I don't feel right about taking from him."

"Oh, come on, Lamb. He's dead. He can't complain. Live a little."

His eyes crinkled in what was almost a grin. "Old habits die hard. Anyway, will you be out all day, do you reckon?"

She mopped up the last of her egg yolk with her remaining soldier and bit into it. "I should be back mid- to late-afternoon. I was thinking of finding a pub somewhere for lunch."

"Ah. Well, then you'll want the Aviemore Arms. On the High Street, just past Craig Na Gower Avenue. They do a nice steak and ale pie, they do. That is, if you like steak and ale pie. You might not, but I do."

"I love steak and ale pie. I'll check it out."

After clearing away the dishes, Emmie dashed out to her Panda. Soon, she was on the road, driving through thick, Highland mist, her headlights and her eyes peeled for stray sheep. She made it to Aviemore in a little over half an hour.

By mid-morning, the sky had cleared up, and the sun came out. It shimmered through the moist air, bestowing the quaint tourist town with an invigorating, dew-kissed feel. The Highland air was so fresh and so fragrant that Emmie found herself inhaling deeply every time she stepped out of a shop.

The locals were friendly, and customer-service was clearly a top priority. Each shop owner invited her in like she was an old friend. They spent time with her, explaining their products, and letting her try, feel, taste and smell them. At one store, a stout, middle-aged lady in a tartan vest took the time to explain to her all the different clan plaids that were represented on pure wool scarves, which were prominently displayed near the front window.

"This one here is Urquhart," she said, pulling one out and showing it to her with soft, short-fingered hands. "My clan."

"Matches your vest."

The woman beamed. "Aye, it does. And see here?" She fingered a small, gold pin anchored to the lapel. "Speak weil, mean weil, doe weil. The Urquhart motto."

Emmie's eyes travelled up the built-in cubbyholes with all the scarves stacked neatly by clan. "What about MacCombish? Is there a tartan for that name?"

"MacCombish, MacCombish." The lady tapped her chin with her pinkie finger, then scurried to the counter at the back of her store on fat, little legs. From beneath the cash register, she pulled a well-thumbed paperback book.

"MacCombish," she repeated to herself as she leafed through the pages. "Ah, here it is. Well, see now, MacCombish was under the protection of Clan Stuart. The Bonnie Prince himself. So they would have worn his colours."

The lady laid the open book on the counter, and pointed to the entry. Emmie leaned over, craning her neck slightly to read the blurb beneath the name.

"And here's the Stuart colours," the woman continued, flipping to a well-used page. In a full-page, glossy image was a replica of the red and black of Clan Stuart. "Is your name MacCombish, lass?"

Emmie hesitated, drawing a finger over the colourful plaid photo. "Yes... well, no, actually. It's Tunstall. But it was MacCombish once."

"Oh." The lady furrowed her brow. "Married?"

"I was adopted when I was six, and my adoptive parents had my last name legally changed to theirs. But MacCombish was my mother's name."

"I see. Well, it is always good to know something about a person's family history."

"And now I do."

The woman nodded proudly. "Aye. Now you do."

By the time Emmie left the shop, she had a bag of hand-knit lamb's wool mittens, a wool scarf in the Stuart colours, a leather bookmark with the Stuart motto embossed in gold Gaelic script, and a tin of organic heather balm.

At one in the afternoon, she took Lamb's advice and headed over to the Aviemore Arms for a late lunch. It was a cozy little pub, the décor not dissimilar to any of the pubs back home in Corner Brook. But the creaking, wide-planked floors, the smoke-stained beams, and the distinct scent of centuries-old wood gave the place an authenticity that no New World establishment could fabricate.

When the barman came to take her order, she asked for the steak and ale pie.

It was delicious, just like Lamb said. The meat was tender, and the gravy thick, almost buttery. On the suggestion of the barman (a good-looking man, though a little old for her taste, in his mid-forties, maybe), she paired it with a nice, dark half pint of a locally brewed stout.

As she sat by the open window overlooking the leisurely bustle of the high street, Emmie savoured her meal and enjoyed some more of the book she'd brought along. She felt at peace. Happy. In the whole of her life she never felt like she belonged anywhere. From what she remembered of her childhood before the Tunstalls, she and her mother moved around a lot.

After the Tunstalls, she felt like an outsider. To be fair to them, they provided her with much-needed stability, and all the love and support they had to give. But she never really felt like she was "one of them." She was always curious if her brother, Chase, felt the same way, too. He'd been adopted by the Tunstalls also, from a First Nations reserve in the Yukon. She never asked.

The happiness, though. It was being here in Scotland, being at Tullybrae... it just felt right. Like whatever watered-down Scottish heritage that had made it into her blood was singing now that it had been called home.

She laughed quietly to herself. A historian's fancy.

"Something funny, love?" The barman had come over to see if she wanted anything else.

"Oh, no. Just thinking to myself."

"Pie was okay?"

"Yes, thank you. It was delicious. Actually, a friend recommended it to me."

"Oh, aye? And who might your friend be? I know all the regulars."

"Harold Lamb. Up at Tullybrae House."

"Ah, yes. Good old Harold." The man nodded, his full head of salt-and-pepper hair catching the afternoon light from the window. "He's a top bloke, he is. Been around forever, it seems. And the stout, how'd that go down for you? Not too strong, I hope."

"It's delicious. Stout's my beer, actually—when I drink beer, that is."

"Of course it is. It's my job to read the punters, guess what their flavour is. I saw you, and I said to myself, 'Now that lass likes a dark pint. She's got a bit of the Celt in her, she does.'"

"Are you reading my mind? I was just thinking something like that." She clapped her hands together lightly beneath her chin.

The barman winked flirtatiously. "That's my secret, love. I'll take this plate away for you, then."

Emmie watched him go, his lithe, trim body gliding effortlessly between the close-packed tables. She smiled a secret, private smile. Too bad she wasn't looking for a relationship just now.

When she returned to Tullybrae late in the afternoon, the aroma of roasting meat greeted her like a warm hug. Still clutching her shopping bags, she followed the scent down to the kitchen. There, she discovered an elaborately set table, with fresh-cut, late-bloom toad lilies from Tullybrae's back garden. Lamb stood at the oven in one of his serviceable aprons, where he had a roast beef dinner with all the trimmings going.

"Lamb," she chastised. "It's still my week to make dinner."

He eased open the stove door and removed a pan with a roast sirloin tip in it. "T'was no bother. It's been far too long since I've had someone to have a proper roast beef supper with."

Aw, the old darling.

"When there were more servants in the house, Mother used to have Cook do a roast for the staff on Saturday nights," he continued. "Lord Cranbury, you see, he wanted his roast with the family on Sunday."

"I'm flattered." She looked around the kitchen which, in contrast to Lamb's intensive labour, was still immaculate. "Is there anything I can help with?"

"If you wouldn't mind taking the puddings out of the muffin tins, that would be kind."

The puddings, of the Yorkshire variety, were a sunny yellow in the centre, and golden brown around the edges. She breathed deeply the sweet steam that fanned out when she pulled each one from its tin. It was heavenly.

"I haven't had much Yorkshire pudding, but I remember liking it the once or twice I did have it."

"I do hope so. These are from Mother's recipe."

"Another famous Mrs. Lamb recipe? You'll have to show me some of them sometime."

"Er, well, I don't have them written down. They're... they're all in my head, you see."

"Didn't you say you had a cook?"

"Oh, that was in the very old days. Back then, Mother was the head housekeeper, and there was a separate cook. Mrs. MacGuffy was her name. She and Mother got on famously. Mrs. MacGuffy passed in 'sixty-four. By that time, the girls—that is, Lady Camille and Lady Anne-Marie—they had married and moved away. After that, his lordship saw no reason to employ a new cook."

"I hope your mother got a raise for taking on the extra work."

Lamb shrugged. "Well, Mother's no' one to complain. She does love Tullybrae so. Do you have the bottle of red?"

Emmie reached into the tote hanging from her bent arm. "So this is why you wanted it, you sly devil."

Stuffed full of roast beef, mashed potatoes, two Yorkshire puddings, and the best apple crumble she'd ever tasted, Emmie retreated to the third floor. Tonight would be an early night, preceded by a nice, long soak and more of her book. Her head was warm with the wine, just enough to make her feel exceedingly content, yet not so much that she would feel poorly in the morning.

It was as she was lumbering up the servants' stairs, watching thin patches of clouds brush across the moon through the window, that a niggling thought pricked her brain. Something Lamb had said.

He said his mother does love Tullybrae. *Does*—present tense.

The thought brought her to a halt, one foot suspended in the air to take the next step. Lady Rotherham said the house was haunted, and Lamb said his mother loves Tullybrae.

Could it be...?

"Oh, don't be silly," she chided. Lady Rotherham clearly said there were two ghosts: the sixth Countess of Cranbury, and the young girl Clara. No mention of any others, and certainly not of Lamb's mother.

Fun to think about, though.

In her room, Emmie changed out of her clothes. Even for a day out she'd made the effort to dress up. Her favourite slim-cut, dark denim jeans were folded neatly and put back in their drawer. Her black ballerina flats were lined up precisely beneath her bed, and her white tunic-style shirt went into the armoire on its hanger. The delicate gold bracelet and her teardrop silver earrings came off piece by piece and were returned to their designated places in her jewellery box.

It was a ritual she never missed—putting each item back where it belonged. It was like a book end. She started the day in a state of order, and she finished it that way.

Swaddled in her plush bathrobe, with her gentle curls twisted into a clip, Emmie padded down the hall to the bathroom, with a scented candle and a box of matches in one hand, a jar of bath salts in the other, and her book tucked beneath her arm.

She turned the taps onto full blast, sending up a rich steam. Once her candle was lit and her salts liberally sprinkled into the churning water, Emmie perched on the edge of the tub, untied her robe and lowered the collar over her shoulders. For long moments she sat there, skimming her fingers over the rising surface of the water. The bath salts effervesced at the bottom of the tub, filling the room with the pleasing scent of vanilla, which mingled with the sandalwood from the candle. Her book lay atop the sink counter, but now that she was here, she didn't much feel like reading.

When the bath was full, she twisted the knobs shut, hung her robe on the hook on the wall, and stepped into the tub. The water caressed her bare skin. She sank completely beneath the surface, held her breath a few counts, then rose languorously back up. Laying her head on the rim, she closed her eyes and enjoyed the silence, the relaxation, and the scents.

With no windows, the air in the bathroom was still. The candle sent up a steady, strong flame, infusing the room with a warming glow. No draft disturbed her tranquility here, not like in the rest of the servants' wing, where it whistled and whined and grated on her nerves at times. The scents of vanilla and sandalwood thickened the air, wrapping her like a lover's embrace.

Better than a lover's embrace. It offered comfort without wanting something in return. Emmie let herself slip into a deep state of contentment.

She sighed, her voice low and resonant.

Then another sigh, one that lingered on her lips.

And then another sigh which turned into the stirrings of a melody.

One note whispered after another, unbidden, uncalculated. What the melody was, or from where inside her it came, she did not know. But Emmie didn't mind that. The melody seemed to rise up from some hidden place, like a forgotten memory. Her voice trilled over the notes, creating a forlorn, pensive tune.

She closed her eyes, and gave herself over to it.

When the last note left her throat, she opened her eyes again, and looked around the room as if she'd woken from a dream. A heavy scent of rose hung in the air, the sandalwood and the vanilla of her candle and salts overpowered by the phantom perfume.

In the corner, the candle flickered... though there was no draft.

Emmie heard herself speak. "Countess?"

The candle flickered in answer.

The countess was here. In this room. Watching her. Emmie should have been frightened. It did occur to her that she would be frightened if she'd met a ghost under any other circumstances. But now, here, like this... she wasn't.

In fact, she was glad to have met the countess. It felt like an introduction, an intimate first encounter.

Like she had found a secret friend.

It was nice to have a friend.

FIVE

AN ARCHAEOLOGICAL CREW from the University of Edinburgh had been contracted by Stannisfield Films for the episode of Digging Scotland that would feature Tullybrae House. The day they arrived was the first time Emmie ever encountered the presence of the unknown Highlander.

Not that she knew, at the time, who or what it was she encountered. She knew only that it felt nothing like the countess. And from what Lady Rotherham described, the little girl Clara was mischievous.

This presence, this energy... it certainly didn't feel mischievous.

That Monday morning Emmie spent an extra half hour getting ready. She chose her outfit, then re-chose it, then re-chose it again. Nothing was right. The ballerina flats were too cutesy. The booties were too cutting-edge. And the sensible nude pumps—well, they were positively matronly when paired with the oversized, retro-style blazer that had been meant to go with the booties. In the end, she settled on a pair of tight-fitting tan slacks, which she tucked into her knee-high riding boots and topped with a soft, white cable-knit sweater. The ensemble made her feel unaccountably underdressed, a state of being which she attempted to offset with her hair.

When she was certain that every wave and curl was exactly where she wanted it, that her outfit was as right as it was going to be, and that her makeup was skillfully invisible, Emmie left the sanctuary of the third floor to face the men and women of Stannisfield Films.

She made it as far as the study, where she spent the rest of the morning hiding like a hermit.

It was there that Lady Rotherham found her, head buried in a chest of old papers, just as the trucks pulled off the main road and onto Tullybrae's gravel drive.

"There you are," she exclaimed breathlessly. "What are you doing in here? Come out and meet them. They're *here*."

"Yeah, I... yes. In a minute. Maybe."

Lady Rotherham tisked. She strode into the room and examined the papers from over Emmie's shoulder. "God, almighty! That's my tenth form social studies paper. Throw it away, there's no value in that."

"Of course there is," Emmie insisted, placing a manicured hand protectively over the stapled, yellowing assignment. "Maybe not now, but seal it up in a dry place, leave it for fifty or a hundred years, and scholars are going to be really interested in this."

"If it's going to be around in a hundred years, then you can leave it alone for five minutes and come and meet Dr. Iain Northcott. Oh, he's such a handsome young chap, I could just eat him up!"

"I promise, I'll come out in just a minute. Five minutes," she repeated when the lady gave her a stern look.

"All right. Five minutes, and if you're not out there, I'm coming back to drag you out myself."

Lady Rotherham trotted off like an over-excited puppy. She wouldn't give Emmie a second thought once she was in the presence of the famous Dr. Iain Northcott. Emmie was counting on it.

She left the documents in an orderly pile on the floor, and drifted to the oriel windows to watch the spectacle outside.

Lady Rotherham made an odd picture out there. Perfect, but not. Wrong in her perfection. Emmie chewed her lip, considering. The lady's perfume still hung heavy in the room. It was a cloying scent to begin with, and she'd applied it far too liberally. Her shock of red hair had been curled at the ends so that it swooped back in a hairspray-stiff dovetail at the base of her neck, from which hung an elongated chain of large, irregularly shaped brass pendants. That one, bold item of jewellery was her statement piece, tastefully paired with a demure coral pantsuit which was perfectly tailored to her trim figure. She accentuated that figure with perfect posture. Borne of a lifetime of practice, no doubt. A pair of coral peep-toe slingbacks completed the ensemble.

Lady Rotherham was well put-together. A little too well. Constructed might be a better word for it. The whole effect came across as an older woman who was trying too hard.

Emmie wondered if *she* gave that impression to anyone. If people thought she tried too hard. Strange that the thought should occur to her now, when it never had before. Perhaps because she'd never seen the same kind of effort on another person until now.

Good God, Emmie hoped she didn't look *constructed*.

Next to Lady Rotherham, husband Oliver, Lord Rotherham, looked as though he couldn't care less who was coming to Tullybrae. Tall and lean, he played the quintessential Englishman in his lightweight sport coat, tan slacks and tweed Gatsby cap.

Emmie hadn't officially met the Earl of Rotherham yet. Not that she was especially eager to meet him or anything.

"He couldn't give a fiddler's fart what I'm doing with the house," Lady Rotherham had declared earlier. "He's not so rude under better circumstances. I'll have to convince him to introduce himself to you at some point."

Emmie had smiled appreciatively. Inside, *she* couldn't give a fiddler's fart if the Earl of Rotherham introduced himself or not.

Outside, the white, unmarked vans came to a halt, and the crew hopped out. With no more than a nod to the noble family, they set to work unloading, pulling out sound boards, microphones, lights, stands, and electrical cables.

When Dr. Iain Northcott jumped down from the passenger side of the last van, Lady Rotherham danced forward to meet him. Clad in faded jeans, well-worn hiking boots and a dark blue hoodie, the archaeologist-turned-television-personality looked washed out next to his hosts. Emmie wondered if the lady was disappointed by this real-life version of the man. If she was, she hid it well behind a radiant, zoom-whitened smile.

Dr. Iain Northcott looked younger than his forty-odd years. He smiled a boyish smile at Lady Rotherham, and ruffled a hand through his shaggy hair. As they conversed, Lady Rotherham gave the archaeologist an animated overview of the house. Her arms swept wide, her head turned in this direction and that, and she beamed that star-struck flash of teeth so intently, she looked a bit like a snarling dog. Dr. Northcott scanned the horizon, nodding with polite interest—feigned, probably—at every small detail the lady had to give.

"Careful over there," the earl shouted to one of the cameramen who had ventured away from his comrades. His voice came muffled to Emmie's ears through the glass.

It was all so unnervingly ridiculous. She scowled and folded her arms across her chest. There was Lady Rotherham, flirting with Iain Northcott, Lord Rotherham barking orders lest a blade of grass be trampled on land that he didn't even legally own, and these foreigners, these *English bastards*, romping over Scottish soil as if they owned it...

Emmie stiffened.

Where in the hell had *that* come from?

As she searched her brain, dredging its depths for the source of that unprecedented flood of animosity, a soft, almost undetectable draft tickled her right side. The hairs on her arm stood up, and a shiver trilled down her spine.

Someone else was in the room with her.

Fear locked her body. Her heart picked up to a gallop. Her skin prickled all along the right side of her face, her neck, her arm, her waist, and right down to the outer edge of her foot.

There was definitely someone there. It was male.

And it was angry.

That anger infiltrated Emmie's brain, pulled at her thoughts. Changed them.

Her mind, her precious mind, the one thing that belonged to her and her alone... had been violated.

Then in a single breath, it was gone. *He* was gone. She was alone again.

Her fingers twitched, she shifted her weight. Her breathing hitched as the magnitude of what had happened sank in.

The study closed in around her, stifling and stale. Desperate to escape, she hastened out of the room, and up the main staircase to the servants' passage on the second floor. The painted eyes of Tullybrae's nobility followed her, watching silently from their gilt frames.

In her room, she sat on the edge of the bed and wrapped her arms around herself. A chill which had nothing to do with the cold coursed through her body. She shivered, and rocked herself. The bed creaked rhythmically as she pressed the balls of her feet into the floorboards again and again.

Lady Rotherham had made the ghosts of Tullybrae House sound like old friends. And the countess (if in fact it had been the countess Emmie encountered that night) had been warm, friendly, a comfort.

This... this thing, this person in the study—it was not friendly.

For the first time since coming to Tullybrae, Emmie felt threatened.

SIX

EMMIE NEVER TOLD Lamb what happened. She stayed in her bedroom until the crew from Stannisfield Films left the property. When the old butler called up the stairs to let her know that dinner was ready, she feigned a headache and called back that she was going to bed early.

Not long after, he was at her door with a tray. Homemade beef stew and a slice of rye bread with margarine.

Emmie was lying on top of her covers, with her back to the door. The only light in the room was from her bedside lamp. She turned her head when Lamb approached.

"Are you sure it's just a headache?" he inquired. "You look pale."

Emmie shoved herself into a sitting position and slumped against the brass rail headboard. "I feel guilty now. If I'd have known you were going to bring something to me, I would have come down."

"Of course I was going to bring something to you. I couldn't let you waste away."

"I don't need you wearing yourself out waiting on me."

Lamb moved slowly into the room, and placed the tray on the night stand. "It was no trouble, really."

"Yeah, sure. Those stairs with your old knees?"

"Nonsense. Is there anything else I can get for you? A paracetamol perhaps?"

"No, but thanks. I took one already," she lied.

"All right, then. I'll leave you be. Good night, dear."

"G'night, Lamb. Thanks."

He left, casting a troubled glance over his shoulder before he disappeared down the hallway.

Later that evening he stood at the kitchen counter, wrist-deep in bread dough for next day's breakfast.

"I don't like it," he murmured. "I don't like it one bit. He shouldn't have done it."

"Oh, leave him be," sighed Mrs. Lamb, who hovered at his right shoulder.

"What right does he have to frighten her like that? What possible *reason* could he have?"

"He didn't mean to. He didn't even know she was there. Don't be so hard on him— No, no, you're doing it wrong. *Fold* the dough, don't squish it."

"I *am* folding it, Mother."

"You're no'. You're squeezing it to pieces. Oh, you are a useless lad."

Lamb turned sharply to the empty air. "If you think you can do better, then by all means."

"Don't get smart," Mrs. Lamb clucked. "Anyway, he didn't mean to frighten her. He's frightened, himself. The young man hasn't quite accepted his death, you know. Poor thing's still convinced he shouldn't have died."

"What good does that do, to be stewing over something he cannot change?"

There was a sharp tug at Lamb's ear; he swatted ineffectually.

"Look at you, all high and mighty," Mrs. Lamb admonished. "Wait until you step over onto *our* side of the line. You may just start to think a bit differently."

Lamb went back to his kneading. "I still don't like it. You saw the state of her. He frightened her something terrible."

Mrs. Lamb drifted to his other side. "He did do that, aye. Perhaps I should keep an eye on her tonight."

"I reckon it would be good if you did." Lamb shaped the dough and pressed it into the waiting pan on the counter top. Once it was the right shape, he covered the dough with a damp cloth, and popped it into the refrigerator to rise slowly overnight.

"I've been meaning to check in on her at night anyway," Mrs. Lamb continued. "That Clara's been getting curious again."

"I thought you told her to stop bothering her. I won't have her doing what she did that first night, pulling the covers off and disturbing her sleep."

"I did tell her," Mrs. Lamb insisted. "As much as you can tell a five-year-old anything. You know how they are. Tell them something one day, and the next they've completely forgotten about it. You were far worse when you were that age, you know."

Lamb harrumphed. "Well, tell her again. That poor girl needs her sleep, needs to recover from what happened today."

"I'll go up as soon as I'm sure that dough's rising right. I have my doubts, what with the way you were squishing it to pieces."

Lamb rolled his eyes. "Yes, Mother."

THE FIRST FEW days of the dig were noisy and chaotic. The primary archaeology crew were the ones doing the grunt work. Dr. Iain Northcott came out only twice more after his first visit, and stayed only long enough to make a few on-camera appearances. It would give the impression that he was there in the fields, working alongside his colleagues for the benefit of the show.

On his third visit, he was close enough to the open nursery window that Emmie could hear what he was saying for the cameras.

"It's day three of our dig, and we're making substantial progress. The weather's been cooperating so far. The rain's held off, so we've been thanking our lucky stars that we have dry conditions to dig in."

"We?" Emmie muttered from two stories up.

For the initial stage of the dig, a backhoe was brought in. The job of the operator was to scrape up the top soil, one thin layer at a time, which covered the direct areas where the ground-penetrating radar had picked up disturbances. There was a cluster of these areas, which Lady Rotherham had explained were thought to be the outbuildings. A more distant disturbance, farther east of there, was thought to be the burial site for the murder (assuming, of course, that's what it was).

Normally, this kind of activity excited Emmie. In her fourth year of university, one of her undergraduate professors had taken her class to a dig site at Fort Henry in Kingston, Ontario. She'd been fascinated by the process, by the possibilities that these men and women were helping to uncover. They hadn't actually uncovered anything while her class was visiting, but still, the idea that they *might* find something was what captivated her imagination.

Now, though, the work going on outside made her feel uneasy, like it wasn't right.

Like whatever was buried there, out in those fields, should remain buried.

She stayed inside those first few days, avoiding the crew. It was easy, since they didn't come inside. They had their tent set up close to where they were digging, with a generator rigged to it. Inside the tent the excavators had a hot plate to boil water for tea, and their laptops, paperwork, and other technical equipment. They even had a port-o-potty onsite, so they weren't traipsing in and out of the manor house all day.

Thank goodness for small mercies.

Emmie's cataloguing and research kept her occupied, and by this time she was beginning to feel like she was making progress. She used her progress as a justification for why she needed to stay indoors, rather than go out and meet the dig crew—she was just too busy. She knew Lamb went out, though. With clockwork precision, he brought biscuits and tea to the excavators every morning at ten, and again at three in the afternoon.

They knew she was in the house, hiding from them. Lamb mentioned it at every meal.

"They're eager to meet you, you know."

"I know, I will. Soon."

She couldn't avoid going out forever, though. Emmie Tunstall may be a bit of a wallflower, but she was no hermit. Wherever this aversion to the dig came from, whatever had sparked it… it was simply all in her mind. It had to be.

This wasn't like her.

So she went.

It was just before noon. She finished up with a collection of random buttons which she'd found buried in a cardboard box in one of the main bedrooms (several of which buttons she'd traced to the officers' uniforms of the German Imperial Navy of the late eighteen hundreds), closed her laptop, and went outside.

At first, she stood on the edge of the driveway, one hand hugging her middle and the other shading her eyes. Above, the clouds chased each other across the sky, intermittently blocking out the sun, like giant search lights sweeping over the hills. A light breeze ruffled the sleeves and the hem of her sheer, cream-coloured blouse.

They looked peaceful out there, the crew, digging quietly within the perimeters of the grid they'd marked off with yellow nylon string and pegs. Doing what they loved to do in contented silence. Emmie didn't doubt that this was how she looked to others when she was knee-deep in cataloguing and tagging. There was a comfort in doing these kinds of repetitive tasks. She recognized that same comfort in the excavators working in the field now.

She hadn't been there long before one of the archaeological crew spotted her. It was a young woman, tall and svelte. Her light brown hair was pulled back into a ponytail, which was tucked through the snaps of a pastel blue baseball cap. A neon yellow reflective vest hung from lean, strong shoulders. Denim shorts, cut off just above the knee, were dirty from days of digging in the Scottish soil.

She waved and stood. Hopping up out of her shallow trench, she loped towards Emmie in a graceful stride.

"Are you Emmie?" she asked when she was close enough. She spoke with a slight accent. German, maybe? Or Swedish?

"Yeah, hi." Emmie extended her hand. The woman removed one of the heavy-duty work gloves she was wearing, and gave Emmie's hand a firm shake.

"Hello, I'm Famke. Famke Bomgaars. Mr. Lamb has mentioned you. And also Lady Rother-ham—am I saying that right? Rother-ham?"

"Rother-um" Emmie corrected. "Do you mind me asking what your accent is?"

"It's Dutch."

Emmie nodded appreciatively. "Far from home, then."

"As are you, I understand. Canada, is it?"

"Born and raised."

"And you are curator here?"

Emmie tipped her head back and forth. "Er ... that's the official title. There's so much stuff here, though, and none of it is catalogued, so mostly I'm doing a lot of junior stuff that would already have been done before a curator would typically be brought on board."

"Oh. I'm sorry to hear that."

"No, no. Don't get me wrong, I'm okay with it. I knew what I was getting into before I came out here. It's good experience."

"Yes, I suppose it would be," Famke agreed. "I've been in a similar position myself."

The two women smiled at each other, slightly awkward in their new acquaintanceship.

"Would you like to come and see what we're doing?" Famke asked.

"Sure, I'd love to. If you don't mind, that is."

"Of course not." Famke motioned with her head, then set off across the field.

Emmie trailed behind, stepping carefully over the nylon string and into the grid. There had been a rain last night, and the ground was spongy beneath her feet. Her low-heeled leather booties weren't the best footwear for this kind of terrain, even when it was dry. She was relieved when she made it out to the dig site without overturning an ankle.

"Here is where I'm working." Famke pointed to her trench. "I've not yet found anything."

"Do you think you will? Find something here, I mean?" Emmie peered into the trench.

"I hope so. I think I will. Some of the others have found a few things already. Nothing very exciting, of course. Pottery shards and domestic waste, mostly."

"Domestic waste is exciting," Emmie argued amicably. "Evidence of lives lived long ago and all that."

Famke beamed. "I think so, too. Usually I'm the only one."

VERONICA BALE

She brought Emmie farther into the field where the rest of the team was working. A young woman and a late-middle-aged man were in the trench closest to Famke. Both were equally dirty, and both were blissfully content scraping away layer after layer of compacted soil.

"Sophie, Ewan. Emmie Tunstall has come out to see us."

The man looked up from beneath a khaki bush hat to reveal a face covered with a full, brown beard. "Ah, yes. The elusive Emmie Tunstall" he noted in a Northern English accent. "We almost came to bets on whether or not you actually existed."

Emmie glanced sheepishly to Famke. "Oh. I… Sorry, I didn't mean to be rude, I—"

"You're awright. I'm just teasing, love. Ewan Brown." He extended his dirt-caked glove.

"Emmie." She smiled and shook his hand.

The girl next to him clucked her tongue. "C'mon now, Ewan. Look at the state of you. You can at least take off your dirty glove." She removed her own glove, and extended a short-fingered hand with chewed nails. "Sophie Miner," she said in a thick, cockney accent. "Pleased to meet you."

"It's all right. I don't mind." She shook Sophie's hand as well. "I've been hearing that backhoe for a few days now. It's nice to have the quiet back."

"I'll bet," Sophie acknowledged.

"So how do you know when to stop with the backhoe and start on the manual excavation?"

Ewan's eyes lit up. "That's a good question. You see here?" His hand swept over the far wall of the trench. "This ridge of discoloured soil? That's usually our cue to switch gears and start with the more delicate hand work."

"Don't ask him too many questions, you'll be here all day," Sophie warned.

"I'll behave," Ewan promised. "You should come out to see us more often."

Emmie surveyed the field. "Yeah, I don't know about that. I'm kind of avoiding the cameras."

"They don't come out too often," Famke explained. "And they call before they come out anyway, so you won't be caught by surprise if you are here and they do show up."

"And besides, you need to sign a waiver before they'll use any footage of you," Sophie added. "That Rotherham lady was quick to sign, wasn't she?"

Ewan huffed. "Thought she'd scratch right through the paper, she was so chuffed."

"She's a right piece of work, she is."

"Soph," Ewan chastised.

44

Sophie ignored him. "I mean, really. Did you see her prancing about with Iain, flirting and laughing? I swear, she couldn't get enough of us when he was here, and now that he's gone, we haven't had even a whiff of her."

"She's…" Emmie pursed her lips, searching for the word, "unique."

"That's one way of putting it," Famke agreed. "I think she's nice. Flaky, but nice."

"She's awright," Sophie admitted reluctantly.

Their conversation was interrupted when the last two members of the crew came bounding over. Both were young men, in their late twenties, Emmie guessed. She smiled hesitantly as they approached, waiting politely for an introduction.

"Who've we got here, then?" asked one of the young men in the same cockney accent as Sophie.

Famke sighed. "Behave yourself Adam. This is Emmie Tunstall. Emmie, this is Adam Flett and Dean Walker."

"Cor, if I'da known you were hiding in there, I woulda found a reason to check the place out sooner," Adam guffawed.

"For the love of shite, man, you have a girlfriend," Sophie complained.

Adam fixed her with a charming grin. "Only fun, love. Only fun. You're not offended, are you?"

Emmie shrugged dismissively.

"See, Soph? She's a good'un."

"Well then, move over and let the man who doesn't have a girlfriend have a chance." The one called Dean shoved Adam out of the way, and offered Emmie his hand. "Dean Walker."

Emmie took his hand. "American?"

"Texas, born and raised, ma'am." He winked.

Famke and Sophie rolled their eyes.

"Laying it on a little thick there, aren't you, Deano?"

"Why you gotta call me out like that, Soph? You can never lay it on too thick, you know that."

"And on that note, why don't you go put on some cologne," Adam put in. "You reek, man."

Dean swung a toned arm around Adam's neck, and pulled his head down for a good, firm knuckle rub.

Their boyish, over-eager banter was infectious. Emmie found herself laughing along with the others while Adam and Dean rough-housed playfully.

"I'm Emmie Tunstall," she offered, when they were finished and standing upright again. "I'm curator here at Tullybrae."

"Oh aye, we know," Adam nodded. "We were wondering when you were going to come out and see us. We were starting to think we'd frightened you away, or summut. I know we're dirty now, but we clean up good, love. I promise."

"I'm sure you do. Anyway, I don't want to keep you guys from your work. I just came out to say a quick hello."

"You can keep me all you want, love. I don't mind."

"Oh would you shut *up*, Adam." Sophie chucked her spade at him. He dodged it easily.

"Ah, I'm only teasing. You don't mind, right?"

"In small doses, no," she relented. "I'll let you guys get back to it. See you soon."

She started to turn but Famke called to her. "Emmie, what are you doing this evening?"

"The usual, dinner with Lamb. Why?"

"We're all going to have supper at the pub in the village. You know, being Friday and all. Would you like to join us?"

Emmie's hesitated. Her first inclination was to say no, to go back to hiding now that she'd gotten the introductions out of the way. But the thought of spending time out with people closer to her own age (with the exception of Ewan, who was likely closing in on sixty) was suddenly appealing.

"Um… yeah, sure. That sounds good. Thanks."

"Great. So seven o'clock, then, at The Grigg?"

"Where's The Grigg?"

"Just up the road that way a bit." Famke pointed in the direction of the road. "Turn right at the end of the driveway, and go straight for about ten minutes. You can't miss it."

Emmie nodded. "Ok. I'll see you there."

SEVEN

T HE FIRST THING Emmie did when she got back inside was find Lamb. Going out with the dig crew meant she'd be skipping out on their dinner routine for the first time since she'd been here, and she wanted to make sure it was okay with him.

She was sincerely coming to enjoy their quiet meals together.

"I can cancel if you don't want me to go," she added once she told him.

Lamb's bushy white brows drew sharply together. "Don't you dare. I'll not lie, I've grown fond of your company in this short time, my dear. But I won't stand in the way of your night out. You young people need time to let loose every now and then."

Emmie was touched. "Aww, that's the first time you said you enjoy my company."

He gave her a bashful glance. "I would have thought it was obvious."

"You big softie." She pulled him in for a quick hug. He hadn't expected it, and his arms bent stiffly at the elbows, not embracing her but not resisting. His wrinkled face was notably pink when she stepped back.

"Okay, then I'll go. But we're still on for roast beef tomorrow, right?"

"That we are."

At five o'clock, Emmie retreated to the third floor to shower and change. Even her 'going out to a pub' outfit was mindfully selected. A casual plaid fitted shirt, slim-cut denim jeans, and clean-as-a-whistle Ugg boots made the perfect statement. Casual, but composed. After a final primp in the mirror to make sure her hair was still secured in a purposely messy top knot, she transferred her personal effects to a canvas satchel-style purse, and was off.

She took the main staircase from the second floor, traipsing past the portraits of Tullybrae's dead. Perhaps she was just imagining it, but she

47

thought their eyes held a measure of approval. Like they were pleased for her that she was getting out for a night. In fact, the entire house was intangibly lighter, even though the sun was starting to set and Lamb hadn't yet turned on any of the corridor lights.

She climbed into her Fiat Panda, and made the short journey into the village. Famke was right. Emmie couldn't miss The Grigg if she tried—it was the only pub in sight. The Grigg was a one-story building with a Tudor-style front, and a chalk-board sign on the curb outside announcing the night's specials.

She parked on the street across from the establishment, climbed out of her car, and smoothed the wrinkles from her shirt. The night was crisp, but not unpleasant. Somewhere in the vicinity, someone was burning a wood fire. She pulled in a deep breath, savouring the smoky fragrance. The same sense of contentment she'd felt on her Saturday off in Aviemore came over her again.

"I could definitely get used to living here," she whispered to the night.

Inside, the air was thick with cigarette smoke. Wooden benches with high backs and long tables lined the walls of the lower seating area, which was reduced to half its size to accommodate a live band. It was more crowded than Emmie expected for a remote village pub, and the people who were there looked like they came out specifically for the music. The band was good, an older group of gentlemen playing traditional Scottish tunes. The audience nodded their heads and tapped their feet along with the familiar melodies.

Two shallow steps, located about halfway into the building, led to a raised seating area at the back with individual tables and chairs. At the far corner, next to a narrow, stained-glass window, were the excavators from the University of Edinburgh.

"There she is," Adam called happily. He flung his arms into the air like he was signaling a touchdown.

The others turned expectantly. Pints of ale in various hues occupied the surface of their table.

"Hope you don't mind," Sophie said, flicking a finger at her pint glass. "We got here a bit early."

"Of course, no worries." Emmie took the empty seat next to Famke at the end of the table. She glanced back over her shoulder to the bartender. He was as thorough a Highlander as one could want, with ruddy, weathered cheeks and a mane of shaggy, graying hair. Catching her eye, the man acknowledged her with a tip of his chin, then sent one of his three waitresses over.

"You eating, too, love?" inquired the middle-aged woman, pre-emptively handing Emmie a laminated, four-paged menu. She had bleach blonde, spiky hair, a tight, black tee-shirt, and the look of someone who was perpetually tired.

"Thanks." Emmie took the proffered menu. "I'll have a pint of Kilkenny, please."

The waitress gave a listless nod and left.

"Kilkenny," Dean noted approvingly.

"I had you down as a cider drinker," Sophie put in.

Emmie tilted her head. "Cider's okay. But I like the strong stuff better."

"I'm with you," Famke agreed. She lifted her pint of stout in salute.

Ewan snorted. "The only Dutch woman in existence who doesn't like Dutch beer."

"So tell us," Dean said, leaning forward. "What's it like working with that Lady Rotherham?"

"We already had this conversation," Ewan answered, swallowing the last of his pint. "I'll have another," he told the waitress, who had come to deliver Emmie's Kilkenny.

"I didn't hear this story," Dean protested. "So? Lady Rotherham?"

Emmie took a sip of the thick, creamy red ale. "She's... enthusiastic."

"Cor," Adam exclaimed. "She'd barely shook my hand before she was off, scampering about like a dog being let out of the house. Totally dismissed me, she did. I was like, 'Eh, careful lady. Don't wanna go pissing me off, or I might just cut your water line while I'm digging in your yard.'"

Sophie scoffed. "Give over, man. You couldn't cut through chicken wire with those bony arms of yours."

"She's really not that bad," Emmie insisted. "Just excitable."

"My nephew's excitable. Wees himself when he gets worked up."

Emmie laughed at Adam's quip despite herself. "I think her plans for the house are different than the late Lord Cranbury's. She's eager to get started on it all, now that she's free to do what she wants with the place."

"Cranberry?" Famke asked, confused.

"Cran-*bury*. I know, I thought she was saying 'Cranberry' when I talked to her on the phone, too."

Adam took a long swallow of his Tennent's. I say 'Cranberry' anyway. I want to see if she's paying attention. She never is."

"Just don't say it to Lamb. He caught it when I first met him. He may look old, but he's sharp as a tack."

"Oh, he's a sweetheart," Sophie declared. "I like that man. Makes the best shortbread bickies, he does."

Emmie smiled tenderly. "Yes, he is a sweetheart."

The waitress came back to take their orders. Emmie hadn't yet looked through the menu. While the others were ordering, she opened the laminated pages and quickly scanned her choices. They all looked like possibilities, but in the end, Famke's order piqued her interest.

"I'll have the Thai curried beef, too, please," she told the waitress when it was her turn. "Can I get my rice on the side, though?"

The waitress bobbed her platinum head as she scribbled on her notepad. Then she collected the menus and returned to the kitchen. Ewan's eyes followed her retreating backside.

"Ewan, you dirty old man." Sophie, who was sitting next to him, shoved him lightly in the arm.

Ewan didn't miss a beat. "I am not old."

Emmie listened to their easy banter appreciatively. Together, this group had found the kind of comfort that came from years of working together. She envied it a little; she had never been close enough with any of her previous teams to know this kind of effortless company. She was glad to be a part of it tonight, though. Their high spirits raised her own. They were a lot of fun, this eclectic mix of archaeological excavators. And they made an effort to include her in their conversation. Even if it was just making eye contact to let her know they were speaking to her, as well. She began to settle into the group, and by the time the food came, she'd even allowed herself to be pulled into their good-natured bickering.

"Ooh, that looks good. Why didn't I get that?" Dean leaned over the waitress as she placed two Thai curries in front of Famke and Emmie.

"Shoulda, woulda, coulda, mate." Adam eyed his own plate of loaded nachos with an eager grin.

Just as he was reaching for his first chip, Dean's hand shot forward and snatched the cheesiest, meatiest chip from the top. Before Adam could protest, he pushed it into his mouth.

"Eh, get off." Adam pulled his plate away, cradling it like a child. "Touch my crisps again and I'll kill you in your sleep. Just watch, mate."

Dean grinned at Emmie through a mouthful of nacho.

"Don't even think about it," she warned, pulling her own plate close to her.

Sophie barked a laugh. "He wouldn't dare. He's still trying to impress you. It's you, Famke, that's gotta watch your plate."

"So when's someone going to ask her about these ghosts we keep hearing about?"

Emmie's hand stilled over her rice. She stared at Adam, who chewed a mouthful of nacho with a glint of humour in his eyes. When he saw the expression on her face, he sobered.

"Eh, you okay, love? Sorry, did you not know about the ghosts? I thought you did."

"I— Um, yes, I know about them."

"Are you all right, Emmie? You look very pale." Famke studied her with genuine concern.

Emmie shook her head and forced a smile. "Yes. I'm fine. Sorry about that, you just caught me off guard."

"So then? Tell us about them," Adam prodded.

"Adam, have some tact," Ewan grunted.

"What?" He shovelled another cheese-and-bean-laden taco chip into his mouth.

Sophie tossed him a disgusted look. "Could you be any more of a pig?"

He grinned sloppily. "That a challenge?"

"Really, *really* no."

Emmie laid her fork down on her plate and folded her hands in her lap. "Why don't you tell me what you've heard, and I'll tell you if it's true or not."

"We were told on debriefing that there were two ghosts at Tullybrae," Famke answered, somewhat chagrined by her own curiosity.

"That's it?"

"That's it."

"Yeah, they didn't say much," Dean added. "Only that there were two, and that they were friendly."

"Is it true? Have you seen them?" Sophie leaned over her plate, eager to hear more.

"It's true. I haven't *seen* them, exactly. I may have... I'm not really sure how to describe it. I may have *encountered* one. At least I think I did."

"Really?" Dean leaned forward, too, mirroring Sophie's wide-eyed awe. Then, as quick as lightning, his hand snapped out and snatched a few French fries from her plate.

"Deano!" She slapped his hand, and scooched her chair away from him, dragging her plate with her.

Dean laughed. "I totally had you, Soph. Seriously, though, Em. What happened?"

"Not much happened. Just that a candle flickered when there was no draft. It had been burning for a while and hadn't flickered once. That's not a big deal, I know. But it happened at the same time that I smelled a rose-scented perfume. I don't know where it could have come from. I didn't have anything *rosy* around, and I know Lamb uses lemon-scented cleaners religiously. But that's what I was told happens when the Countess of Cranbury is around. People smell roses."

"Do they know which Countess of Cranbury it was?" Even Ewan was engrossed in her story. His hands rested around his half-drunk pint, and he listened just as intently as the others.

"The sixth, I'm told. She lived at Tullybrae through the sixteen hundreds."

Sophie sat back and exhaled through puffed cheeks. "Wow, that's fantastic. Man, if I were telling this story, I'd be right into it, with voices and sound effects and I dunno what. I don't know how you can be so nonchalant about it."

"Nonchalant," Adam teased. "Look at you, using big words."

Sophie pulled a face. "You'd know some big words, too, if you ever read anything other than Playboy."

"I read it for the stories," he guffawed.

"What about the other one?" Dean interrupted. "Do you know anything about him? Or her?"

"Her," Emmie nodded. "A little girl named Clara. She's supposed to be mischievous, but I couldn't say from experience. Lady Rotherham said she died in the seventeen-eighties."

"Is there any historical documentation to show that these people actually lived here?"

"Of course you'd ask that, Ewan," Dean joked. "C'mon, dude. She's just told you she's seen a ghost, and you want to know what kind of a paper trail there is?"

Ewan shrugged.

"Provenance is important," Emmie agreed solemnly. "Of course, they know who the sixth Countess of Cranbury is, when she lived and when she died and all that. Although there is nothing concrete which proves that's who the ghost is."

"If you can even prove there is a ghost in the first place," Adam put in.

"True."

"And the girl?" Ewan pressed.

"Yep. They do have a record of a little girl by the name of Clara dying on the property. Or, at least, she is the only recorded child's death, so that's why they think it's her."

"What did she die of?" Famke asked.

"Tuberculosis."

They all nodded and murmured in unison. Historical diseases like tuberculosis, syphilis and the bubonic plague were all ones with which the crew was familiar.

Famke sat back in her chair. "I wonder why they would not have told us that in the debriefing. We should know about what kinds of diseases have been recorded."

Ewan took a sip of his beer. "Now, Famke. You've been in the field long enough to know that people who *aren't* in the field have a funny way of deciding what information is and isn't important to share."

Adam nodded. "Her ladyship is only interested in the bones at the bottom of one grave. That's the one what's gonna make Stannisfield Films happy. We find that, it'll make for a good television show."

"Is that the murder?"

Adam levelled a serious look at Emmie, more serious than she would have though him capable.

"Murders, love. Plural."

"More like a massacre," Ewan corrected.

She looked from one to the other. "Massacre? What massacre?"

"Haven't you heard?" Ewan put a piece of his shepherd's pie into his mouth and chewed thoughtfully. "There's supposed to have been a dispute between clans that was settled in these parts. Nearly a dozen men slaughtered in ambush."

"I heard a hundred," Adam challenged.

"You did not, you wanker. It was a dozen, or thereabouts."

"I didn't know that," Emmie reflected. "Lady Rotherham talked of murder, and the victim was supposed to be buried on the property, but I thought it was only one."

"Oh, if the stories are true, then it's a hell of a lot more than one. The disturbance the technician found with the ground penetrating radar certainly corroborates the legend."

Emmie suddenly felt unwell. Her palms began to sweat, and her skin felt clammy. "What clans were they?"

Ewan laughed, failing to detect the wobble in her voice. "I'm sorry to tell you, lass, but we don't know. I know this is probably going to eat away at your historian's curiosity, and I'm sorry for that. But there's nothing recorded. Not one scrap of written account—or not one that survives to this day, anyway. All that we have is legend passed by word of mouth. That, and now this disturbance."

Adam raised his arm to the waitress, who was on the other side of the room, and caught her eye. He made a circling motion with his finger.

"'Nother round, love," he said through a mouthful of chips.

"Your girlfriend is one lucky woman," Sophie drawled when a gob of chewed-up chip fell onto his plate.

"She counts her blessings every night," Adam parlayed, stretching his arms above his head languorously.

Emmie forced a laugh with the others, though her hands still trembled in her lap. Tales of murder, mayhem and mass disease always piqued her interest. But never before had she been so overwhelmed by a story that it affected her physically. Especially not a story that was nothing more than a vaguely recalled legend which might not even be true.

This story, though, this particular massacre…

She couldn't say what it was, exactly. But it frightened her.

EIGHT

"E MMIE, SWEETHEART! YOU certainly took your time about calling."

Emmie was tucked away in the alcove under the grand staircase where one of the manor's three landline phones were plugged in. It was an eighties-era dial-up, ivory plastic with a spiral cord, which stood on an antique cherry wood pedestal table. A padded walnut armchair was placed next to it. Emmie sat in the chair, with her knees pulled up to her chin, and her fingers winding nervously around the phone cord which was misshapen from decades of fingers pulling at it.

"Sorry about that, I've just been busy is all."

"Why aren't you calling from your cell?" Gratuitous concern laced Grace Tunstall's voice. It was one of Emmie's pet peeves about her adoptive mother: Everything out of the norm was a reason to fret. That Emmie never voiced her dislike of this particular idiosyncrasy required a conscious effort.

"It's just logistics."

"Are you sure? Do you need us to send a new phone over for you? We got Chase a Samsung last week."

"That's a tablet, not a cell phone," Ron, her adoptive father, barked from the background.

"How come he can talk through it then?" Grace barked back.

"Really, it's not necessary," Emmie insisted. "My cell still works, and even if it didn't, I can buy a new one here."

"So why are you calling from a landline?"

She took a breath, willing herself to remain calm. "Because calls home are included in my living arrangements, and it's just easier to put it on

55

Tullybrae's phone bill directly, instead of expensing my cell bill at the end of the month."

"All right. If you're sure."

"Yes, I'm sure."

"So tell me all about your big adventure. Have you had a chance to take any pictures of the house yet? Your dad is dying to see the place."

She sounded so excited. And so genuine. Whatever Emmie's personal reservations were about her adoptive parents, she couldn't say they didn't love her. She felt bad that she hadn't called sooner.

"It's beautiful. Better than the pictures Camille sent over before I left."

"Camille?"

"Lady Rotherham."

Grace glowed with pride. "Look at that. My little girl on a first-name basis with the British upper crust. That's going in the monthly newsletter."

"Oh, no. Don't, please. It's no big deal."

Grace clucked her tongue. "Now honey, I've got a daughter that's a curator all the way over there in Scotland. If that's not fair bragging rights, I don't know what is."

Emmie was already getting that itchy, squirmy need to end the call. She had never been quite at ease with Grace's fawning, and the thought of being plastered into the church newsletter made it worse. She changed the subject. "How is Chase doing in his new job?"

"Oh, you know your brother. He could charm garden gnomes and grizzly bears into following him home if he had a mind to. He's already Mr. Popular out there in Toronto."

"I'll bet."

She could just picture her brother in the big city, swanning around all the night clubs and upscale patio bars in a swanky suit, letting loose after a fast-paced day at the office. The rich, honey colouring and the jet black hair of his Aishihik heritage on his biological father's side, combined with the crystalline blue eyes of his French-Canadian mother, always had women drooling over him everywhere he went.

"You'll never guess," Grace continued. "He got rid of his truck. And he's found himself a girlfriend."

"About time. So Carly's gone, then?"

"Gone, gone, gone. Can't say I'm sorry to see the back of that one. Far too young. Twenty-two, Em. Twenty-two, and two children from two different fathers."

"Yes, yes. I know."

"This new one's a few years older than him. Gillian, he called her. She's an account manager at a marketing firm, apparently. On the up-and-up. And she's got a condo of her own in the Distillery District... whatever that is."

"Stop it," Emmie warned, good-naturedly.

"Stop what?"

"I hear that tone of yours. He's just met her. Don't go planning the wedding yet. Give it a year at least before you get your hopes up."

"I have no idea what you're talking about—what's that, dear?—Oh, really, Ron!" Grace blew a pained sigh into the receiver. "Your father wants to know if the pubs are as great as they're made out to be—Yes, I heard you, and no I'm not repeating what you *actually* said."

Emmie laughed. "Go easy on him. You can tell him that I've been too busy to do a real pub crawl, but the two I've been to so far have been top-notch. If not better than anything back home, then at least as good."

"You hear that, Ron? Em says you're a cretin, and you wouldn't know a good pub if you fell down drunk in one."

"How the hell would I hear if she said that? You're on the damned *phone* with her, woman."

"You're evil," Emmie told Grace.

"I hope you're not spending all your time in bars, sweetheart."

"You don't need to worry. It was just to eat both times."

"Mmm hmm. Are you getting enough to eat?"

Emmie's foot began to tap impatiently. "Plenty. Lamb takes good care of me."

"Lamb?"

"He's the butler here. A really nice old man. You'd love him."

"I'll take your word for it. And how is the work going?"

"It's just a lot of cataloguing and researching right now. Nothing terribly thrilling— Oh, I forgot to tell you. There's a crew here filming an episode of Digging Scotland. They have a team of archaeological excavators out in the east field. And there's a camera crew, too, that shows up every once in a while."

"Is that so?" Grace's pitch rose a notch. "What channel's it going to be on? I'll have to watch it, see if I can find my little girl."

"Don't try too hard. I've been avoiding the cameras. Plus, the excavators told me I'd have to sign a waiver for the producers to use any footage with me in it, and I'm not going to do that."

"Oh, Emmie! Such a shrinking violet. What are they digging for?"

"They—they're digging... for..."

Emmie's throat suddenly constricted, and she couldn't get the words out. Didn't want to get the words out. Like what was beneath that field was not everyone's business. Not yet, anyway, not until the episode aired at least.

"Just... you know, household stuff. There were outbuildings on the property at one point. So they're looking for artefacts. To tell them how people lived back then, you know?"

"You make sure to keep us in the loop. Let us know if they find anything really extraordinary."

"I will. So… anyway, I'd better go. The long-distance must be costing a fortune."

"Oh. Oh, yes, of course." Grace's disappointment was audible. "Well, sweetheart, you take care of yourself out there. Make sure you're getting enough to eat, and drinking enough water. Are you sleeping well?"

"I'm sleeping great. Everything's great. Nothing for you to worry about."

"And you're not working too hard?"

"No, I'm not. I promise."

"Okay, then. I guess, good bye. Don't wait so long to call next time."

"I won't."

"All right. You take care, Em. I love you."

"Love you too… Mom."

Emmie cradled the receiver and slumped against the backrest. For a long while she sat, staring into space.

"Pardon me, Emmie," came Lamb's soft voice from around the corner.

Startled, she leaned forward and poked her head out of the alcove. The old butler was standing off to the side, looking slightly uncomfortable.

"What's up?" She gave him her best disarming smile.

"I didn't mean to intrude, but I'm making hot chocolate and biscuits. I wondered if you wanted some."

"That would be lovely. Thank you."

Lamb hesitated, his feet shifting indecisively.

"Tell me to mind my own business," he said, "but I was wondering if I might ask you something."

This was unlike Lamb. Emmie raised an eyebrow. "Of course you can ask."

He fidgeted, clasping his hands in front of him, and fiddling with his wrinkled fingers. "It's only that… well… and I know this is none of my affair, but it sounded like you were uncomfortable calling your adoptive mother 'Mom.' I probably only noticed it because you did say you were adopted. And, well, I was curious."

Emmie was touched. His concern for her never ceased to warm her heart.

"That's fine. I don't mind talking about it. You're right, I guess. I'm not sure I'm really okay with calling them 'Mom' and 'Dad.' When I came to live with them, Grace invited me to call her 'Mom,' and I didn't have the heart to turn her down. She wants so much to be a real mother to me."

"And that makes you uncomfortable?"

Emmie tilted her head. "It… it doesn't feel natural, you know? I came to them when I was six, so it's not like I grew up knowing her as 'Mom' until that point. Ron, he's better about it. I don't often call him 'Dad.' Neither does Chase, come to that. We usually just call him 'Ron.'"

Lamb nodded, contemplating. He was a man of few words. But then, he didn't need many words. He was one of those rare individuals, she was coming to understand, whose silence spoke volumes.

"You're a sweet man, Lamb. I probably say that too much, and I'm sorry if I'm making you uneasy. Tell me to stop if I am."

He inclined his head, his white hair catching the glow of the wall lamp behind him. "I suspect it's much like your mother. Your adoptive mother, that is. It may make you uneasy to receive her open and unabashed affections, because it is no' something that feels natural to you. But you would certainly be sorry if she ever ceased to offer them."

He was right. Of course he was right. Grace loved Emmie with her whole heart. And just as Lamb was not entirely comfortable with Emmie's display of affection for him, it would hurt terribly if Grace ever stopped telling her that she loved her.

"I'll be off to fix that hot chocolate, then."

"Thank you," Emmie echoed, after he'd left.

Later, when she was full of warm milk, cocoa and sugar, Emmie climbed the stairs to her bedroom. She made no attempt to change out of her wool slacks, shell-pink blazer and wedge heels, into her pyjamas. Instead, she sat on the edge of the bed and stared at the photograph of her mother.

It was the only photograph she had, the only one her real grandmother had given her before she passed away. After she passed, Emmie was too late. Her grandmother, her last living blood relative that she knew of, died three months before the Tunstalls found out. By that time, all her possessions had been sold, given away, or destroyed.

Ron and Grace had tried. For Emmie's sake, they tried desperately to recover something. Anything. But there was nothing left to recover. Every last piece of evidence that proved her mother had existed at all, had been on this earth, was gone. Except for the photograph that smiled back at her. And, of course, Emmie herself.

"Am I like you at all?" she asked the image. "On the inside, I mean? I don't think I look like you. I've tried so many times to find the similarities between myself and your face, and I never can. Sometimes, I think it might be there in the smile. Other times I don't see it."

The woman continued to smile enigmatically from behind her glass frame.

"Do I look like my father? Do you even know who he is? Does he know I'm alive? Is *he* alive?"

They were all questions she'd asked the photograph before. There were no answers this time. Just like every other time.

"Did you even care about me?"

Every now and again these stirrings of self-pity would surface. Emmie never had anyone she could talk to about it. Chase was the closest option, but even he couldn't empathize. Not truly. He'd come to the Tunstalls as an infant. He didn't have the six years that she did of knowing another life, another existence.

Chase was also in touch with his birth family. He'd found them when he was eighteen. It hadn't been the reunion he'd hoped for, but it was something. He learned the story of his conception from his mother, the daughter of a CN Rail engineer. When her father was transferred to an outpost in the Yukon, he dragged his reluctant, teenaged, city-reared daughters with him. Bored by the lack of entertainment, Chase's mother, then fourteen years old, had made her own entertainment with the local Aishihik boys. Chase's relationship with his mother now was strained, polite, distant. But it was there.

He'd found his father, too, and every now and then he'd travel north and stay for a few days. What they had in common other than DNA, Emmie couldn't imagine. But through his father he found grandparents and cousins and uncles and aunts. They enveloped him in their Aishihik community and culture. And while Chase was not legally able to claim First Nations status, since the lineage did not follow the maternal line, his father's family were the anchor that kept him connected to his heritage.

Emmie had nothing like that. From what she did know of her mother, it was unlikely she'd find her father or any of his family. Not in this lifetime.

She was lonely. It was overwhelming. And she was desperate for a friend. A kindred spirit that would understand the very depths of her soul.

"Countess?" she called into the empty room, which was dim with only the gentle glow of the bedside lamp. "Countess, are you here?"

Her call went unanswered. If the countess was here, she was not making herself known.

She probably wasn't here, anyway. Hauntings didn't work like that.

NINE

THE EXCAVATING WAS starting to become a bit too much for Emmie. In fact, it was damn near doing her head in.

Day after day the team came in from the village, driving their two white-panel Renault Kangoo vans which the studio rented for them. Wherever she was in the house, as soon as she heard the crunch of those tires on the gravel outside, Emmie stopped what she was doing and scurried up to the nursery.

It was not that she didn't like the team, or didn't want to see them. She couldn't explain what it was, really, except that their constant presence out there, digging away at the Scottish soil, made her anxious. Uneasy.

Occasionally, their voices would waft in through the open window. Their friendly conversation, Adam and Dean's perpetual bickering, a shout of excitement when something of particular significance was unearthed—on these occasions, Emmie would feel the urge to shut the window and retreat to her bedroom. Then she'd stop, rub her face, and ask the question that had become a daily mantra.

"What is *wrong* with me?"

In the few short weeks they'd been at Tullybrae, the team had unearthed a number of utility items, broken pottery, rusted gardening tools and the like. But so far, they'd all been from the last hundred years. It was encouraging, yes, but not the find they were hoping to make. Although, just yesterday, they'd made a breakthrough when Ewan and Sophie uncovered the outline of the old kitchens which went back to the time the house was built.

Emmie's avoidance of them didn't seem to bother her new friends much. In fact, it hardly seem to register with them. Ever since their night at The Grigg, they pulled her into their folds. It was no matter that she never came outside to see them, they were perfectly comfortable seeking her out in the house. With every discovery, they ploughed into her sanctuary, full of enthusiasm. And Emmie, not wanting to put a damper on their excitement, would force herself to adopt an air of eagerness, and follow them outside to see what the fuss was about.

Really... what was *wrong* with her?

This particular morning, she woke up feeling very off. The kind of "off" where there was an edge of the surreal to everything, like when a fever first makes itself known. Except that she was not suffering from a fever. On the contrary, she was fighting fit. Physically, at least. Her temperature was fine, she had no aches or chills. Nothing.

She just felt spacy. Unaccountably, inexplicably... off.

An early morning gloom had cleared, and a tentative sunshine struggled through the haze of fresh fog. Cool, dewy moisture pillowed the hills and the house. Emmie threw open the windows of the nursery and pulled in several deep lungsful of the Highland autumn air (an act which went against her curator's instinct to preserve the house and its artefacts from moisture damage). It not only had a scent, the air, it had a taste, too. It was clean, restorative. Invigorating.

She couldn't get enough of it.

She was still there at the window, absorbing as much of the Highlands as she possibly could, when Dean's voice, then Adam's, brought her back to the nursery. They were in the house, barreling down the corridor.

Good Lord, please let them have wiped their boots this time.

Not wanting to let them find her with her head hanging out the window, Emmie flung herself across the room and into her desk chair. She had just opened her laptop and was pretending to type furiously when they burst through the door.

"Em, we need you."

She looked up into the flushed, beaming face of Dean. "What's up, guys?"

"We've found something," exclaimed Adam, shoving Dean out of the way, even though the latter was a head taller and substantially less scrawny. "We need your opinion. None of us are sure what it is."

"Um... yeah, sure. I'll be down in a bit. Give me a half hour?"

"Nuh-uh. We need you now." Adam grabbed her hand across the desk and gave her arm a tug.

They ushered her out, pulling her along the narrow hallway nearly three abreast. Adam held tight to her hand, and Dean kept his hand on her lower back. Neither of them wanted to give an inch to the other in the battle for her attentions. She tolerated their overtures with humour. Adam was more overt than Dean. To hear Sophie tell it, the man was a hopeless flirt by nature.

"It drives Kim nuts," she said, referring to Adam's girlfriend. "She's so insecure and clingy. It drives her crazy to let him go off by himself like this, not knowing what he's getting up to."

"That's… sad," Emmie commented. "Do you think I should put a stop to it with me? I never bothered before because I thought he wasn't serious."

"He's not serious. You could try putting him in his place, but you'd be wasting your time. Adam flirting is like dogs pissing on trees. He can't help himself."

"I feel bad for his girlfriend, though."

"Yeah, I guess." Sophie pursed her lips. "She's really nice, too. Not quite sure how those two ever got together in the first place, though. Don't tell him I said so."

As for Dean's overtures, they were more disconcerting to Emmie than Adam's. For the most part they, too, were innocuous. But every now and again, she detected in them the underlying hope that she'd return his subtle advances. He was a nice enough guy, but not her type. Too down-home redneck… in a charming way, of course. Besides, it wasn't the right time for her. She dreaded the day she would have to come out and say it for certain. She'd regret having to disappoint him.

Adam and Dean led her out to the east field. Their original trenches had expanded and deepened. A truck from the University of Edinburgh came out daily to cart away their finds for examination and storage. Laid out on a long, plastic workbench that was set up beneath the tent were today's artefacts, those that had been found since morning.

There were only four small pieces. Emmie gave them a cursory glance, but they were so encrusted with dirt, she couldn't tell what they were.

A heavy churning had begun in her belly at some point after leaving the nursery. It had started off slow, like a huge turbine struggling to pick up speed. Now that she was out at the dig site, it was turning steadily, and had spread to her legs, weighing them down.

It was as though her body instinctively knew that, whatever it was they'd found, she did not want to confront it.

"Emmie." Famke waved enthusiastically. Emmie waved feebly back.

Ewan was farther beneath the tent. He came to the edge of the table when Adam and Dean ushered her by the elbows to the things they'd pulled from the ground.

"Sorry to disturb you," he said, "and I say that on behalf of Thing One and Thing Two, here, because I know they didn't bother to apologize for strong-arming you away from you work."

"I was going to," Dean insisted, letting go of his grip on her.

"Not me, mate," Adam countered, throwing an arm around her shoulder and pulled her close for a cheeky kiss on the temple. "Didn't even occur to me. Sorry to bother you, Em. Shoulda said."

Ewan shot Adam a disapproving look. "If you're willing, we'd love to get your opinion. We're not sure what it is, exactly, but it's intriguing."

Emmie hadn't noticed that Ewan was holding something in his hands. When he thrust his palm forward, the object on it made her wince.

It was small, only the size of her index finger. A slender, silver protrusion was topped by a dirt-crusted ornament the size of a dime. They were right to be excited about it. The moulded design was elaborate. She couldn't quite tell what it was, but it was Celtic. Probably dated to before the time of the Jacobite rising in the early seventeen hundreds, if she had to guess.

"Have you ever seen anything like it?"

Emmie swallowed thickly. "It's a kilt pin."

Famke, who had drifted closer, peered over Emmie's shoulder. "A kilt pin? What's that?"

"A pin to keep your kilt together," Adam scoffed. "You know what a kilt is. Them funny skirts blokes wear in Scotland?"

"Oh, yes. A *kilt*. I thought she said a *killed* pin."

"Look at that detail," Dean pressed. "Is that a clan ensign, do you think?"

Before she could say anything, he had snatched the pin from Ewan's palm and tossed it at her. Emmie reacted without thinking, catching the pin in both hands. She barely heard Ewan say, "She should be wearing gloves, Deano," before she was hammered by a wave of emotion.

It was the strongest rush she'd ever experienced. Rage. Pain. Grief. Anguish. It all rolled over and through her, constricting her lungs, her heart, her throat.

Sophie was the first to notice something was wrong. "Hey, Em. You okay? Your hands are shaking."

"Emmie?" Famke repeated when she didn't answer.

"Yes—I... I just haven't been feeling well lately," she forced herself to choke out. Her voice was strained, hoarse. "I think I need to go back inside."

"I'll help you," Dean, insisted. Ewan stopped him.

"No, Deano. You stay here. Emmie, let *me* help you."

He took the pin from her trembling hand, and put it back on the table. Taking her gently by the elbow, he led her back to the house. He was patient, letting her walk at her own pace, and Emmie was immensely grateful that he didn't try and talk to her. What would she say?

He stopped at the front door, and looked into her face. His eyes, which Emmie hadn't before noticed were a clear green with gold flecks, searched her face beneath that full, brown beard.

"Do you need help inside? Or can I get Lamb for you?"

Emmie shook her head. "I—I just need to sit down, I think."

"You're not diabetic, are you? A low blood sugar? You look as pale as a sheet and you're sweating."

"No, it's nothing like that. I don't know what happened, really."

Ewan breathed deeply, and glanced up at the sky. "Sometimes it just happens. You're fine one minute, then the next you feel like you've been hit by a lorry. If you haven't bounced back in an hour or so, make sure you tell Lamb. I'd feel better if he knew you were poorly."

"I will. I promise. Tell the others I'm sorry."

Ewan snorted. "Adam and Deano? They don't deserve it."

He waited while she went inside. She thanked him once again before closing the door. His concern for her well-being caused the corners of his eyes to crinkle, but he raised a hand in farewell and let her go.

Safe behind the walls of Tullybrae House, Emmie climbed the main staircase on heavy legs, and hauled herself to the servants' stairs. But once she reached them, her legs would climb no further. Instead, she sank pitifully onto the first stair, leaned back against the wall, and pulled her knees to her chest.

Burying her face in her arms, she lost the fight against a torrent of tears—tears which she could not account for. They consumed her. The anguish she'd first felt upon touching that kilt pin squeezed her heart until she thought it would stop. Great, heaving sobs poured out of her into the empty air. She tried to staunch them; she didn't want Lamb to hear. But it was no use. Her nose ran, her mascara tracked down her cheeks, and her face turned a bright shade of crimson. It was ugly, angry crying. Helpless grief.

The more she cried, the more her sobs echoed back to her. They bounced off the walls in stereo, coming back in unsynchronized rhythm. Her own voice...

Wait... *not* her own voice.

Not an echo.

Emmie sniffled, and quieted. The sobbing quieted, too.

Rubbing her eyes into focus, she scanned the second floor landing. There was no one there. Yet, she felt certain that someone *was* there, in the stairwell with her. Closer to the door.

She peered. Squinted. Strained. Tried to make sense of the discrepancy between what she saw, and what she felt. The longer she stared, the more the air by the door began to shift. To shimmer, like heat rising from pavement.

Then slowly, the shifting, shimmering air took on the vague outline of a person.

It was not a definite outline. She could not see a face, or even discern if it was man or woman. It felt like a man, though. The same male presence she'd felt that day when the camera crew had come for the first time.

She watched the shimmering air, amazed. And it watched her.

It saw her. *He* saw her.

For a long time she sat motionless, staring at the entity in the corner as it stared back at her. But unlike before, she didn't feel that same invasive fear, didn't feel threatened.

She felt at peace.

Later that night, as she lay in her bed staring at the ceiling, Emmie thought about what happened in the stairwell. Thought about what it felt like.

It felt like comfort, like she was understood. The anguish which had overwhelmed her when she touched the kilt pin hadn't been her own. It had come from him. But when she'd received it, his grief had mingled with her own, grief that had been pent up inside for years which she hadn't allowed herself to acknowledge. It converged and changed.

And when it poured out of her... somehow, he'd felt it, too.

Whoever he was.

TEN

THE HIGHLANDER. HE had noticed her that day in the stairwell. He'd become aware of her, knew of her existence. And he was curious.

From that day on, Emmie was rarely alone. There was always that vague knowledge that he was hovering somewhere nearby. When she was in the nursery, working on her laptop, he would be in the hall outside the door. At breakfast, lunch and dinner, the back of her neck would tingle with the sensation of his presence. When she went up to bed for the night, he lingered at the top of the staircase, and when she came down again in the morning, he was still there, waiting for her.

She wasn't sure what to make of his near-constant presence. It might have annoyed her, but for the fact that she got the distinct impression he was trying not to bother her. He was trying, in his curiosity, to fly under her radar, so to speak. It was oddly endearing.

She felt him like a tingling underneath her skin, one that never really went away, though it would fade if she wasn't paying attention. It was a strange sensation. At times during the day, she would find herself stopping whatever she was doing, and assessing the energy, testing its strength or weakness to determine the Highlander's proximity to her.

She wondered if he was aware she did this. She doubted it.

A Highlander he definitely was. How she was so certain, she couldn't say, other than that she could just feel it. A skeptic would argue that she was in the Highlands of Scotland, and that it was a logical assumption—

Scratch that. A skeptic would declare that she was imagining things altogether.

Whoever he was, and whatever he wanted, Emmie found that much of her time was spent absorbed in the awareness of him. It was swiftly becoming a habit, like nail biting or hair twirling. There were times when she didn't even realize she was doing it.

"Are you all right, Emmie?" Lamb asked her one morning.

She had taken a bite of toast, and had paused mid-chew to test out the prickle in her spine. The Highlander was in the corner of the kitchen, over by the old Victorian range. She was so intensely focused on him, on the way his presence moved and dissipated and converged again like fog, that she hadn't realized she'd been staring into space with a piece of toast wedged into her cheek until Lamb's question brought her around.

"Yeah. I—um," she cleared her throat, slightly embarrassed. "Sorry. I spaced out there, didn't I?" She laughed lightly, brushing it off as a momentary lapse.

Lamb was not fooled. He gazed at her, his pale eyes seeing through her sudden brightness.

"My mother says—well, she *used* to say—that no matter what may be bothering you, you'll always feel better if you talk about it."

Emmie searched the old man's placid face. Did he know something? Was he, too, aware of the Highlander? She didn't want to talk about him. The Highlander's newfound interest in her seemed personal, somehow. Something she wanted to keep to herself. But she did want to know more about him, about what kept him here. It occurred to her that Lamb might be able to help her learn about him.

"That's probably true," she hedged. "Can I ask you, Lamb… do you know anything about the massacre that is said to have happened here?"

He wasn't surprised by her question. He put down his fork, and folded his fingers together.

"The massacre, you say. Well, now. I'm no' sure what the history books say. I suppose you've already checked it out on the Internet."

"No, actually, I haven't," she admitted. "That's probably where I should have started, huh?"

"I don't mind telling you what I know, although I'm afraid it's no' much."

"It'll be a starting point, if nothing else." She straightened on her stool, leaning forward and tucking her hands tightly between her thighs.

"As far as I know, the murders predate the house. It had nothing to do with anyone associated with Tullybrae. That is about the only thing I can say with any certainty."

"So it was more than, what, three-hundred years ago?"

"Oh, at least."

"Ewan said it was a clan dispute. Do you have any idea which clans they might have been?"

"Nay, sorry. As I said, I don't know much. But I do know that there was a severe and unforgivable betrayal involved."

"Betrayal," she echoed, her eyes wide.

"Aye. Many men were murdered, sacrificed to facilitate one man's death. From what the servants used to say about him, this man was wronged."

WRONGED. THE WORD stuck with Emmie, echoing in her ears all afternoon. Wronged. Wronged how? By whom? The Highlander was definitely involved in some way—if he wasn't the one man whose death was so highly desired, then he was at least one of the sacrificed in the party of this centuries-old tale. She knew it because as soon as Lamb's old lips uttered the word, the Highlander's presence pulsed invisibly. As if he were silently telling her—*Yes!*

She didn't know it then, but she would come to regret asking Lamb to tell what he knew. That one word—wronged—was like an infecting agent, a wet cloth full of germs swiped over an insignificant skin abrasion. It turned her curiosity from something inconvenient into a thing which she could not stop scratching at.

After breakfast that morning, she buried her nose in her laptop, searching for anything that might illuminate the supposed massacre. Her efforts yielded no results. Keyword searches, drilling down through embedded links, scholarly articles available through the various subscriptions she maintained—there was nothing other than a general history of the clans in the area.

But, if she had learned anything in her training all these years, it was to never discount any piece of information, no matter how unimportant it may at first seem. Emmie scribbled down everything she could find, recording details, possible leads, and points of interest which needed more research. By early afternoon, she abandoned the digital world in favour of Tullybrae's library, which housed a sizeable collection of books on local history.

When Sophie found her a few hours later, the afternoon light was coming low and long through the window, and Emmie had just switched on the standing lamp by the cold, empty hearth.

"There you are," Sophie exclaimed, stopping in front of the open doorway.

Emmie glanced up from her cross-legged position on the floor. A pile of books had accumulated there, forming a moat of pages around her.

"Oh, hey, Soph. What's up?" The words were barely out of her mouth before her eyes were lowering back to her book.

Sophie came into the room. She sat down in front of Emmie and stuck her legs out straight, crossing them at the ankles.

"Everything okay with you?"

"Sure, why do you ask?"

A small, pale hand with short, chewed nails slid over the black-and-yellowing pages. Gently, the book was removed from Emmie's grip.

Emmie looked up, chagrined. "Sorry. What did you say?"

"I asked if you're okay. In general, I mean. You've been kind of out of it the last few days."

"I have been a little distracted, haven't I?"

"If that isn't the understatement of the year, I'll be buggered. Look: I may be a right stroppy mare sometimes, but I care about my friends—even Adam, but don't be telling him that. You haven't come out much to see us, and when we do see you, you look like you're in space half the time. And Lamb says your appetite's been falling off— You're not up the duff, are you?"

"Pregnant?" Emmie balked. "God, no. Nothing like that."

"Okay. Well I'm sure it's none of my affair, and I can keep me nose out of where it don't belong. Just promise me you're really all right, and we'll leave it at that."

She looked into Sophie's eyes. Really looked. What she found was concern that went deeper than the young woman's brash, indelicate East-Ender exterior. Worry wrote itself on her face, creasing her slightly large brow and small, upturned nose.

Emmie wondered—she hadn't been that bad, had she?

She thought back to how she'd been acting the last week or so. To be fair, the encounter with the kilt pin had been alarming at the time, but it had been an isolated incident. Nothing else struck her as unusual... Well, perhaps that one time Lamb had to practically shout her name at the doorway of the nursery to get her attention. And, okay, it might be accurate to claim she didn't have much of an appetite lately. She was going to bed later, and was more high-strung than usual.

Suddenly Emmie felt ashamed. The crew outside had actively sought to keep her a part of their world, and Lamb's concern for her well-being was so genuine. But how could she possibly tell them about the source of her distraction: the Highlander? He consumed more of her focus and energy than was good for her, she didn't mind admitting. She couldn't explain that to them in a way they'd understand.

And besides, she didn't want to tell them. The Highlander was her secret. She didn't want to share him—

It. She didn't want to share *it*. The secret.

What *was wrong* with her?

"I promise, I'm fine."

"Can you tell me what's the matter? Just to ease my conscience?"

Emmie squinted, tipping her head to the side. "Nothing 'the matter' really. It's just that... Well, here. Let me put it like this: Do you ever have a bug, or an itch for something, and you don't know what it is but you can't leave it alone?"

"You're talking to an excavator, love. That's my life. 'C'mon, Soph. Just a little farther down. Just a bit more dirt, just another hour. There's something down there.'"

"Bingo."

Sophie changed positions, leaning back on her hands, and uncrossing her denim-clad ankles. It was then that Emmie noticed she'd had the presence of mind to remove her boots so that she would not track mud through the house. If only Adam and Dean were so thoughtful.

"Nice socks."

Sophie flexed her feet, examining her mix-and-match novelty socks— Ralph the Dog and Doctor Teeth.

"Ta. Two of my favourite Muppets. They don't get enough credit."

"Fozzy Bear's always been my favourite."

They chuckled together. Sophie let her unguarded smile linger.

"Look, we're heading back to the university to unload our finds, and then we're off to Iain's place. He's having a party. Wanna come with?"

Emmie wavered. "Er… I don't know. I've got a lot of work to do here, and I'm kinda tired—"

"Let me rephrase that," Sophie interrupted. "We're heading back to the university and then to a party, and you're coming with, unless you can think of a damn good excuse that I buy. We clear?"

The young lady's demands were met with a long-suffering look from Emmie. "Oh, all right. But just for you."

Sophie beamed, flashing a set of slightly crooked teeth. "Brilliant. Right, then. You go get changed. Something casual. Dress down for once, yeah?"

Emmie glanced down to her trim black blazer and chic button-up white blouse. "Dress *down?*"

"When you're hanging out with a bunch of archaeologists, clean jeans without rips in 'em are as good as formal wear."

A HALF HOUR later, Emmie still had no excuse for why she needed to back out of being dragged along to Dr. Iain Northcott's party. Out of time for a last-ditch attempt, she stood in front of the bathroom mirror, begrudgingly assessing her dressed-down ensemble. A fitted long-sleeve tee-shirt replaced the blazer and button-up, and she had traded her black slacks for a knee-length corduroy skirt, and brown suede slouch boots.

Her friends on the dig crew had already been to their hotel to change, and had returned in slightly better outfits than those in which they typically worked. It made Emmie feel hugely overdressed in comparison. Still, her attempt earned an appreciative once-over from Dean, followed by a slightly less subtle ogling from Adam.

"For God's sake, Adam, give it a rest," Ewan expostulated. Adam's response was a boyish grin and a few deliberate chomps on his gum.

They piled into the Renault Kangoo with Ewan at the wheel. Emmie said nothing as the others began to chatter excitedly. She was too distracted by an unexpected lightening, almost as if a blanket had been pulled from her body. The Highlander, it seemed, would not be following her to Edinburgh. Or couldn't, perhaps. She was struck by the sudden clarity of her thoughts, the sharpness with which her mind focussed on things other than him. It was disconcerting, for she hadn't realized how harnessed her mind had become. Dependent on his proximity, his mood.

The separation from him, though, was also disconcerting. She'd been warm under the blanket. Now that it had been removed, she felt the chill of being alone. Without him.

Him. The Highlander. A man she'd never met and never would meet. Not even a man—a spirit, a presence. A ghost. She gritted her teeth and forced herself to pay attention to her friends, to quell the uncomfortable churn in her belly.

The drive to Edinburgh should have taken more than two hours, but Ewan's lead foot cut the commute almost in half. Other than five sets of white knuckles, the passengers arrived unscathed.

Historic cities never ceased to amaze Emmie, and Edinburgh was no exception. It was a city of juxtaposition: Its castle, seemingly carved into the crown of the ancient volcanic mountain, loomed over a blend of history and modern life that existed side-by-side. She wondered if, in times of quiet reflection, its inhabitants were as awed by the raw beauty of it as she was.

Ewan took them off the South Bridge road, and down a series of side streets that wound around the collection of buildings comprising the main campus of the university. Fittingly, the School of History, Classics and Archaeology was a stately building of yellow stone dating back to the latter years of the eighteenth century. It was housed in the William Robertson wing of the Old Medical School, and proudly displayed a statue of the aforementioned Robertson himself atop a rearing horse in its courtyard.

Having driven around the front for Emmie's benefit, Ewan parked the car outside a rear entrance, where the team proceeded to disembark and unload the cardboard boxes with their carefully wrapped finds. There weren't many. Adam, Dean and Ewan took the lot, leaving Famke, Sophie and Emmie to follow into the building.

"You look very nice tonight, Famke," Emmie offered.

The tall, svelte Dutch woman accepted the compliment with quiet grace. She wore a tailored, tan-coloured button shirt, and slim-cut jeans. Her light brown hair had been straightened, and hung just below her shoulders.

"Thank you," she said. "So do you."

"And what am I—chopped liver?" Sophie put in with mock offense.

"I was getting to you," Emmie laughed. "I started with Famke first because I already complimented you on your socks."

"Smooth." Sophie grinned, pulling the hem of her printed tee-shirt over her denim mini skirt.

Famke tisked. "You're going to freeze in that tee-shirt."

"That's why I've got a cardy in the back of the van, isn't it?—A cardigan, a sweater," she clarified when Famke gave a confused grimace at the slang term.

Famke responded with something in Dutch which Emmie fancied was a lament over the butchering of the English language by native speakers.

They trailed after the boys down a series of clean, modernized hallways. The interior of the building surprised Emmie, given its historic exterior. Pale wood panelling adorned the white and glass walls; the floors were tiled in slate. Classrooms and computer laboratories were still lit up here and there, housing a handful of dedicated students who were choosing to work later than their peers. Her curious gaze met that of a young man within one small study room, and she felt a thrill of nostalgia as she recalled her own days spent in study halls just like this one.

They proceeded towards a rear staircase, where Famke raced ahead to open the metal door for the guys. Single file, they descended the concrete stairs into a basement that was far more institutional looking than the main floor. Corridors, research laboratories, offices and archive storage rooms tracked outwards from the bottom of the stairs.

"Let's get these to Receiving," Ewan ordered. He, Dean and Adam headed down a corridor to the right, while Famke and Sophie proceeded to another room on the left with Emmie in tow. The room, she saw when they unlocked the door and turned on the fluorescent overhead lights, was a workstation of sorts that the team appeared to be using for an office. Waist-high lab-style desks rimmed the walls, their surfaces scattered with computer monitors, paperwork, microscopes and other technological gadgets. In the middle of the room was a stainless steel examining table. Here, too, textbooks and binders full to brimming were stacked precariously on top. The whole room felt like an afterthought, like a place which advertised that great work was done elsewhere.

"Sorry about all this." Famke fanned a strong, slender hand at the mess. "Our department has just gone through a major inventory. The natural history museum at Oxford U was interested in some of our things from Skara Brae for their Neolithic exhibition, so our department head thought it would be a good idea to inventory everything else at the same time."

She perched on the edge of a tall metal stool in front of one computer monitor, while Sophie went to another. Flicking three sheets of pink paper off a mouse, she wiggled the black plastic object to wake her computer up, then logged on to check her email.

"You were at Skara Brae?" Emmie put in.

"Well, no," Famke answered. "We collaborated on the project after more recent excavations. Some of the stuff was sent here for identification and analysis, carbon dating, that kind of thing. We also re-evaluated the artefacts that were carbon dated back in the nineteen seventies. Soph was there briefly."

"Undergrad year. The Bay of Skaill was unreal," Sophie confirmed, still glued to her monitor.

"That's amazing."

Before she could ask anything more about the famous Scottish site, Adam popped his head around the doorframe.

"You birds just about ready?"

"Gimme a minute," Sophie said as she typed furiously.

"Cor, Soph. Whoever he is, the bloke can wait."

"The bloke is Professor Kothari. He wants to know about the black-burnished piece he brought up from storage. So if you don't mind, mate—"

"Yeah, awright."

"Hey, Em," Dean said eagerly, stepping from behind Adam. "While Soph's doing that, wanna come see something cool?"

"Keep it in your pants, mate. She's seen one before," Adam joked.

"Lord give me strength," Sophie sighed to her monitor. Dean cuffed Adam's ear.

"Sure, I'll come," Emmie said. She made a show of shaking her head at Adam as she passed, but could not keep the stern face for long.

"C'mon." Dean snatched her hand and led her down the hall.

The way he was holding her hand, and the fact that he was dragging her away from the others, set her on edge. Dean wasn't trying to make his move, was he? Leading her to a quiet corner to confess something? Until now, none of his overtures had been serious enough for her to worry about. She prayed he hadn't plucked up the courage to step up his campaign tonight.

Her discomfort increased when he let go of her hand, placed his palm onto the small of her back, and guided her into a darkened room. The moment he flipped the light switch, however, she felt a little silly. As she looked into the space, it was clear that Dean had a very good, very thoughtful reason for taking her away.

On several stainless steel gurneys topped with white linen sheets were laid out the bones of four human skeletons.

Her eyes absorbed the scene with amazement. A sense of overwhelming sadness, mingled with a sense of awe, settled over her. Four human skeletons, four people that had once been alive, that had once had hopes and dreams, thoughts and feelings.

"I thought you'd be interested," Dean explained, suddenly shy. "You know, being a historian and all."

"This is absolutely incredible," she breathed.

He stepped farther into the room, beckoning her to follow.

"This is all for the first year criminal forensics students at UWS and Glasgow Caledonian. They come here on field trips to view the bones."

"Ah, forensics," Emmie said, understanding. "Let me guess: There's something about the bones that will tell you how they all died."

"I probably should have asked if you've taken forensic archaeology before," he chuckled. "You haven't seen this kind of thing already, have you?"

"No. Forensic archaeology was one elective which I really wanted to take, but it just didn't fit into my schedule in undergrad."

"I'll give you the condensed curriculum, then." He inclined his head towards the body in the farthest corner.

"This gentleman, we call him John Parker."

"You *call* him John Parker?"

"It's not his real name. At first we called him Parker, but Irene—one of the graduate studies teachers here—her grandson's name is Parker, and she was creeped out by it. So we made Parker his last name and added John."

"Why Parker?"

Dean wiggled his eyebrows. "Because he was found beneath a parking lot down in Dorset. See here?" He traced a finger along the bones of the neck. "That there is a clean break between the second and third cervical vertebrae."

"Not an accident," Emmie speculated.

"Smart girl. Probably not. A fall likely would have resulted in a fractured break, jagged edges. When we see a clean break like this, it usually indicates one thing.

Emmie stared, mesmerized by the separated vertebrae. "A hanging?"

"A hanging. And in this case, there was a bit more to substantiate the theory. The parking lot they found him under was behind Dorchester Prison. They were repaving after it closed, and the workers inadvertently uncovered hundreds of remains. All of them had the same clean break in about the same location of the vertebrae. The official conclusion is that the site is the long-forgotten mass grave for condemned criminals."

"And someone just paved over it." She shook her head, knowing too well the disregard of people for historic places.

"I know, right?" Dean agreed. "But it was first paved back in the nineteen forties. They didn't think about that kind of stuff as much then."

Still captivated by the evidence of the hanging, Emmie let herself be guided to the next body. It was a small frame of bones. A child.

"This is Lucy," he said with surprising tenderness. "Female, between the ages of three and ten."

"Not exactly a precise identification, is it?" She traced a finger along a tiny arm bone.

"Well, Lucy's Victorian. Malnutrition being what it was, it's hard to tell a lot of the time. We think it's malnutrition for a few reasons." Carefully, he picked up a collarbone, which was fractured in the middle. He pulled the ends apart to show her the bone's inner composition. "This is far too porous to be considered a well-nourished child. Also, we think she's somewhere closer to five because of the way the frontal and parietal bones here in the skull have fused. Generally speaking, that's too fused to be any younger than two, but not fused enough for her to be in the pre-teen range."

Emmie nodded thoughtfully, examining the sutures of the skull, and followed Dean to the next body.

"Now this young lady we know. Her name was Mary Vincent, and she, too, was Victorian. Died in eighteen fifty-nine."

"Is that evidence of disease?" Emmie asked, immediately picking out the scarred skull, sunken nasal cavity and deformed jaw.

"Syphilis," he confirmed. "The bones make her a dead ringer for a syphilitic prostitute. That, as well as the fact that she was buried in the cemetery at St. Luke's in London—it's a famous paupers' lunatic asylum from the era. Syphilitics went mad by the end of their life, as you probably know."

She did know. "I went through an Alcatraz phase once. Al Capone is said to have declined in health and mental state there from his syphilis infection. Sad... not about Capone, *specifically*, but you know what I mean. Sad for Mary and her lot."

"I know. It's all sad. And what's even sadder is that Mary was estimated to be about fifteen at the time of death. Now, if you know anything about syphilis, this is an advanced stage we see here. Sufferers of the disease can often go anywhere from ten to twenty years with symptoms coming and going before they're got in the end. So it's quite possible that she contracted the disease at the age of at least—"

"Five," Emmie finished for him, horrified.

Dean paused, then said softly, "It was a common thing back then: Children—girls—being pushed into the trade because men were willing to buy them."

He led her over to the closest body to the door. This one was much larger.

"This strapping man we call Arnold."

76

"Arnold?"

"As in Schwarzenegger," he laughed. "Look at the size of his upper body. Thick arm bones, thick ribs, ridged shoulder plates. See the deep grooves? That's what happens when there's significant and repeated musculature strain. The bone starts to ripple to provide more surface area for the muscles to attach to. You'd probably see that in a competitive body builder today. Now compare the upper body with the legs."

Emmie took note. "They look disproportionate."

"Significantly disproportionate," he confirmed. "A common thing to find in knights back in the medieval period. They trained to use their upper bodies, but sat on a horse all day so their lower bodies were a lot weaker— by comparison of course. He's still a behemoth."

"That's interesting. I mean, I know you can tell a lot from bones, but I never realized how much."

"You can tell more from bones than a lot of people think. See here? This dent in his skull?"

"Ouch."

"Yup. Dude probably took a blade to the front of the skull at one point or another. But that's not what killed him. See? It's begun to heal. Probably went three or four more years after that."

Emmie leaned closer. "So what killed him then?"

Dean grinned devilishly. Gently, he detached Arnold's jaw and lifted it for her to see the underside. "Tell me what you see."

"They've got cut marks on each side."

"Mmm hmm. Pretty deep cut marks to be affecting the bone, don't you think? Evidence that the man had his throat slit."

"Really?"

"Those marks are a surefire way to tell if a person's had his or her throat slit. If you think about it, someone comes from behind and grabs you by the hair. Then they take their knife and drag it from ear to ear. That's bound to make a mark on the bones. With that much force and at that angle? More often than not, victims of a throat slitting have that same mark on the jaw."

"Hey, you guys just about ready?" Ewan appeared at the door, rapping on the metal frame with a knuckle.

"Yep, we're done." Dean turned to Emmie. "Cool, huh?"

Emmie laughed in disbelief. "Only to people like us. I think for anyone else, this stuff would be pretty morbid."

"Thank God for people like us, then. *This stuff* is what helps us solve modern day murders."

"Did you show her John Parker?" Ewan inquired.

"Of course I showed her John Parker. First thing—he's the coolest one in there."

The others were waiting eagerly when they returned to the team's temporary office. As a group, they went back up to ground level and out to their van in high spirits. Emmie tried to show as much enthusiasm as the others. But inside, Dean's story about Arnold and his slit throat made her feel sick.

It was a strange thing. She'd been affected by the stories of the other three, of course. But the sadness she felt for them was remote, tempered by the fact that their circumstances were also intriguing.

The last body, though, was anything but remote. It was inexplicably personal

ELEVEN

THE FAMOUS DR. Iain Northcott's home was a three-storey townhouse. It was newly built, no more than a decade old. But careful attention had been paid to neighbourhood aesthetic, with the end result being that it did not look out of place with the older buildings and homes in the area. A small, well-maintained walking park occupied the land directly opposite Dr. Northcott's row of townhouses, with a working fountain and several large, old oak trees. If the homes themselves weren't an indication, then the prevalence of expensive automobiles parked in the driveways and on the streets were an unmistakable giveaway of the area's significant affluence.

The sky had fallen completely dark by the time they arrived. Mellow interior lights warmed the windows of the homes, and a general air of domestic contentment embraced the street. The crew piled out of the white van and made their way to the most brightly lit house of them all, from which laughter and music could be heard.

In contrast to what she'd been expecting, Emmie was relieved to discover that the party was tasteful without being stuffy. History buffs, in her experience, tended to throw rather stuffy soirees. It was why her first impression, when Sophie had told her about the gathering, was that the still-youngish Londoner had gotten it wrong when she'd instructed Emmie to dress down. But when they stepped through the tall oak front door, there were enough faded jeans and hoodies mixed in amongst the more professionally dressed people that the crew fit right in.

Dr. Iain Northcott was near the door. He was engaged in an animated discussion with a well-dressed older woman sporting short, platinum blonde hair, and a middle-aged man in a blazer and Buddy Holly spectacles.

He, himself, was dressed somewhere in-between, in a button shirt with small blue-and-white stripes, and a clean pair of faded denim jeans. When he saw them enter, he waved enthusiastically, and excused himself to his guests.

"Hey, guys, glad you could make it," he called over the crowd in his tempered Scottish brogue. When he reached them, he clapped Ewan on the back, and extended a hand to Dean. "I thought it might be too far."

"We knocked off early," Sophie admitted.

"As well you should. You lot work far too hard as it is." He turned his boyish green eyes on Emmie. "And who might this lovely young lady be?"

"This is Emmie Tunstall," Dean was quick to answer. "She's the new curator up at Tullybrae."

Dr. Northcott's eyes lit up. "Oh, is that so? Well, I'm pleased to meet you, Emmie. You're very welcome. Now please, all of you, help yourselves to drinks. And there's some fantastic tuck in the kitchen."

"Tuck?" Emmie whispered to Sophie.

"Food."

"Ah."

They all ventured down a narrow hallway, which had gleaming hardwood floors lit up by track lighting overhead. They had to go single file, and skirt around people who were milling about, taking up much of the already slim space.

In the kitchen, more people stood around, chatting happily in groups of two and three. The drinks and "tuck" which Dr. Northcott had mentioned were laid out in abundance on the butcher-block centre island. Cheeses, meats, fruit and vegetable trays, a crock pot with saucy meatballs, plates of chicken wings, phyllo-wrapped appetizers and mini sandwiches—the counter was brimming. In a cluster beside the food were several different bottles of red, white and blush wines, pre-made spritzers and all kinds of spirits. On the floor on either side of the island were two coolers packed full with bottles and cans of beer, which were kept cold by crushed ice.

Some of the people in the kitchen waved to the crew, who waved back. Spotting the beer, Adam went straight for them. He fished a brown bottle of Hoegaarden lager from the ice, cracked the cap off, and took a long swig. "What are you drinking, Em?" he offered once he'd lowered the bottle.

"Um," she glanced at her choices. "I'll have a red wine please."

"Cor," Sophie declared, eyeing the spread with glee. "He's got that cream cheese salsa dip."

She plucked a taco chip from an oversized ceramic bowl and scooped a large chunk of cheesy dip. Her teeth crunched into the morsel with audible satisfaction.

"Here you are, love." Adam thrust an etched crystal wine glass into Emmie's hands. The ruby liquid sloshed inside.

"Wow, this is a lot," she laughed.

Adam winked. "Famke—you're up. What'll it be?"

"White for me, thanks."

Once she had her drink, Famke caught Emmie's eye and inclined her head. "Come on, let's go exploring. I've never seen inside Iain's house."

Like thieves, the pair stole away, leaving Sophie to devour the cream cheese salsa dip singlehandedly. Adam was busy chatting up a stylish zoomer-aged woman, but Dean noticed them sneaking off, and shook his head playfully.

The house was stunning, expertly decorated as one might expect for a well-off bachelor and scholar. White pine fixtures and floors, along with archaeological show pieces, were accented by strategic lighting. Original canvas paintings in bold reds, oranges and blues were hung on the clean, white walls. Despite the number of bodies radiating heat, the atmosphere was comfortably cool and remarkably fresh.

"Upstairs?" Famke suggested when they'd seen all of the first floor.

"You devil," Emmie teased.

"What? Other people are doing it. Let's go."

Indeed, the entire house was occupied by party-goers. There was an upstairs study in which a number of people were mingling, examining books and more artefacts. Famke ran into a few of her former colleagues from her undergrad days at the University of Groningen in the Netherlands, and was pulled into a round of catching up. She made a concerted attempt to include Emmie, who smiled along with the conversation, but let her go when Emmie excused herself on the pretext of needing to use the washroom.

After running into Sophie, then Dean, then Ewan, and engaging in conversation with each of their groups of acquaintances, Emmie felt confident that she'd done enough socializing. Fetching a paper plate of food for herself and another glass of wine, she retreated to the conservatory, which ran off of the kitchen. It was surprisingly empty, as was the back garden beyond. Grateful for the opportunity to be alone, she opened the glass door, and moved out into the night air. At the far end of the small yard was a black cast iron bench. She sank onto the chilly metal and exhaled a delicate puff of vapour into the cold.

"I am not a party girl," she told the rose-coloured fall mums that occupied the planter across from her.

Taking a leisured sip of her wine, she rolled the tart, rich liquid around on her tongue, and savoured the pleasant burn as it slid down her throat. Her thoughts drifted back to the skeletons at the university, and she considered their significance to the students that would examine them. She considered their significance to academics like Dean. To herself, even, and historians like her. Those skeletons were irrefutable proof of the inevitability of death. And weren't they all preoccupied with death in their different ways?

She wondered if Arnold ever savoured wine as she had. If Mary Vincent felt the sting of cold air on her arms as Emmie did now. Those bones were so much a part of why she loved history. Like the artefacts she catalogued and researched and preserved, they, too, were the evidence of lives lived long ago.

It was romantic. In an achingly sad way.

The Highlander, too, made her heart ache. Her thoughts had never been far from him since leaving Tullybrae. The tangible absence of him, the lack of awareness of his presence. He'd been on her mind all this time. She wondered if he knew she was gone. If he missed her the way she missed him—

The thought brought her up short. Missed him? She did not *miss* him. This was not some silly crush, and the Highlander was not a person. He had no form, no face, no physicality whatsoever.

And yet, there it was: She *missed* him.

The realization was unsettling. This was not like her.

Caught up in her fretting, Emmie was startled by the sound of the conservatory door opening.

"Oh, I'm sorry," said a male voice.

She turned to find Dr. Northcott standing on the threshold with a bottle of beer in one hand.

"I didn't realize anyone was out here."

"It's not your place to apologize in your own home," Emmie pointed out genially. "I'm probably not supposed to be out here, Dr. Northcott. *I'm* sorry."

"No, no. By all means. I'll leave the door open for you if you'd like. And please, call me Iain."

"Iain, then. Don't worry about the door, I'm coming back inside. I've been hiding out here for too long."

She rose from the bench and crossed the lawn, but stopped when he crossed his arms and leaned against the door frame.

"I hope you're having a pleasant time. You're not hiding because the party's lame, are you?" He flashed his famous charming grin, but there was genuine warmth behind it.

"I promise, it's nothing like that."

"Not much of a party girl?" he guessed.

"You know, I was just telling your flower pot that."

He laughed, refreshed by her wit. "I've had many a conversation with those mums, myself."

"I was kinda dragged here by Sophie," Emmie admitted. "She basically told me I've been a hermit for too long. Nose buried in historic junk and all that. Don't get me wrong, I'm happy to be here. I hope it's not an imposition."

"I am always happy to meet the friends of my friends."

"Oh good. 'Cause I was starting to feel like a party crasher."

"You were not," he teased.

"I was. So the crew are good friends, then? I wasn't sure—I thought maybe they were just acquaintances."

"Good friends, all of them. "Did you know that Sophie and Adam were both students of mine when I taught at York?"

"No, I didn't," she said, mildly surprised as much by the information as by Iain's down-to-earth countenance. She wasn't happy to admit it, but Emmie saw now that she'd formed an opinion of the archaeologist before she'd met him, and without even realizing. The genuine, friendly man that sought to make her comfortable at his party was far from the snobbish, full-of-himself television personality she'd imagined.

"Yeah, they were a lot of fun, even as undergrads. And I've gotten to know Famke and Ewan and Dean over the years, too—archaeology being the small world that it is. I asked for them specifically for the Tullybrae project."

"Really? I didn't know you got to pick your own team for the show. I thought it was just whoever looks good on camera."

"Ewan? Looking good on camera?"

"He fits a type," Emmie laughed. "Papa bear, maybe."

"Perhaps," he allowed. "But no. I insisted on having them all. They're not always available to drop everything and uproot to a dig site, but when I can get them, I jump at the chance. They're only working out of the Edinburgh U campus temporarily."

She nodded her head, understanding. "I thought their office looked a little transient. Huh—I never thought of that. I just assumed that digging is what they always do."

"It's what they'd always do if the university would let them. But alas, tuition is a powerful motivator. Eager young minds clamouring for knowledge, and the undergrad courses need to be taught. To say nothing of the delegate committees, research grants and other short- and long-term projects." He paused and tilted his head. "Emmie—is that short for Emily?"

"Emmeline, actually." She took another sip of her wine, growing self-conscious.

"Emmeline. That's beautiful. Unusual. A family name?"

"My great-grandmother's, or so I'm told." When he raised a brow quizzically, she added vaguely, "I've never met her."

"It's always nice to see the past carried forward to the future. A nod to those who came before us. But I'm sure I don't need to tell you that. How is it that you came to be curator at such a young age, by the way? That's impressive."

"Not really," she dismissed. "It was kind of a trade-off. Lady Rotherham couldn't afford to pay for a full-fledged curator with the amount of work that needed to be done cataloguing and referencing and all that. So I'm doing all the grunt work in exchange for the title and the experience."

"Sounds like a fair trade."

"I think it is. And so did Professor McCall—he put me up for the job."

"Professor McCall—as in Boomer McCall?" Iain belted a laugh.

"I take it you know him."

"As I said, archaeology's a small world." He shook his head, smiling inwardly. "Boomer McCall. Imagine. Ask him how he got his nickname, next time you see him."

"I've already been given an overview by Lady Rotherham," she answered dryly. "At least an overview of the livestock and … er … *items* that were involved."

"And how do you find Lady Rotherham?"

"She's…" Emmie paused, searching for the right way to express her impression of the lady. "She's okay. Nice, if a little all over the place. But she's great to work for. Doesn't hover, or try to micromanage or anything. She trusts me to get on with my work, and do the job right. So I appreciate that."

"Yeah, she's… ah… she's something else." He chuckled, ruffling his shaggy hair. "Nah, she's got a good heart underneath that high-energy exterior. I really think she cares about Tullybrae deep down. If I thought she were exploiting it for her own gain, or to get herself onto the telly, I wouldn't have agreed to take on the project. Mind, I think there *is* some of that in there, wanting her five minutes of fame. But that's not what's at the heart of it."

"I'd say that's about right," she agreed. "When she told me all about the supposed ghosts, she wasn't trying to hype it up or make a big thing out of it. She simply told me about them like they were part of her family."

"That's what Shelagh said—she's one of the producers over at Stannisfield. She told me Camille mentioned a murder, or murd*ers*, but didn't much hype up the story other than to pitch it as a point of archaeological interest."

"It's a shame they don't know anything about who it was—or who they were, if it's more than one. I looked online and in the manor library, but there's nothing concrete in the written records to substantiate anything."

"One of the frustrating things about history, huh? If it's not in the written record, then there's nothing to carry it forward. It as good as never happened."

Emmie tilted her head. "Not necessarily. I mean, isn't that what you do? Dig up the forgotten past, bring it back to life?"

He nodded once, conceding. "I have hope for you yet, young grasshopper. I like the way your mind works. So many of the old fuddy-duddies in our extended field don't make those kind of leaps. Those that do are the ones that end up making a mark on the historical record. The ones that don't find their careers stalled at regurgitating research papers and teaching undergrad classes until retirement." He paused, a thought coming to his mind. "You know, if you're actually interested in trying to breathe life into the legend, I have a mate down at Glasgow U that has access to a lot of records and documents that no one thought important enough to write about. Lots from your neck of the woods up at Tullybrae. There may be nothing in there, but there could just as easily be something that can give you a bit of a jumpstart. If you want, I can put you in touch with him."

"Really?" Emmie beamed. "I'd love that!"

"Don't get your hopes up. It may be a dead end, but at least it's something."

"That's the thing about history," she replied. "You hit dead end after dead end, but you keep going until one day a dead end turns out to be a hidden door."

Iain laughed, a charming, heartfelt laugh. "Well said." He raised his bottle. "A toast, then. To dead ends."

"To dead ends," Emmie echoed, and clinked her glass against his.

TWELVE

IAIN'S BUSINESS CARD lent a satisfying weight to the pocket of Emmie's corduroy skirt as Ewan drove them back to Tullybrae along the dark Highland roads. It was after midnight by the time they turned through the gates and came up to the house.

Ewan pulled the Kangoo to a stop in front of the main entrance, and turned the engine off.

"I've left my notebook in the tent. Be right back."

Dean unlatched his seatbelt. "Might as well stretch our legs while we're waiting." Adam followed suit.

Famke, who had been asleep until then, jolted awake as Sophie crawled sloppily over her lap. After indulging in one too many Smirnoff Ices, the young Londoner was more than a little worse for the wear.

"Yep, stretch's what I need too, mate," she slurred.

She yanked open the door, stumbling a little when her feet hit the gravel drive, and sauntered off around the side of the house.

"Man, not again," Adam groaned.

"Someone make sure she doesn't go too far," Ewan called to them, halfway into the field. "I'm leaving as soon as I've got my book. She can walk back if she's not ready to go when I am."

"I'll get her," Emmie relented, exiting the van. The offer was received with a grateful smile from a bleary-eyed Famke.

"You want me to go with?" Dean offered.

"No, that's okay—Oh, Adam!" No less worse for the wear than Sophie, Adam was relieving himself against one of the tires.

"Sorry, love. Call of nature," he answered.

"Do you have *any* shame, dude?" Dean admonished.

"Occasionally."

Shaking her head, Emmie trotted off in the direction Sophie had gone.

"Soph?" she called into the empty night. "So-*oph*."

From somewhere at the back of the house, towards where the gardens were laid out in a maze of beds and high shrubbery, she thought she heard quick, light footsteps on the gravel walkways. Picking up her pace, she followed the sound. When she lost the trail, she stopped.

"Soph?" she called again.

A giggle came from her left.

"Soph, where are you?"

She took off again, following the laughter.

"This isn't funny."

Breaking through the rear hedge where the grounds of the manor ended, Emmie slowed. In front of her was a view more breathtaking than the daylight had ever shown. The moon shone brightly, gilding the hills in ribbons of silver. The view was endless. Empty. Yet sublimely beautiful, like Earth when seen from space.

An acute desire to walk out, to become lost in that silver moonlight, pulled her forward, away from the known, safe grounds of Tullybrae. These luminescent hills called to her, promised her that this was where her heart truly lay. It was not in Corner Brook, never there. It has always been here.

She'd gone perhaps a hundred feet before the tingling washed over her right side. A tingling which had been lifted from her when the van left the estate earlier that evening.

He was here. The Highlander.

As if in a dream, Emmie turned to the right. Her eyes tracked across the horizon, taking in the panorama before coming to a halt at a figure in the distance. He was another hundred feet away, but still she knew him. Without ever having seen his face before, Emmie knew it was him.

Immense sadness permeated the space between them and sank deep into her core. He stared at her with an intensity that held her mesmerised. Dark, unruly hair tumbled to his shoulders, and framed a captivating face. Strong, yet graceful in its masculinity. A traditional *feileadh mhor* flapped gently around bare, muscled legs.

He was something she might have seen in a movie, something Hollywood might emulate with the help of makeup artists and costume departments and award-winning directors. Except that he was so much more, so much grander than anything makeup and costumes could ever effect.

He was real. Authentic.

He made no move, did not try to communicate or gesture in any way. He simply stood, looking at her. Waiting, it seemed, for her to come to him.

And she wanted to. Dear God, it terrified her to admit that she wanted to.

Without warning, a pair of arms grabbed her from behind. Emmie yelped, her voice echoing across the landscape.

"Whatcha doin' out here, hmmm?" Sophie drawled into her ear.

"Soph, you almost gave me a heart attack!"

Sophie giggled—a very different giggle than what Emmie had heard only moments before. Her gaze snapped back to the Highlander. He was gone.

Still reeling, she looked to Sophie, who was sloppy grinning at her like nothing had happened. The girl had no idea what she'd interrupted, no inkling of the connection she'd just severed so carelessly. An irrational streak of anger surged in Emmie's chest; words bubbled up from some vile place deep within her, begging to be hurled at Sophie and her foolish, pie-eyed face.

Don't do it. It wasn't her fault, urged the rational part of her that was horrified by her own reaction. And she *was* horrified. Mortified. Emmie was not one to take her frustrations out on other people, even when they deserved it.

Sophie did not deserve it now. Emmie breathed. Breathed again. Smiled, and threw an arm around Sophie's shoulder.

"Come on, sweetie. Let's get you back to the van."

She looked back one last time to the empty hills. There was no one there.

Once the van turned onto the road and drove out of sight, Emmie closed and bolted the manor's front door. The darkened, oil-painted eyes of Tullybrae's dead followed her up the main staircase.

She felt very strange as she changed into her pajamas and retreated to the washroom to prepare for bed. Rattled, more like. If she had any doubt before now of whom or what she'd been sensing, those doubts had been vanquished. He was a Highlander. He was *the* Highlander. And his interest in her went far beyond curiosity.

It had been no accident that she'd been led away from the group and into the open land. Neither had it been a coincidence that she'd come upon his apparition. He'd meant for her to see him.

He did not look like anyone she'd seen before. Despite this, Emmie had the inexplicable conviction that she knew him. Or maybe not that she *knew* him, exactly, but that he was important to her somehow. That he was, and always had been, an integral part of her existence.

How the hell did that make any sense? It didn't. The fact that it didn't, and the fact that she couldn't shake herself of the conviction, frightened her. It was because she couldn't control it. It had no place in her ordered, careful life.

The night passed restlessly. The child's laughter that lured her away from the gardens plagued her dreams. Incessant laughter. And his face, the face of the Highlander, plagued her dreams, too. In sleep, he was closer than when she'd seen him awake. Close enough that she might reach out and touch him. But she couldn't—her arms would not move.

In her dreams, he wore a tortured expression. "Save me," he would say. Nothing more, just "Save me."

"I can't save you, you're dead," she called.

"Save me" was his only whispered response.

"Save you from what?" she cried. "Save you from *what?*"

Somewhere in the back of her consciousness, the part that lingered between awake and asleep, she was aware that she was tossing and turning. Aware of the strong scent of roses, and of a hand upon her hair.

When the dim light of a rainy morning pulled her from slumber, she found that the covers had been tucked in around her during the night, and roses still hung in the air.

It was after ten when she was ready to head down to the kitchen for breakfast. Instead of her usual stylish ensemble, she wore jeans and a college hoodie. Her hair, still wet from a hasty shower, hung lank around her shoulders. There wasn't a spot of makeup on her face, and she hadn't even bothered with shoes. Instead, it was her slippers.

When she caught sight of herself in the full-length, enameled Rococo-style mirror at the top of the main staircase, she cringed.

This is not me, she thought, and waited for the familiar panic to surface—the panic which always accompanied the knowledge that she was not at her best. That the leash on her life which she held tightly at all times was slipping.

It never came. Apathy was all she felt as she looked at herself. Apathy, and the Highlander's presence.

"Late night?" Lamb remarked when she joined him at the wooden work table and listlessly plunked herself onto the sea-green stool.

"I thought you'd be upstairs already," she answered. "Aren't you usually hard at work this time of the morning?"

"It is my turn to cook the breakfast," he said simply.

Emmie dropped her head into her hands and rubbed her squeaky-clean face. "I'm sorry, Lamb. I didn't realize you'd be waiting for me. I should have been up earlier."

"Nonsense. You young people are entitled to a night of fun followed by a lie-in once in a while."

"I wouldn't call it 'fun' exactly."

Lamb quirked a white brow. "Did you no' have a nice time?"

"I shouldn't say that, it's not fair," she amended. "I did have a good time. It was nice spending an evening with the dig crew. They're all great, and they each tried so hard to make sure I felt included. Even Adam, if you can believe that."

"Oh, aye. Adam. That one." Lamb chuckled.

"He's not so bad once you get to know him. There's a good heart beneath that male-chauvinist exterior. He actually served us all drinks. I mean, took the time to ask us what we wanted and pour it for us."

"You don't say."

"I know. I wasn't expecting it. But I think it proves that he's thoughtful. Deep down, at least."

"I'll remember that in my dealings with the lad. Was there something about the party itself you didn't fancy?"

Emmie reached for the silver thermal coffee pot in the centre of the table, and poured its contents into her cup.

"Cream?" Lamb offered, passing her the white jar.

"Thanks." Emmie accepted it and poured. "I'm not really big on parties. I'm a wallflower, to be honest. I find keeping up conversation in a big group exhausting. Does that make sense?"

"It does." Lamb helped himself to a piece of toast. "I'm much the same. I prefer good conversation with one or two friends rather than stilted or superficial conversation with many people. Especially when most of those people are all trying to talk over one another."

Emmie smiled sadly. "And you feel like you've got to keep up or risk fading away?"

He tipped his head knowingly, and they lapsed into silence. Emmie spent the lapse staring blankly at her coffee cup.

"Why don't you go back to bed for a while, hmmm?" Lamb suggested. "You look knackered."

"No." Emmie plucked some bacon and a slice of toast from their platters, and munched without enthusiasm. "Too much to do. It's just a bad night of sleep, that's all. Everybody has those."

With a last sip of her coffee, which she'd only half drunk, Emmie took her dishes to the sink and gave them a scrub. Then, approaching Lamb from behind, she gave his shoulders an affectionate squeeze. "Thanks for brekkie, it was delicious."

He watched her go.

"I assume her bad night of sleep had something to do with *him*?" he said when she was out of earshot.

Mrs. Lamb sighed, troubled. Her starched dress rustled as she materialized in the seat Emmie had just vacated. "I daresay it does."

"Should I be worried? He seems to be around her a lot. He doesn't mean to do her any harm, does he?"

"Oh, nothing like that. He's fascinated by her, though, I'll say that. Drawn to her. I don't know why yet, I haven't been able to puzzle it out.

And no' for lack of trying, mind. But there's something between them. Something that goes beyond a chance encounter." She paused, at a loss to explain the inkling she had. "I'll keep an eye on her, and on him. In the meantime, *you* can work on getting her to eat more. She's all skin and bone as it is. Half a piece of toast and two rashers of bacon does no' a breakfast make."

"I can't make her eat, Mother. If she doesn't want to eat, she doesn't want to eat."

"She doesn't want to eat because this bacon is overcooked. I tell you and I tell you—you have to take it off the skillet *before* it's done, for it will continue to cook in the grease after it's been removed from the heat."

Lamb sighed. "Yes, Mother."

EMMIE DID HAVE lots of work to do, it wasn't a lie. But when she reached the library, which was the next room on her "to catalogue" list, the thought of poring over dusty old books all day wasn't terribly appealing— highly unusual for someone who loved old books so much. Instead, she retreated to the nursery, where she stared unenthusiastically at her laptop while it booted up.

The dig crew hadn't arrived yet. With a heavily overcast sky threatening rain, it was unlikely that they'd come at all today. To be fair, it had always been unlikely that Sophie was going to come. She must be hurting something fierce after last night's excess.

The first thing Emmie did when her laptop was warmed up was log on to her email. The archives at Cambridge had gotten back to her about some inquiries she'd fired off last week—complete with invoice. She cringed at the amount when she opened the .pdf document. But at least it was exactly what had been quoted, no more.

No less, come to that.

Lady Rotherham had approved the expense when Emmie explained the necessity. "Oliver will moan and groan about it, but you leave him to me," she had laughed over the phone.

There was also an email from Dean. The time stamp on it said it had come in at a quarter to ten that morning. Yep, if they were logged on and sending email this late in the morning and they still weren't at Tullybrae, then today was a write-off.

She opened the email, for which the subject line read, "FW: E-120463-C55 Kilt Pin, Silver, Tullybrae."

Hey Em,

Thought you might be interested to know that we got an ID on that kilt pin we found a while ago. We were able to clean it up and History was able to identify the insignia as belonging to Clan MacDonald. Haven't done any digging yet to see that clan's footprint on the area. I'll leave that to you history types to figure out.

We likely won't be out to Tullybrae today. The forecast calls for heavy rain. And besides, Queen Sophie spent all last night yacking in the bathroom, and hasn't yet graced us with her royal presence. We've taken an over-under on what time she'll emerge — Adam's going for broke and says she won't come out at all.

Hope you're feeling okay this morning, and we'll see you soon.

Deano

Dean Walker, MSc, Archaeology
Associate Professor
Dept. of History, Classics and Archaeology
University of Edinburgh

"Hold my beer, while I kiss your girlfriend." - Brad Paisley

Below that was the original message which had been sent from the history department with the details of the kilt pin.

Emmie smiled at Dean's unorthodox email signature. It was so unprofessional, yet something only someone as naturally charismatic as Dean could get away with. She found it easy to forget that the crew—Adam and Dean especially—were highly educated scholars. When they were working on site, they looked like carefree children digging in the dirt. She tended to forget that theirs was a highly specialized field which took a lot of school and a significant degree of intelligence to earn.

As for the content of his email, the name MacDonald had set a bell ringing in her head. Like the melody that had come to her that night in the bath when she first encountered the countess, she knew the name without knowing why.

Opening an Internet browser, she looked up Clan MacDonald. While she searched, Clunie stalked into the room, settling himself on top of her slippered feet beneath the desk.

"Hey there, fella," she murmured, wiggling her toes against him. Deep, rumbling purrs were his response.

Emmie conducted her Internet search as methodically as her training had conditioned her to... specifically: experimental keyword searches, occasional hyperlink clicking, and general, all-round hunch following. What she found was a fairly standard history for a Highland Scottish clan, much of which glossed over a long-standing conflict with Clan Campbell. According to the maps on her computer screen, the MacDonalds inhabited a wide swath of land on the western edge of the Grampian mountain range, on which land Tullybrae now sat. Cameron clan land separated that of Clans MacDonald and Campbell, but nothing about their triad interactions through the centuries sparked a similar recognition as that which she'd had for the name MacDonald itself.

She sat back in her swivel chair and folded her hands across her belly. Clunie, ignorant of her inner turmoil as house cats typically are, continued to purr contentedly at her feet.

The search had been disappointing. It shouldn't have been, for the simple fact that Web searches were always disappointing. They were best regarded as a starting point, a sort of digital muse, where inklings began their tickle and led to deeper, more meaningful searches elsewhere. But when she read Dean's email—no, the second she saw it in her inbox—she realized she'd been hoping her search would mean something. Would trigger... *something*.

What, though?

She re-read the information on the last website she'd landed on. None of it was significant—MacDonald, Campbell, fighting—nothing meant anything to her.

For some unaccountable reason, this absence of meaning was frustrating. And on some level, it occurred to her to wonder why she was so frustrated. It was as though the frustration wasn't coming from her, as though someone else's frustration was rubbing off on her...

The Highlander.

She recalled that sudden and inexplicable burst of anger that invaded her thoughts the morning when the digging had started. As surely as she knew that anger wasn't hers, she knew this frustration wasn't hers, either. Or not entirely, at least.

She dropped her head to the desk, and softly banged it against the surface several times. *Get out of my head, get out of my head, get out of my head,* she chanted. But the Highlander would not back off.

A distraction. That's what she needed. Sitting up, Emmie pulled up her email again. The next message was from her brother, Chase. She began reading, mouthing the words to keep her attention on them and off of the frustration. Soon, the reading came more naturally.

Hey there, Em-bo-bem,

I spent Thanksgiving weekend at home, and as you can imagine, Mom was at me non-stop to get in touch with you to see how you were doing. Actually, she was at me to *call* you, and expressly forbade me to email, but who the hell calls anybody anymore, right? I know you get it, and you agree with me, so I know you'll forgive me for disobeying orders.

Emmie's heart warmed, picturing her brother's Thanksgiving weekend with the 'rents. The house was likely done up in fall colours and the pumpkins lined up on the porch, at the ready for Hallowe'en like orange soldiers.

So I hear that things out there in brave old Scotland are going well. I hope they are, anyway, and that Mom isn't exaggerating. Of course, Ron keeps going on about the pubs, and about how, first chance they get to come and see you, he's going on the pub crawl of a lifetime. Which, knowing him, means having a pint in the closest dive he can find, then picking up a six-pack from wherever they sell beer over there, and retreating to a La-Z-Boy for the rest of the night.

Things are great with me, in case you're wondering. And Mom says you *are* wondering — in fact, to hear her tell it, you're dying of curiosity and inconsolable that I haven't provided you with an update sooner. She says she's told you about Gillian already, so I won't bore you with that except to say that things are going well. And contrary to what she might tell you in one of her spells of wishful thinking, no, we have no plans to get married, no, I have not moved in, and no, grandchildren are not "just on the horizon." The job's way too crazy to be worrying about a family. But good crazy. I'm at the bars three or four times a week after work, hanging with some of the top sales execs. And these bars, they're so upscale, nothing like the pubs back home in Corner Brook, I can tell you that.

From what I hear, Mom's also told you that I sold my truck. . . 'nuff about that, it's still a sore spot, lol.

I've had a bit of news. I wouldn't call it bad, exactly. Maybe sad is a better word for it. My mom — my real mom, that is — passed away two weeks ago. I'm not sure that I'm really sad about her going, more sad about the whole thing. Turns out she's had cancer for the past few months, and I never knew about it. She and I don't really keep in touch, as you know. It was her family who got in touch with me after she passed. They invited me to the funeral. Mom and Ron offered to go with me, but in the end, I went alone. It was just something I had to do by myself, to face them all and let them know that I turned out just fine on my own. They were glad I came, but I wasn't enveloped into the folds of their family like a long-lost son. I'm glad about that. They let her give me away, after all. No point in pretending like I'm happy to see them now.

Anyway, all this got me thinking, and I wanted to tell you something. It's something that I've been thinking about for a while now, and I've never said it before. But I think I should, just to know that I've said it. My mom's death has reminded me that life is finite, and you never know when you're going to be out of it.

I wanted to say that I envy you a bit, Em. I know the circumstances of your adoption were horrific, and no kid should ever have to go through that. But think of it this way: You weren't given up as though you didn't matter. Your mom and your grandmother died. My mother could have kept me, could have loved me, and chose not to. And before you start in on me, I know you're going to say that I had no idea what choices she had to face, and what battles she had to fight. I know all that, and in my head I agree. It probably was for the best that she gave me up. Grace and Ron have been wonderful. They are my mom and dad, and I can't imagine life without them. But somewhere in the back of my heart, I can't help but be angry for my own sake. Because I can't get past the deep-down feeling that my mother's choice was selfish.

I know that all this doesn't make what you went through any better. But at least you know that you were always loved. By someone.

I won't take up too much of your time, but just promise me you'll take care of yourself out there, and come home soon. We all miss you.

Love, Chaser.

Her brother's message hit Emmie like a lead ball to the stomach. She hadn't been expecting something so deep. Not from him. Water off a duck's back. Butter wouldn't melt. All the clichéd expressions one could think of—that was Chase.

He'd been right—she would argue that he could never know what his mother had had to face, he had no idea of the choices she had been forced to make at so young an age. Emmie understood his feelings and where they came from. And though she thought he was being unfair about his own adoption, she didn't resent him for what he was saying about hers. He had a good heart, and she understood the logic behind it. In telling her this, he meant well.

But he was wrong. His feelings were based on *his* experience. He was an outsider to what Emmie had gone through, would never understand what it was to be not enough, not worth it to fight for.

Defeated by feelings she thought were long buried, Emmie pushed away from the desk, shut the screen on her laptop, and retreated to the hidden door to the third floor. The leaden sky broke outside the unadorned staircase windows just as she began to climb, and a flash of lightning, followed by a heavy grumble of thunder, gave way to rain patter on the large, slanting roof.

In her room, she turned on the bedside lamp and sat carefully on the edge of the bed, on the side that faced the dresser. The antique brass frame groaned under her weight.

The framed photo of her mother smiled back at her from behind the glass. Emmie stared at it, trying to divine its secrets.

"Chase thinks you didn't have a choice in giving me up, but you did," she accused. "You didn't have to die—you chose to. You *chose* to let yourself die."

Silence.

"Did I not mean enough to you? Did my future, my happiness, mean *anything* to you?"

More silence. The frozen smile looked today like an apology.

"An apology isn't enough," Emmie told the photo. "It's too late to be sorry about it."

Then the grief broke. Grief which she'd dammed up, reinforced with the concrete and steel girders of a tightly controlled, perfectly lived life. Emmie turned her back to the photo, lay her head on the pillow, and cried. She cried long and deep. Sobbed with a heartbreak, the equal of which she'd felt only once in her life—the day on the stairs when she and the Highlander had cried together.

Above, the rain continued to pelt the roof. She cried until she was light-headed, until her gasping sobs began to lose momentum. Her sleepless night caught up with her, and she began to fade into slumber.

Somewhere in the twilight of half-sleep, she slipped into another level of consciousness. Vaguely, she detected the invisible weight of someone laying down behind her. Warm, strong arms wrapped around her in a comforting embrace.

It was the Highlander. Just as his rage had affected her those weeks ago, her sorrow was affecting him now. He knew it, could feel it. And was offering what little comfort he could in that hazy space between the living and the dead.

Emmie took solace in the comfort he was offering. Willingly, gratefully, she let it lull her into a sense of peace.

Save me, were the whispered words that carried her into a dreamless sleep.

THIRTEEN

Tuesday, October 14 **7:35 pm**
From: Emmie Tunstall <E.Tunstall2325@freemail.com>
Subject: Would Like to Request a Meeting
To: protenfeld@webspot.co.uk

Dear Mr. Rotenfeld,

My name is Emmie Tunstall, and I am curator at Tullybrae
House, which is just south-east of the town of Aviemore. I
was given your contact information by Dr. Iain Northcott.
He is hosting an episode of Digging Scotland in which
Tullybrae is being featured.

I hope you don't mind, but Dr. Northcott suggested that you
might be able to help me better understand the clans that
historically inhabited the lands in and around the Grampian
mountain range. If you had some time for me, I'd love to
come down to Glasgow and speak with you at a date and time
that suits your schedule.

If, however, you are unable or uninterested, then please
accept my apologies, and I thank you for your time.

Sincerely,

Emmie Tunstall
Curator, Tullybrae House

Thursday, October 16 9:24 am
From: Rotenfeld, Paul <protenfeld@webspot.co.uk>
Subject: RE: Would Like to Request a Meeting
To: Emmie Tunstall

Hello Emmie,

Thank you so much for your email. Yes, Iain and I go way back. It is no trouble at all, I'm glad he pointed you my way.

I'd be more than happy to entertain you with all the stories I have on the clans of the Grampians if the trek to Glasgow from Aviemore isn't too much for you. How does next Thursday suit? Say, 1 pm? I have a committee meeting in the morning, but am free the rest of the day. Looking forward to meeting you.

Best,

Paul Rotenfeld
History, University of Glasgow

FOURTEEN

THURSDAY MORNING BEGAN with a gentle, almost tentative sunshine. A low-lying fog had settled over the Highlands in the night, bringing with it an unusual warm front. The effect on the land was enchanting, like a veil of gossamer had been laid down by the faeries.

Emmie woke early, roused by the drone of her alarm clock. Despite how she had been feeling of late, she wanted to look her best for the trip to Glasgow. Her now frequent outfits of sweatshirts and yoga pants would not be making an appearance today.

Today, she was feeling much more "on." A sharp sense of purpose put an extra bounce in her step. She got herself showered, paying particular attention to the finer points of her personal hygiene routine that had slipped over the last little while. Her sunny curls were straightened with a flat iron so that they fell in long, silky tresses. To celebrate the burst of fall warmth, she dressed in black leggings and a light-weight sweater dress in baby pink. Simple ballerina flats completed the ensemble.

With a delicate gold charm bracelet on her wrist and fresh-faced makeup lightly applied, she hurried down to the kitchen, where Lamb was enjoying an early cup of tea.

He straightened on his stool, surprised to see her. "I wasn't expecting you this early, my dear."

"And why should you?" She rounded the table and hugged him affectionately from behind. "You stay there, I'll cook breakfast this morning."

"But it's no' your turn," he objected.

"That's okay, I want to. Besides, I might not be back in time for supper tonight."

"Yes, well, you take care on those roads down to Glasgow. And mind you call if you're going to be later than nine. Give an old man some peace of mind that you're no' in any kind of trouble."

"I'll be fine, you worry wart," she chastised.

"Promise me, though."

"I promise, so long as *you* promise not to wait up for me."

"All right, I promise."

He was lying, of course. They both knew it.

After a breakfast of bacon and scrambled eggs, Emmie headed out to her car. The Highlander followed her. He'd been with her since she opened her eyes, and he was just as excited as she was.

Or perhaps he was feeding off her excitement… or perhaps his excitement was intensifying hers…

Either way, it didn't matter. They were both in a good mood.

Once again, though, as she left the grounds of Tullybrae, his presence pulled away from her. She tried to ignore it, to lose herself in the scenery. But the absence of the Highlander made her feel disconcertingly alone. Exposed. Abandoned.

Abandoned?

She didn't remember feeling abandoned since she was a little girl, since coming to live with the Tunstalls. They'd given her every material thing she ever wanted, and as much love as they had to give. And it had never been enough because all she wanted was her mother. But her mother hadn't wanted her. Not enough to stay alive, anyway.

More feelings rising which she thought were well and truly buried. She'd convinced herself that the problem had been her mother's, not hers. And while the child Emmie had been longed for her mother, and blamed her, and cast a whole host of other emotions upon her, Emmie the grown woman had been sure that abandonment long ago ceased to be one of them.

Now, here it was once more, rearing its ugly, cold head and throwing her back there all over again. And it was the Highlander who brought it about.

As much as she wanted to, though, she couldn't be angry with him for it. She did try, too. As she drove, she clutched the steering wheel and worked at seething over what he was doing to her. But the seething simply didn't take; she soon gave up. It was odd, but she had the sense that he knew how she felt. Even though he wasn't with her just then, she could still identify that they shared the knowledge of what it was to be abandoned.

Her face must have betrayed her thoughts, because when she stopped for coffee and a nibble at a small restaurant outside of Crieff, the heavyset, elderly waitress gave her a motherly pat on the arm.

"You look like you have the weight of the world on your shoulders, poppet," she said as she approached Emmie's table.

It surprised Emmie to hear. Was she that transparent?

"Oh, yeah. Well, nothing a coffee and a muffin won't fix," she answered lightly.

"We do have a nice selection of muffins," the woman offered. "Some double chocolate and some blueberry. But if I'm guessing right, you look like you might enjoy one of our burnt butterscotch."

"Mmmm, burnt butterscotch. I'll try one of those."

Pleased by her own intuition, the woman bustled to the counter. She was soon back with the muffin, coffee, and an extra plate.

"Raspberry butter drop scones. On the house, poppet. Sweeties and cakes never make anything better, but they sure do help."

A half hour later, Emmie was on the road again. Half her muffin was wrapped to go, and the woman had given her a fresh takeaway cup of coffee. She arrived in Glasgow shortly before one in the afternoon, and located the university with little trouble.

Thanks to the helpful young man at the information desk, she found Dr. Paul Rotenfeld's office in building D15 off a street called University Gardens. A tall, lanky man with salt-and-pepper hair slicked stylishly to the side, he looked like he'd just returned from his committee meeting. He stood at his desk, sorting through a stack of papers. A vibrant, sky blue dress shirt was open at the neck and tucked into dark, slim-cut jeans. Trendy, narrow-toed oxfords of burnt orange leather made a prominent accent to his ensemble. The man was the polar opposite of Iain Northcott.

"Dr. Rotenfeld?" she inquired politely, tapping on the door frame.

He looked up. His distracted expression broke to a pleasant, attractive smile. "Paul, please. You must be Emmie." He abandoned his stack of papers and stepped towards her, hand outstretched. His grip was firm when she extended her own hand, and he spoke with an American, slightly New Jerseyish accent. "Please, won't you come in and have a seat?"

She followed him into the office and took the grey padded armchair he offered.

"I must admit, when I saw that you were curator, I wasn't expecting someone so young."

"It's an incentive title," she dismissed.

"That's the best kind. Means you know something about ambition. You look like you know what you want, and aren't afraid of a little hard work to get it."

"Thank you." Emmie blushed at his praise.

"So, Emmie. What exactly are you looking for? You wrote in your email that you'd like to know a little bit more about the clans in the Highlands—stuff that you can't find on Wikipedia." He winked knowingly.

"Yes, I Wikied already," she grinned sheepishly. "Never enough detail, no matter how far down those hyperlinks you drill."

"Iain was right to refer you to me. You'd be hard-pressed to find anyone that knows more about the Highland clans than I do—just don't tell my colleagues that."

"My lips are sealed."

"Good, good. Swollen egos around here. Is there anything in particular you'd like to know more about, or is it just a general inquiry?"

She tipped her head back and forth. "Yes, and no. I'm not sure how to put this... would it make sense if I said I have a vague idea about something specific?"

"Don't we all? I'd say that's the bane of our existence."

"I have a starting point, at least. So, apparently, there was a murder, or murders, on the estate where Tullybrae is, in the Cairngorms."

"Another clan murder?" he groaned in jest.

"I know. Big surprise, right? Anyway, a kilt pin was unearthed by the excavators that are working there. A rather elaborate one, actually, and the insignia on it was identified as MacDonald. So of course I went online to see what I could find. There's lots about the legendary hatred between the MacDonalds and the Campbells, but unfortunately there's nothing specific enough to link it to murders on Tullybrae land."

"Was Tullybrae around at the time of these alleged murders?"

"I don't know for sure, but the story goes that the murders predate the house."

Paul templed his fingers under his chin and crossed an ankle over one knee. "It's not a lot to go on, but bigger discoveries have been made on less."

Emmie shrugged. "Let's just say I won't be holding my breath. I simply want to start rooting and see what I come up with."

He tilted his head to the side, smiling thoughtfully. "You remind me of Iain. He gets curious about things and can't let them go. Even though he knows it will in all likelihood lead to dead ends and a lot of frustration."

"It's funny you mention that. We had a conversation about dead ends when I attended a party of his recently. That's where I met him."

"And hopefully was the start of a long and fruitful acquaintanceship. He's a good guy. A great friend." Paul slapped his palms on his thighs. "Well, Emmie, I do think I can help you. But I'd much rather do it somewhere else than this stuffy old office. How about we go out for a bit to eat and we can talk more? You hungry?"

She wasn't. Not in the least. But the prospect of sitting in a pub or a restaurant instead of a college office was far more appealing.

"I could eat," she evaded.

"Excellent! Let me just send an email off to the wife that she'll have to pick up the rug rat, and we'll be off."

"Aw, you have a wee one?"

"A daughter," he beamed, and passed her a framed photograph which he took from the shelf above his desk. "This is them."

Emmie took the pewter frame and looked at the faces as Paul typed. A beautiful, statuesque woman with rich, chocolate skin smiled out at her. In her arms was an adorable little girl who looked to be about two years old. She smiled shyly at the camera in the way children do. Her skin was lighter than her mother's, the colour of milky coffee, and she had clear, hazel eyes like her father.

A pang of jealously stirred at the sight of this child. She was clearly loved. Unconditionally. By both her parents. She didn't know how lucky she was.

Emmie set the photograph on the edge of the desk. "They're gorgeous."

"I think so. But of course, I'm biased."

With an exaggerated click of his index finger on the mouse, he announced, "And that's that."

He stood, and ushered Emmie out of the office. With a quick pause for an introduction to the head of the department as they passed on their way out, Emmie and Paul were off at a brisk walk down University Gardens.

"Warm today, isn't it?" he noted when they reached a small, unassuming pub a block away.

Being so close to the university, Emmie expected a dingy college bar. So she was pleased when Paul pulled open the heavy door to find a neat, if slightly smoky, traditional pub. Complete with brass taps and oak. It was also, thankfully, empty. Devoid of rowdy college students.

"Why don't we take that seat up there?" he suggested. He pointed to the back of the pub, where a row of tall tables were lined on a narrow, raised strip.

Not long after they'd seated themselves, the bartender came out from behind the bar to take their order.

"Good to see you again, Paul lad," the man said.

Paul looked up at the tall, thick man with an unruly mop of grey hair. "And you, Neil. How's Suze liking her time off?"

"She's bored as shite. Driving me radge in the process. Can't wait until the woman's off bed rest."

"I'll bet. Sorry to hear. I'll have the pork pastie special."

"And for you, love?"

"Um," Emmie scanned the leather-bound menu quickly. "May I please have the breaded shrimp bites and a pint of bitter?"

Paul raised an eyebrow approvingly. "Add a pint of bitter to my order, too, Neil."

The barman bobbed his large head once, and left to place their order.

"His wife, Suzanne, has just had an operation," Paul explained when he was out of earshot. "Nothing major, but she's on bed rest for six weeks. The pair of them don't get along at the best of times, so I can only imagine how they're both feeling now."

"Ah."

"So, back to you. You said Tullybrae is in the Cairngorms?"

"It is. About a half hour south-east of Aviemore."

"Lovely area. I'm always in awe of those hills every time I'm through there. And I've lived in Scotland for over ten years now."

"It is amazing," she agreed. "I'm in awe every time I drive through there, too—well, the few times I've driven around, anyway. Those rock outlines that you can sometimes see in the open spaces are fascinating. They're just out there in the middle of nowhere."

"The foundations of centuries' old houses and dwellings."

"They really are houses, huh?"

"They certainly are—cheers, mate," he said to the bartender when their drinks were brought. "Yes, there would have been people all throughout these hills, living their lives over the centuries. They probably would have been Camerons in your area of the Cairngorms. Maybe Campbells, possibly MacDonalds. But more likely Camerons."

"Can you tell me more about the feud between the Campbells and the MacDonalds?"

"Feud is putting it lightly." Paul took a pull of his bitter.

"They didn't play nice in the sandbox?"

He barked a laugh. "They destroyed the sandbox."

"What was the feud about? I mean, the condensed version. Not Wikipedia condensed, but the historian's condensed."

"Historian's condensed." Paul thought. "I suppose you'd have to start in the times of Comyn and Bruce. From that day and generally forevermore, the MacDonalds were always seeming to throw their lot in with the reigning king's opposition, while the Campbells sided with whichever king was on the throne."

"That'll do it."

"Indeed. See, the MacDonalds dreamed of an independent Highland kingdom, and despised having to bow to the lowland Scots. Unfortunately, with being on top of each other in terms of territory, the years and the centuries brought lots of grievous offenses, the worst of which was probably the Massacre of Glen Coe."

He paused in his story, pleased by Emmie's rapt attention.

"You know, I usually bore people stiff when I start rattling on about clan history. I'm not used to people looking at me like I'm a rock star when I'm talking—and that includes my undergrad classes."

"Sorry," Emmie laughed lightly. "I hadn't realized I was gawking. I get caught up in history."

"A girl after my own heart—just teasing. But there are so many good stories about the Campbell-MacDonald feud. I'd talk your ear off if I tried to tell you all of them."

"I don't mind," she assured him. "Give me one. Your best one."

"My best one, eh?" Paul leaned back in his chair. "What about the Piper of Duntrune? Have you heard that one?"

"No."

"There are a few versions of this story, but here's the one I like best." He took another pull of his bitter.

"The legend goes that back in the first half of the seventeenth century, the Campbells and the MacDonalds were fighting over Duntrune Castle, which is on the north shores of Loch Crinan in Argyll. It was a defensive fortress that overlooked the loch, so in the wars of the clans it was strategically desirable. It changed hands back and forth over the centuries, but at the time we're speaking of, it was held by the Campbells. Of course, the MacDonalds mounted a savage attack and drove them out, killing many who fought to defend it. With the castle secure, the MacDonald chief, Sir Alistar MacDonald—also known as Colkitto—sailed away to continue his campaign. He left behind a small force to hold Duntrune, including his loyal piper."

"Colkitto?" Emmie queried, curious by the non-Celtic-sounding name.

"The anglicized version of *Col Ciotach*. It means 'left-handed,'" he explained. "If you know anything about clan history, you'll know that the piper held a privileged position. So when the Campbells launched a counter-offensive to retake the castle in Colkitto's absence, every MacDonald not killed in the fight was put to the sword—every one, that is, except the piper."

His voice dropped dramatically, and he leaned closer.

"Day after day, the piper kept vigil on the wall walk of Duntrune."

"Wasn't he a prisoner?"

"Remember I said pipers were privileged. That extended to his captivity. Kind of like the minimum-security prisons of today. He was allowed certain freedoms within the castle. But the piper knew that Colkitto would be coming back, whereupon he would be ambushed by the Campbells lying in wait. So he used that limited freedom to watch for his chief's return.

"One day, Colkitto's boat appeared on the horizon. Desperate to warn his chief, the piper began to play his pipes. It was a loud, boisterous tune that he hoped would reach Colkitto over the waves. But as the boat drew nearer, the piper realized that Colkitto must think he was playing a tune of welcome. So he changed the melody, and played a sadder tune instead."

"And?" Emmie demanded as Paul paused for effect.

He leaned even closer, which prompted Emmie to follow suit. Quietly, he said, "If I never told you how the story ended, how pissed off would you be?"

"You wouldn't dare." She swatted playfully at his arm as he snickered.

"You're right, I wouldn't. The warning worked. The message was heard by Colkitto and understood. The boat turned, and the MacDonalds sailed away to safety. But the Campbells understood the warning message in the tune, too. As punishment, they cut off the piper's hands so that he could play no more. The piper bled to death—the price of loyalty in the time of Scotland's clan wars."

"Wow," Emmie breathed, and slumped back in her chair.

"Yeah. Wow for sure. But the story gets better. For centuries, it was passed down as nothing more than a legend. After all, no written account of the event exists. But then, in the late eighteen eighties—I can't remember the exact date; eighteen eighty-seven or eighty-eight, or something like that—the contemporary owner of the castle was having repairs done to the courtyard. When workers pulled back one of the flagstones, they found a human skull staring up at them. By dusk, they had uncovered the full skeletal remains of a man."

"Let me guess—his hands were missing?"

"At the wrists. And here's the icing on the cake—pardon the cliché. I don't know if you're one of those that believe in ghosts and ghoulies, but Duntrune is said to be haunted. Strange occurrences, sounds, things moving about by themselves, that kind of thing. Could it be the piper looking for his lost hands?"

It was fortunate at that moment that the barman returned with their order of food, because Emmie needed a minute to recover from this last part of the tale. Something in what Paul had said struck her. The Highlander—he wasn't *looking* for something, was he?

"So, you said there was a MacDonald kilt pin found?" he inquired when they'd each started into their food.

"Yes. Here, I can show you."

She fished through her purse for her mobile device. Scrolling through her emails, she located the one from Dean, and pulled up the picture he'd sent of the pin after it had been cleaned. Accepting the phone from her outstretched hand, Paul gave a low whistle. "That is a beauty."

"I know. I've seen kilt pins before, but never one so ornate. They're usually utilitarian. It looks like this one might have been commissioned by a laird or a chief. A show of wealth, maybe."

"Or as a gift, perhaps? To commemorate something special?"

"Could be. I hadn't thought of that."

"Ah, now see here." He tilted the screen so Emmie could see. "This is the insignia of the MacDonalds of Keppoch. It's almost eroded away, but that shield is the fish, the ship, the lion and the cross. Do you see them? I'd bet my doctorate on it."

Emmie scrutinized the image. "Oh, yeah. Yes, I can see it."

"That is an interesting find. The MacDonalds of Keppoch were wiped out in fourteen ninety-five by the Campbells." He paused, and pinched the bridge of his nose. "Oh, you've apparently caught me on an off day. I don't remember the particulars off-hand. But there was a dispute over whether the MacDonalds of Keppoch or the MacIntoshes legally held the land. It was physically held by the MacDonalds, but by force. The MacIntoshes were intent on taking it—I believe the Crown had officially granted the lands to them. If I remember correctly, the MacDonalds of Keppoch appealed to the larger branch of the clan, the MacDonalds of Clanranald, for protection. What they didn't anticipate, though, was that the Campbells would take this as a threat. Or perhaps it was the MacIntoshes who convinced the Campbells it was a threat. Anyway, for whatever reason, the Campbells thought that the two MacDonald branches were joining forces, and so they teamed up with the MacIntoshes, and flanked the MacDonalds of Keppoch. When the clan was annihilated, and its chieftain, Angus MacDonald the second of Keppoch fled, the Campbells and the MacIntoshes split the land between them."

Emmie swallowed the shrimp she'd been chewing, which had somehow turned to concrete in her mouth. That story—it was familiar. Too close to home.

Why?

"But I'm catching you on an off day," she said with forced humour.

Paul did not seem to notice the change in her. "Tells you just how big my ego is. You know, we have archives of the MacIntoshes that came from Moy Hall in Inverness. It's the seat of the current clan chief. They were donated to the university a decade ago. I don't think they've all been categorized and reviewed yet, or their significance determined, but there were references to the MacDonalds of Keppoch, I believe. And documents that came from Keppoch Castle. You're welcome to have a look sometime. Maybe when you're down for a weekend or something. It will take you a while to go through them, I think."

"I'd like that," Emmie was quick to answer. "I'll have to take a look in my calendar and see when I can clear some time."

They spent the rest of the meal in companionable conversation. Paul, as Iain promised, was a wealth of information. Each story and anecdote he told held as much intrigue as if it were a Hollywood tabloid. Emmie gave the appearance of listening—really, she did *want* to listen—but her mind kept returning to the story about the MacDonalds of Keppoch. Could the graves that her friends on the dig crew were trying to uncover be those of victims from that massacre? Had the Highlander been murdered by a plotting MacIntosh, or a greedy Campbell?

Whatever the answer, she needed to find it. This meeting with Dr. Paul Rotenfeld had planted the seed—

No, that wasn't right. It was the Highlander's mere presence, his interest in her, that had planted the seed. This new information from Paul was the water that had let it take root. Emmie needed more information, more water. Answers. But what she feared, as was so often the case with the historical record, was that there would be no answers to find.

At least none that had been put to paper for the benefit of future generations.

FIFTEEN

"EMMIE, LOVE—I don't mean to be overbearing, but I really wish you'd try to eat a bit more."

Emmie looked up from her plate, on which she'd been pushing her mashed potatoes around. "Hmm?"

Lamb pointed his fork at her uneaten roast beef dinner. "You've hardly gotten any of that down you."

She dropped her fork onto the table, and her shoulders slumped. "I'm sorry, Lamb. Look at me: I'm making a pig's ear of our Saturday roast."

"Stuff the dinner, I'm concerned about you. And it's no' just the dinner. You're on your third glass of wine. That's more than I've ever seen you drink before."

"It's not that much," she argued unconvincingly.

"It is for you. And I daresay, you're no' your usual fastidious self—I'm no' criticizing, mind. Just worried about what's behind it all."

Emmie sat back, reflecting on Lamb's accusations. He *was* concerned for her; even she could see that. She wanted to allay his concerns, but how could she possibly tell him what was going on in her head?

"I don't know what's wrong with me lately," she admitted after a while. "I feel so... off kilter."

"You're working too hard, I think."

"That's just it—I'm not working hard enough. I haven't made half the progress I did when I first started. I can't seem to find my steam."

"Too fast out of the gate, perhaps?"

That wasn't it, either. But it was a better answer than the truth. "Yeah, maybe." Reaching for her wine, she tossed back the last of what was in her glass and poured a fourth.

"Careful," Lamb warned. "You don't want a sore head in the morning."

111

"I'm from Newfoundland. We know how to drink over there. Besides, I'm not having full glasses."

That wasn't the truth, either. Newfoundlanders knew how to drink, and were, by unspoken rule, fond of a good kitchen party. But it was a cultural pastime to which Emmie, not a Newfoundlander by birth, had never acclimatized. By the time she went up to bed, she was feeling the wine.

When she finished brushing her teeth, she lingered over the sink, staring at herself in the mirror. She looked haggard. The Highlander was wearing her down. His constant presence was more than curiosity, she understood now. He wanted something from her, something which she couldn't decipher.

The story of Duntrune's piper played over in her head. His brave sacrifice for his laird. The skeleton under the flagstones. She remembered Paul's words: *Could it be the piper looking for his lost hands?*

Gripping the sink with both hands, Emmie looked deliberately at her reflection in the mirror, and spoke to the Highlander.

"You're not expecting me to find your lost head, or your leg, or something like that, are you? Because I'm telling you now, I don't have the stomach for dismemberment."

For a few seconds there was nothing. Then, out of nowhere, laughter bubbled up from her belly. It was so powerful that her shoulders shook. The Highlander was laughing, too. They were laughing together.

It felt so good to laugh.

Still a little tipsy from the wine, she slipped easily into dreams. But those dreams were not peaceful. The giggling was there again. The strange, high laughter of an unseen child mingled with the Highlander's echoed whispers: *Save me.*

Emmie tried to follow as the whispers moved away, but her feet were weighed down by slumber. "Save you from what?" she wanted to cry, but her voice would not come.

Save me...

She awoke with a start. It was black as tar in the room, which was unusual. Normally there was at least a little bit of moonlight from the skylight above her bed. Not this night. Disoriented, she lay on her back, opening and closing her eyes, listening to the sound of her own breathing.

Odd, though—she didn't feel herself breathing. She felt neither hot, nor cold. The blankets beneath her did not seem to be touching her. She felt nothing.

Nothing except...

The bed shifted, as though an invisible body had risen from beside her. Emmie's heart picked up speed as something caressed her cheek. A hand? A cobweb? A breath?

Why could she feel that and not her own breath?

The unseen form moved across the room. She heard the rustle of cloth, and soft-soled footsteps. Then a door creaked, and a sliver of light stretched across the darkness. Emmie's eyes slid along the sliver, which widened as the door opened more.

Against a warm glow from beyond was silhouetted the Highlander. He was only a dark mass, his features undetectable against the light at his back. He was waiting for her, though. Waiting for her to join him.

To describe herself as entranced would be wrong. Emmie rose from the bed of her own free will. Her thoughts were her own, they were not held captive by some unearthly force. She knew what she was doing. Yet everything around her was surreal, dreamlike. She could feel the cold air on her skin without actually feeling it. Her fuzzy flannel pajamas were soft against her legs and arms and body, even though she had no physical perception of them.

Was this what the dead felt? Remembered sensations affecting the body because they affected the mind?

With her heart hammering in her ears, she put one bare foot carefully in front of the other, crossing the black space. The Highlander moved away from her, into the light. Emmie reached the doorway, took hold of the time-smoothed oak door, and with a breath for courage, opened it.

It was torchlight, the warm glow. It flickered against the stone walls of an ancient-looking hallway, illuminating the Highlander's face. The same face she'd seen in the moonlight beyond Tullybrae's gardens. He held her gaze as if he wanted to say more than he could express with words. Warm brown eyes that were both sad and haunting. The same dark, thick hair tumbled to his shoulders, and a stray lock hung over his forehead. She wanted to reach up to him, to brush that lock away with a fingertip. But she didn't dare.

He looked into her face, his own expression holding a measure of expectation. He held out his hand, inviting her to come with him to whatever was beyond.

Wherever they were, this place wasn't Tullybrae.

She glanced down at the hand he held out to her. Emmie knew instinctively that if she took his hand, if she accepted his invitation, she would be consenting to something. Acknowledging him. Allowing him to be more to her, to demand more *of* her. With an outstretched hand, he was asking for a commitment.

The prospect terrified her.

Then why did she want so desperately to take that hand? Why did she *need* to take that hand?

She was at a precipice, like on a rollercoaster at the peak of the track before it plummets to earth. She reached out, saw her own hand slide into his. Watched as his strong, sure fingers closed around hers.

There was nothing surreal about the shock of warmth that radiated from her palm and up her arm at his touch.

And so began the plummet.

Emmie let herself be led away from the room and into the castle beyond. It was a castle! Voices swarmed around them, sent a dozen different ways by the stone walls. They were behind her, above her, below her—a jumble of laughter and happy conversation. It was like being in a carnival funhouse.

Gradually, as the Highlander led her on, the noise began to come together, and she was better able to identify its source, to pick out individual sounds. A woman's voice tittered above the din briefly, followed by a chorus of male laughter.

He continued to guide her forward, sometimes looking back over his shoulder, sometimes looking ahead. Emmie's eyes mostly stayed on him, on his broad shoulders and his *feileadh mhor*—his great belted plaid.

The corridor opened up into a wide landing which overlooked a great hall. A rather crude wooden balustrade skirted the edge of the landing, and pitched downward along a flight of stairs that led to the ground floor. Overhead, wooden chandeliers, lit with more than a hundred candles, dangled from a soaring wood-beamed ceiling. Trestle tables were set on three sides of a central fire pit in which a sizeable blaze was going.

At the tables, people ate and laughed and drank. Dogs scampered about their feet, snatching up scraps of food wherever they were dropped. Or tossed. The people ate off bread trenchers with knives and fingers, and had none of the manners Emmie knew in her own modern life.

She nearly rubbed her eyes at the sight. Scottish castle life in what looked to be the Middle Ages. Right there in front of her. Everything from the clothing to the hall's décor to the food was more or less as contemporary scholars imagined it.

It was the very thing all historians wanted: To glimpse first-hand the past. To see it, smell it, hear it. It was gritty, earthy. Honest.

And frightening. The people, the men especially, looked rough. Hardened and dangerous. Instinctively, she edged back towards the corridor. The Highlander tightened his grip on her hand, and pulled her so that she was in front of him. He placed one hand on her waist, and rested the other on her shoulder. Emmie's stomach somersaulted at his touch.

Together, they looked down from the landing on the people below.

At the head table, which was on a raised dais, were seated ten people. Amidst the merriment, the man in the centre, presumably the chief (or chieftain or laird), stood. He held his hands up to silence his people. A hush fell over the crowd within seconds—such was the unquestionability of the chief's (or chieftain's or laird's) orders.

He spoke Gaelic in a commanding voice. It was not so much deep as it was authoritative. Emmie knew not a word of Gaelic save "slainte." Yet she understood what the man was saying as if the language were her native tongue.

"My friends," he began. "Ye ken well the events of this past winter have devastated me. Wi' the loss of Ennis—" at this he, along with everyone in the hall, made the sign of the cross upon themselves, "my second eldest son, Lawren, now holds the place as heir to my chieftainship, which was rightfully his brother's."

So he was a chieftain, then. Head of a branch of a clan, as opposed to ruler of the clan as a whole. The chieftain nodded to the youth on his right, who remained seated. The young man, short in stature but robust as a boulder, straightened a fraction, though he did not smile.

"But in such times of sadness, there be small joys. I have considered at length something I'm sure ye've all been wondering for a while now. And I feel 'tis time—high time—that I officially acknowledge young Cael as my son. Cael, lad, come here." He held out an arm, beckoning the anointed one.

Applause erupted from the people at the tables. Playfully slapping at a few young men seated around him, the one called Cael rose and made his way to the front of the hall.

Emmie gasped—the one called Cael was the Highlander.

He was younger than the man that stood behind her now. Not much, but enough that he still retained the baby-faced softness of his late teen years. His cheeks were a healthy pink—perhaps from the ale that the people were drinking in copious amounts, or perhaps from the excitement—and his dark hair was shorter, coming to the base of his neck and falling in wayward strands into his eyes. He grinned, the way young men do when they are immensely proud but trying not to show it. As he passed the tables on his way to the dais, he fended off more playful slaps, and submitted to an onslaught of congratulations from the more seasoned men and women in the hall.

Just as she was wishing they could get closer, the room spun, and Emmie found that her view had changed without having moved. Now she was on the dais. The Highlander was still behind her, one hand still firmly planted on her waist and the other on her shoulder. In front of her, the young Cael approached the chieftain, and bowed low. When he righted himself, the chieftain wrapped him in a fatherly embrace.

"Ye're a bastard nae more, Son," he said for Cael's ears only. "Ye can now well and truly call yerself a MacDonald."

Pride lighted the chieftain's face as he pulled something from his breast pocket. Emmie narrowed her eyes, peering through the dim light.

It was a small drawstring leather purse. The man opened it, and out tumbled a kilt pin.

The kilt pin. The very one that had been pulled from the earth by the dig crew hundreds of years into the future. It gleamed under the candlelight, its newness breathtaking. The chieftain fastened it to the young Highlander's *feileadh mhor.* All the intricate detail as she'd seen it in Dean's photo, worn away by time and exposure to the elements, was now crisp and clear. There, on the bottom, were the fish, the ship, the lion and the cross which Paul had identified as the coat of arms belonging to the MacDonalds of Keppoch.

She could feel the happiness emanating from the young man in front of her as surely as she felt the unspoken question coming from the man behind her.

Why was I killed?

Why *was I killed?*

Why?

The patter of rain roused her. Emmie opened her eyes to the leached colours of a dreary morning. They were the colours of her bedroom—*her* bedroom at Tullybrae. And she was tucked up under her covers, with her pillow beneath her head.

The great hall was gone. The people were gone. The Highlander was gone.

Yet, he wasn't gone. Not really. He was still there, still in the room with her. She could sense him, his constant presence.

In her head, he whispered the only two words she ever heard him say:

Save me.

SIXTEEN

"SHE'S AWAKE. I know she's awake." Lamb paced in his shuffling gait around the large worktable in the kitchen.

As soon as he heard Emmie up and moving around, he'd hurried downstairs as fast as his stiff legs would carry him and started the meal. When a half hour passed and she hadn't come down, he covered the plates of hot food with tea towels. When another half hour passed, he gave the now cold food up as spoiled.

One man's loss being another's gain, Clunie was delighted to have been tossed a full strip of bacon. He munched contentedly by the stove, where he'd been enjoying the warmth.

"She should have been down by now."

"Hush now. You can't force the child to eat with you," replied Mrs. Lamb from somewhere near the door. "Perhaps she's just no' hungry."

Lamb furrowed his snowy brows. "You're a terrible liar, Mother, and a hypocrite. When I dared to suggest something similar, you gave me what for. You're just as worried as I am, admit it."

Emmie's behaviour since coming back from Glasgow had taken a turn. Her cataloguing, which she'd taken so seriously at first, had become completely neglected. Instead, she spent her time pouring over her computer, trying (he learned, from the brief conversations he'd had with her) to find information about the wars between the Campbells and the MacDonalds. Why she was so intensely interested, though, stumped him. Tullybrae was Cameron land. Everyone knew that.

Emmie had also made two day trips to two different libraries. One to the University of Aberdeen, and one to the local archives in Inverness. Both times she'd come back with armloads of books which she read voraciously when she wasn't at her computer.

Her appearance had taken a dramatic turn, too. Once remarkably neat and composed, she now looked downright frumpy—not that Lamb cared; she looked lovely either way. Her hair was always pulled back into a messy top-knot now, she rarely put on any makeup, and her unlaundered yoga pants and hoodies had as good as become a uniform.

If those thing weren't worrying enough, then the fact that the poor thing looked bone-weary was deeply concerning. It was as if she was being burdened by an unbearable weight. And the dark circles under her eyes betrayed that she hadn't been sleeping well.

"Aye, I am worried," Mrs. Lamb admitted. A shadow of her outline flickered in the corner of the kitchen, revealing that she was watching through the windows into the corridor with her arms crossed over her withered breast.

"I daresay that Clara is making things worse. Leading her to him like a lamb to the slaughter. Does he make her do it? Are they in cahoots together?"

"How many times, lad? I hate when you use that phrase—*lamb* to the slaughter. Your father would be turning over in his grave if he heard you." She shuddered visibly. "Deeply unsettling. Use 'goat.' Or 'cow.' Anything other than 'lamb.'"

"I'll use whichever animal I please, you old bat," he muttered under his breath.

"You cannot blame Clara," Mrs. Lamb continued. "She's a naturally curious child. She's drawn to them both. She's not leading Emmeline so much as she's simply enchanted by the sheer strength of her and the Highlander's connection to one another."

Lamb shook his head. "I still don't understand what he might have in connection with Emmie."

"Nor should you. 'Tis no' for you to understand. Any more than it is for me to understand. But for one reason or another, they are a part of each other's story—*if* they can overcome whatever obstacle is between them."

"Obstacle?" Lamb sputtered. "He's dead. How much more of a bloody obstacle does one need?"

Mrs. Lamb ignored her son. She continued to stare out the window, still worried. "Perhaps it's time the countess and I stepped in. I'm no' convinced he's worth the strain he's unwittingly causing her."

"Do you think that will help?"

"At this point, it couldn't hurt."

Lamb thought on it a moment. "Then do. For now, I can bring breakfast up to her. She needs something in her stomach either way."

EMMIE WAS SITTING at her desk with one of the volumes she'd borrowed from the Aberdeen University library open in front of her keyboard. It was the genealogy of the MacDonald clan. But so far, she was not finding much on the MacDonalds of Keppoch.

As to what she had found, everything about this branch of the clan had been relatively superficial—births, marriages, a cattle raid here and there—and all culminating in the line being wiped out over a land dispute between them, the MacIntoshes and the Campbells.

All she had to show for her research, which she was currently trying to fill in with Internet sources, was that her mystery probably took place sometime before fourteen ninety five.

It was maddening. And she couldn't dislodge the obsession to find out. The Highlander needed her to solve the mystery. *She* needed to solve the mystery, for herself as much as for him.

This despite the fact that she was very aware of how badly she was slipping. Worse than slipping, to be honest—she was falling apart, losing control. It terrified her, and yet she couldn't stop the downward slide.

She looked up when Lamb knocked at the door. In his hands was a silver tray.

"I thought you could use something to eat."

She stared blankly at him for a moment, the MacDonalds of Keppoch still rolling around in her brain. Shaking her head, she forced her mind into the present.

"Breakfast. Oh, Lamb. I'm so sorry. I completely forgot to come down for breakfast."

"No need to apologize, surely." He scuffled into the nursery-slash-office and placed the tray on the corner of her desk. "Promise me you'll eat it. The last thing I want is for a lovely young woman in the prime of her youth to wither away to nowt under *my* watch."

Her shoulders slumped, and she gave a weak, apologetic grimace. "I promise."

An hour later, the tray was only a slice of bacon and a nibble of toast lighter.

Her back was growing cramped. So she decided to take a break and go outside. She hadn't been outside in ages. Not properly, anyway.

Well into a Highland autumn now, the air was crisp. Emmie stopped by the hall closet where she'd taken to keeping a thick cable-knit cardigan for the infrequent times she did need to venture out. Slipping her arms into the garment and hugging herself, she stepped through the front door and onto the drive. Her Uggs crunched over the gravel as she headed to the east field.

She hadn't seen much of her friends on the dig crew lately. They'd come in looking for her a few times just to say hi, and see how things were going. And she'd felt bad for neglecting them every time. But their visits had trailed off of late. The last time she stopped by, Famke had told her that they were collectively making an effort not to bother her. They could see how busy she was, the Dutch woman had said. Which made Emmie feel doubly guilty because that wasn't exactly true.

It was Famke who was the first to spot her as she came into view.

"Emmie, hey." She waved cheerfully.

Alerted, the rest of the crew popped their heads up from where they were digging like prairie dogs. Except for Ewan, who was in the tent bent over his laptop.

Emmie crossed the field gingerly, taking care of her steps once she reached the gridded dig site.

"Long time, no see," Famke teased, meeting her half-way.

"Sorry," Emmie apologized. "I haven't been a very good friend lately, have I?"

"Don't be silly. We're just happy you're here. Want to come see the progress we've made?"

"Sure."

Famke led her to the heart of the dig. The Highlander went with them, hovering over Emmie's right shoulder. He was agitated. Anxious about what these strangers were doing. Where they were digging and what they might disturb.

Famke led Emmie to Dean's trench first. He smiled up at her from his crouched position. "Thought you'd forgotten about us."

"Never," Emmie insisted warmly. "Whatcha working on?"

"We found the foundation of one of the outbuildings. See here?"

He pointed, and indeed Emmie saw a long row of brick.

"We're not sure what it is yet, but it's exactly where lady Rotherham thought it would be."

"That's cool."

"It is," Famke said. "Sophie has come across something interesting, too. Let me show you."

Emmie gave Dean a friendly wink before leaving him. She knew his eyes were on her when she walked away. So did the Highlander. His presence flared suddenly, as if he was trying to get her attention. It felt... suspicious. Distrustful.

Was he suspicious of what Dean was doing? Where he was digging?

The possibility didn't feel quite right, but rather than dwell on it, she pushed the Highlander aside and focused on Sophie.

"Another midden heap," she was saying. "But earlier than the buildings, we think."

"Oh? How can you tell?"

"I'm much farther down than Dean. He started working in his trench after uncovering that kilt pin we found, but I've been working in mine longer. Because this trash is farther down than the brick foundation of the building, it's likely to be earlier."

"I see. And what's Adam working on?"

"Bloody nowt," he called from his trench.

Famke grinned when Emmie raised an eyebrow. "He's... oh, what's the word... cross?"

"Peeved?" Emmie suggested.

"Pissed off," Sophie answered.

"Peeved," Famke chose. "He's *peeved* because nothing's turned up in his trench. He thinks we did it on purpose."

"Ewan's the lead on this dig. It were his call," Sophie added.

"It's a bloody conspiracy," Adam insisted, still working. "You lot have got me shifting a bloody load of dirt so you can keep the good finds all to yourselves."

"No one's organized any kind of conspiracy against you, Adam," Famke responded.

"Ballocks."

Emmie laughed, and for a second, she felt lighter. That was, until the Highlander re-exerted his feelings of mistrust on her. He was urging her to leave. This time, she had no desire to fight it. She'd done her duty, visited her friends. Besides, she was getting cold.

"I'd best get back inside. Not dressed properly for this weather."

"Awright," Sophie responded. "But you come back and see us soon, yeah?"

"Count on it," Emmie promised.

She turned to leave, and had gone a few yards when Dean called after her.

"Hey Em, wait up."

She spun slowly around and waited as he loped towards her, tall and handsome. The Highlander didn't like this. She could feel his displeasure.

Did he not trust *Dean*?

"What's up?" she asked innocently.

Dean looked back to the team, where Sophie was gawking playfully, while Famke nudging her with the toe of her boot to get back to work. He laughed self-consciously, and passed a hand through his windblown hair.

"So... how you been, really?" His Texas drawl was unusually thick. Perhaps because he was nervous.

Emmie was immediately wary.

"I've been okay," she lied. "Nothing to worry about."

"That's good. Hey, listen. I was wondering if maybe I could convince you to come out for a drink sometime. You know, just to hang out, away from this place."

"Um, sure. What are the others thinking? They up for it?"

"Oh. I, er, meant just the two of us."

Just the two of us. She'd known that's what he wanted, and hoped she was wrong. The nervous smile on his face was, as always, boyishly charming. He was a good-looking guy. She wished she was attracted to him. She did like him, too—just not like that.

The Highlander's dislike grew stronger. It pulled her away from whatever true feelings she might have for Dean. Or could learn to have. She wasn't sure.

"Oh. Dean, I'm flattered, really. And I think you're great. It's just... well... I'm not really in the right headspace to be going out on a date."

His face fell a fraction, but he remained undeterred. "That's okay, no worries. What about just as friends, then?" When she wavered, he hastily added, "C'mon, it'd be fun. I think you're a lot of fun to talk to, and, heck, I need a night off. Away from these guys." He jerked a thumb over his shoulders.

Emmie eyed him skeptically. A part of her wanted to say yes, knew she would have said yes if she'd met him under different circumstances. If the Highlander wasn't doing everything he could to dissuade her.

My goodness, he *really* didn't trust Dean.

Was Dean dangerous in some way that she didn't know in her limited mortal capacity of understanding? He didn't drown kittens, or stick pins in voodoo dolls, did he?

"C'mon," Dean cajoled again, giving her his full Texan charm.

"Okay," Emmie relented, deciding that the Highlander must be wrong—whatever it was that he thought. "But just as friends, right?"

"Yes, ma'am," he said, giving a two-fingered salute. "What about Friday? You'll probably be busy tomorrow and Thursday, with the guys from Haunted Britain coming and all."

"Oh, my God. I forgot all about that," she exclaimed.

Dean gave a startled laugh. "You forgot? How can you forget something like *that*? You sure you're okay?"

"No, not at all sure." She passed a hand over her makeup-free face. "Oh, I am *so* not looking forward to that."

He shrugged. "Chin up. Think of it this way—at least you'll know for sure if the place is haunted or not."

LATER THAT NIGHT, as Emmie lay in bed trying to read, Dean's words kept circling in her head.

He didn't have it right, didn't understand. She already knew Tullybrae was haunted. The constant presence of the Highlander proved it—a presence which was currently at the foot of the bed, watching protectively.

The reason she wasn't looking forward to Haunted Britain coming was because she didn't want to find out just how haunted the house was.

Or perhaps, more alarmingly, that it *wasn't* haunted. That the Highlander wasn't real. After all, no one else seemed to know of his existence.

What if her worst fears were being realized: that she was losing her mind? That she was weak? That she truly was losing her iron-clad grip on herself? It didn't matter how hard she'd tried before now to keep herself together. She was destined to fail, just like her mother.

She gazed across the room to the face on the dresser. Today, that smile told her nothing. It wasn't even a smile. It was just photo ink on paper. A glossy finish. That was not her mother in that frame. It was no one.

"I hate you," she told the photo. And she meant it.

VERONICA BALE

SEVENTEEN

AUNTED BRITAIN WAS scheduled to film the Tullybrae House
episode in two parts over two days. On the first day, the show
would interview Lady Rotherham, and host Elena Seaton-Downs
would talk about the history of the house and the hauntings. The first day
would also be when one of the show's three regularly featured psychic
mediums would be brought on location to give her supernatural impression
of who or what was haunting it, and why.

The second part would be filmed at night, when the "ghost hunting"
crew would try to catch evidence of the hauntings. For this they would use
a combination of hand-held cameras and stationary ones that had been
rigged around the house in strategic locations. They would also use
electromagnetic frequency detectors, infrared equipment, audio recorders,
and a generous dose of exaggeration at every bump and creak.

Emmie spied the show's host, Elena Seaton-Downs, from the drawing
room window when the crew arrived, and watched her covertly for a
minute or two. She reminded Emmie very much of Lady Rotherham. Both
were high-energy and more than a touch flaky. But Ms. Seaton-Downs had
none of Camille's genuine warmth. Deciding she wasn't Elena's biggest fan,
she retreated to her nursery.

Lady Rotherham soon ferreted her out.

"Sweetheart! What are you doing in here?" she demanded, breezing into
Emmie's sanctuary.

For a brief moment, Emmie resented having her privacy invaded.

Get a grip, Em, she quickly chastised. *It's her house, she can go where she wants.*

"I'm working, *boss*," she answered laughingly instead.

"Oh, pshaw. Don't worry about all that now. Come and meet the
medium. It's so exciting—a psychic medium here, at Tullybrae. She's a nice

lady. Carol is her name. Carol Bowman. You wouldn't think she's anything other than ordinary to look at her."

"I promise, I'll come in a bit. You look great, by the way, Camille."

"You think?" Lady Rotherham plumped her stiff coif. Blood red nails gleamed in the morning light from the nursery's oriel windows. "I've had my makeup done by the show for my interview. I've been 'in Makeup'— Oh, I've always wanted to say that." She clapped her hands gleefully. "Oliver can't take his eyes off me. And between you and me, my dear, neither can some of the young chaps from the camera crew."

Waggling her fingers in a farewell gesture, she glided from the nursery. Emmie shook her head. Well, at least the lady was optimistic.

"In a bit" turned into an hour. Contrary to what she had been hoping, Lady Rotherham did not forget about her. "Emmie, come out here," she'd called from the other end of the second floor hallway, rather more commanding than Emmie was used to.

Reluctantly, Emmie rose from her desk, pausing at the door. The Highlander was with her still. She was glad of it. As long as he was with her, she wasn't alone.

As if reading her thoughts, his presence strengthened. She imagined he had embraced her, offering her encouragement and assurance that it would all be okay. There was no reason to fear the medium.

That's what it was, she realized—fear. Emmie was *afraid* of the psychic. She was afraid the woman would see the Highlander. Emmie didn't want anyone to know about the Highlander. He was *her* secret.

But it wasn't just that. Emmie was deeply afraid that the woman would see more than just the spirits in the house. That she would be able to see her, Emmie. She was afraid that the medium would cut right through her fragile exterior into her soul.

Would she see that Emmie was losing her marbles?

With the Highlander trailing her down the hallway, Emmie caught up to the camera crew. They were in one of the bedrooms-turned-storage rooms. She hung back, observing from the hallway, though she couldn't see much of what was going on inside, since the (notably rotund) sound guy was blocking the door. Nevertheless, she caught a glimpse of the medium. Carol Bowman, Lady Rotherham had called her.

She was heavy-set, but tall. Her short, fluffy hair was dyed a uniform apricot colour, and her face was round and soft and unassuming. It was obvious that she'd been to Makeup for her on-camera appearance, yet the makeup artists had not done much other than to smooth her already smooth complexion with foundation. Looking at her, Emmie had the feeling that this had been her choice, not Makeup's. Other than a pair of beaded earrings that looked hand-crafted, the woman was unremarkable.

No wild costume jewellery, no flamboyant scarves or loose skirts. In essence, not the caricature fortune teller Emmie had in her head.

"This was her bedroom," the woman was saying. Her hands were in front of her, palms down and fingers splayed.

"*Hers*—you mean the woman spirit?"

This was Elena Seaton-Downs, and the question was said with something akin to sheer amazement. The same amazement she showed for every show. In every bedroom and every hallway and with every statement of psychic "fact."

Having watched the show before, Emmie knew what the host of Haunted Britain looked like. Elena Seaton-Downs was a slim woman in her mid-forties. She had dark hair and a heavy fringe bang which accented large blue doe eyes. Those eyes looked good in the night vision cameras when they were wide with fright. Emmie suspected the host knew this of herself, and knew how to play it up to elevate the drama.

If anything could be said of her, Elena certainly knew her job.

"She was very proud of the window in particular," the medium continued. "Used to stand here each morning and look out over her land. I feel like she's a motherly figure. A nurturing figure."

"Can you imagine?" Elena Seaton-Downs exclaimed.

"I always felt like she was watching over me," Lady Rotherham piped up, and the cameraman panned to the left. "When I was a girl I would often feel at night that someone was tucking me in and stroking my hair."

The statement gave Emmie pause. She recalled her own similar experience, and wondered if the medium could actually see the countess. If she was here, in the room with them.

Could she see the Highlander?

Chillingly, at the exact same time as the thought popped into her head, the medium, Carol Bowman, stopped suddenly, and turned to look at her. An odd expression crossed her plain, pleasant face.

For a fraction of a second that felt like an eternity, the woman and Emmie stared at each other.

No, thought Emmie. *Don't tell my secret. Please. It's mine. They can't know.*

"What is it? Are you sensing something?" Elena touched the medium's arm, her voice expertly hushed.

The medium opened her mouth to speak. But then, she shook her head, and looked away. "This energy, this motherly woman, she was also partial to the gardens. Can we go see?"

"Yes, of course," Elena stated, as if the house were hers.

"And cut," announced the director in a very lackluster way. The camera crew lowered their gear, and suddenly all the pretense was dropped. Where the television personalities had moments ago been absorbed in the house and its ghostly inhabitants, now stood nothing more than a group of people, crowded together in a bedroom packed with centuries' old stuff.

"I feel like my hair's doing something funny," Elena complained in a much less flimsy voice than the one she used on camera. "Can I go see Cindy before we go down?"

"I need the loo," put in the sound technician.

"All right, everybody, take ten," the director relented. "We'll meet in the back garden."

Emmie flattened herself against the wall to let the crew pass. Lady Rotherham shot her an excited smile, pencilled eyebrows raised, and squeezed her arm as she went by. No one else seemed to notice her. Carol Bowman was dictating a list of orders to a woman whom Emmie guessed was her assistant. "Then call Roger and tell him I can do five. But don't let him know I've got Puff for the weekend, or he'll lose his junk. Do they have any more of those shortbread bikkies?"

Emmie let out a breath as they retreated. She'd been afraid the medium would stop, and would say whatever it was she'd been about to reveal.

I shouldn't have come, she thought. *I should have stayed in the nursery. In my room. Anywhere but here.*

She fled the corridor for the safety of her nursery, despite a peculiar tug from the Highlander to follow the crew.

"You don't control me," she hissed. She regretted it when the Highlander let go, let her flee. She had the notion that her slight had hurt him. It hurt her to know she'd hurt him.

Ten minutes later, Emmie was finishing off a response to an email from Paul Rotenfeld. He was wondering when she might want to come back down to Glasgow to go over the archives. As she clicked the send button, there was a knock on the open door.

It was the medium. She hovered on the threshold, a tentative smile fixed on her lips.

"Hi there," she hedged. "It's Emmeline, right?"

Emmie's stomach plummeted even as the Highlander's spirits picked up.

"Emmie, yes." She smiled pleasantly back. "What can I do for you Carol?"

"I see I don't need to introduce myself," the medium quipped lightly. "I hope you don't mind the intrusion."

"Not at all." Emmie gestured to the empty chair across from her desk. She cursed herself for not being able to tell the truth: *No, I want you to go away and leave me alone.*

Carol entered the nursery, but instead of taking the chair, she settled herself on the window seat. "I love these windows," she declared, gazing out the glass at the view. "I can see why you chose this space to work in. Light from three different directions. All-day natural light."

"When there's not much sunshine, you take as much as you can of whatever you can get."

Carol settled her gaze on Emmie, studying her curiously. The Highlander was practically bouncing—in a spiritual sense, at least.

"I'm sure you know that I want to talk to you."

Emmie nodded, resigned. "But do you have time? Didn't the director say you only had ten minutes? That was five minutes ago."

"Oh, don't listen to Greg. No one else does. When he says to take ten, it means we actually have thirty. Rule of thumb with him is to triple whatever he tells you. You looked a little startled earlier when I saw you in the hallway. You didn't want me to start talking."

"Maybe," Emmie admitted.

"Sometimes, when I'm listening—sensing, reading, whatever you want to call it—I tend to blurt out whatever I'm picking up without thinking about how it might come out, or who might not want to hear it."

"Oh...kayyyy," Emmie drawled when Carol paused, looking quizzically at her.

"Do you know about the woman? The one who follows you around? She's attached to this house."

"The countess?"

"No, not her. Although she does like to hang around you, too. No, this is a little old lady. Wiry thin, black dress, grey hair worn in a finger wave style."

Emmie raised an eyebrow.

"I wouldn't quite say the nineteen twenties. Maybe thirties or forties was her era. No? You don't know who that could be?"

For a moment, Emmie wondered if the woman might be her grandmother. But it didn't seem likely. From what she could remember, her grandmother had been quite tall and heavy. And her hair had had the thin, white, wispy look of a cirrus cloud. Far from anything one could call a finger wave.

"Sorry, can't think." Teasingly, she added, "Aren't you supposed to be able to tell me that kind of stuff? You're the psychic."

Carol gazed fondly at Emmie. "If they want me to know, then yes. But this one, she's blocking me. Telling me, in her way, that she's not important to the house's story. I get the impression that she doesn't consider herself an active haunting—although, I think there's one person in this house that would disagree." She laughed and shook her head when, again, Emmie lifted a brow. "Never mind. What I can tell of her is that she belongs to the house, and she follows you around. Kind of like a mother figure, or a guardian. Back in the bedroom, when I went to speak, she was there, standing in front of you in my mind's eye. And she told me to leave you alone, to not talk about you while the cameras were rolling. She's very protective of you."

Emmie sat back in her chair and folded her hands in her lap. She contemplated the woman, chewing on her lip as she thought. "Okay. Well, the cameras aren't rolling right now. Have you come to tell me what you were going to say?"

"Only if you're okay with it, sweetheart. If you're not comfortable, I can walk away and we can leave it at that."

The fact that the medium was giving her a choice took Emmie aback. She took a minute to absorb the offer, to think about what she wanted. It surprised her, but she found that she actually *did* want to hear what the woman had to say. The Highlander certainly did. Or he knew what the woman was going to say and wanted Emmie to hear it.

"I'll hear it," she said evenly.

"Oh, good," Carol breathed. "Because ever since I picked up on it, it's been getting louder and louder. You are aware, then, of the young man that's been hovering around you?" When Emmie blanched, Carol concluded, "I see. Yes, you are."

"Can I ask—why does he hand aground? Why is he so interested in me?"

The woman looked at her oddly. After a moment, she spoke, evading Emmie's question. "You're an old soul. Did you know that? People like to use that expression far too often, but they're rarer than you'd think, those old souls. You're one of them."

"What does that mean?"

She shrugged. "Oh, nothing. Most of the time. But I wanted to tell you—this person," she gestured up and down at Emmie herself, "this is not you. It's not going to change anything. You will become what you're meant to become, no matter how hard you try to be something else."

Emmie's brows drew together, somewhere between confused and defensive. "And what does *that* mean?"

Carol shook her head, undeterred by her reaction. "I'm sorry, sweetheart. I don't always know. It's just the impression I get. Anyway, back to what I picked up on earlier. The young man, he's hanging around you for a reason. I think you've already worked out that he wants something from you, but you don't know what it is."

"Do you know?"

"I don't. But I can say that, whatever it is, it is in your power to give him. I'm getting that very strongly. You *can* do what he wants you to."

Emmie's voice was small. "Do I *have* to?"

"Of course not. No one has to do anything. It is also within your power to choose not to, always."

Finished with delivering her message, Carol smiled encouragingly. Then she stood, and started towards the door. As she was leaving, Emmie called out.

"Wait."

She stopped and turned back, waiting patiently as Emmie grappled with the right words.

"I feel like... I don't know, like he's protecting me. Or watching out for me. Like he knows something about what's dangerous—or who's dangerous—that I don't. Does he think... I mean, is Dean somehow dangerous, or a threat? Or he's not good for me or something?"

For several seconds, Carol stared at her, confused. Then she broke into a laugh.

"Oh, dear me no, sweet child. He's *jealous*. How have you not figured it out? Your Highlander is absolutely smitten."

Emmie nearly fell out of her chair. "Smitten?"

"Mmm hmm," Carol nodded emphatically. "Head over heels, and not shy about it. And by the way, he wishes you would stop thinking of him as 'Highlander.' He's telling me quite clearly that he gave you his name for a reason."

EIGHTEEN

CAEL. HIS NAME was Cael. And he *wanted* her to know his name.

He was real. She was not imagining him, wasn't going mad. Which, surprisingly, made the whole thing all the more frightening.

A ghost. A dead person. He had... what? The hots for her? A crush on her? Somehow, those terms seemed too dismissive, too juvenile.

Emmie had been shocked when Carol told her. But it was not because she hadn't know. She had known—on some level that her conscious mind preferred to ignore—that his feelings for her were deeper than the platonic interest of one sentient being in another. The shock came from having it confirmed by an outsider, by someone who did not belong to the inner, private world which she'd thought, until then, was the only place in which Cael was real.

With that confirmation, the subconscious narrative which she'd constructed for herself to validate his existence was pitched sharply into the forefront of her brain, made all the more real because it was real to someone else, too.

Now it was all obvious to her. Of *course* his feelings were deeper. When he watched over her at night, when he followed her around the house. When he wanted her to feel the things he felt and see the things he saw—

Even worse was the fact that her conscious mind was forced to consider her own feelings for him. To admit that those feelings... were reciprocated.

She had feelings for the Highlander. For Cael. *That* scared the hell out of her most of all.

He was dead. How could one have feelings for one who was dead? What did that say about her, about her state of mind? About her *stability* of mind? If she thought she was going mad before, now madness seemed the better option. At least when one was crazy, it was all in one's mind.

No, no. She, Emmie, had to do one better than crazy. She was falling apart over something real, something that frightened her and drew her in at the same time. It tightened its grip on her, squeezing her more and more each day, and yet it wasn't enough to cause her to turn away.

This was what had happened to her mother. Emmie *was* destined to end up just like her after all.

Cael seemed to recognize that Emmie's anxiety had reached new heights. Unless she was imagining it, his hovering took on a possessive quality. He probably felt the anxiety rolling off her like heat from a convection oven. She could not pretend that she didn't know why he was protective of her, nor could she pretend that she wasn't aware of how he felt about her. It was all out in the open. They were looking at each other now with no pretense.

She knew. And he knew she knew.

She wandered about the house aimlessly, arms wrapped tightly around herself, unable to shut Cael out. Unwilling to shut him out.

The second day of filming, the camera crew went about setting up their equipment for the night's "ghost watch," snatching covert glances at the waif that drifted from room to room, pale and drawn. When she was out of ear shot, they tossed one another snide comments.

"She all there?" quipped the sound guy to the electrician outside the dining room.

"Does it matter? Admit it, mate: you'd do her even if she wasn't."

This uncouth comment was the proverbial straw that broke the camel's back. Mrs. Lamb's hackles rose so high that Lamb was worried his mother would topple the ladder on which the electrician stood.

"That's it! It's got to be tonight," the woman declared later that afternoon.

Lamb, who was getting one last polish of the drawing room furniture in before filming would commence, tipped his chin in the general direction of her voice.

"What about the cameras? Is it the wisest idea with all this fancy gear in the house? It's here to catch evidence of you and your spooky friends, you know."

"Do you have a better idea?"

Lamb pursed his lips, then shook his head. "No' offhand. I'll defer to your judgement, then. But whatever you do, be subtle."

Mrs. Lamb's image flickered in the corner, just briefly. Her small, pert nose was raised, and she was smoothing down her skirts with both hands.

"I'm always subtle," she sniffed, and disappeared again. "Besides, I spoke to the countess, and she agrees 'tis high time we took matters into our own hands. Since you've clearly shown yourself incapable of making things better for her on your end."

"And how was I supposed to do that?" Lamb paused in his vigorous polishing. "Besides, if that Highlander is as persistent as you seem to think, what makes you think you can convince him to leave her alone?"

"Convince *him*?" Mrs. Lamb snorted. "No, my dear lad. It's *her* we're going to have a chat with."

"Emmie? You're going to talk to Emmie herself?"

"Indeed I am. We are, the countess and I. Together."

"Lamb gave a long-suffering sigh, and continued his polishing. "Heaven help the lass if you start talking to *her*, too. You've driven *me* mad enough as it is."

IT WAS CLOSE to midnight. The farce which Haunted Britain called a ghost hunt had been going on for three hours. The process was a curious mix of start-and-stop filming that, once completed, would be edited into a smooth fifteen minute segment—complete with room for commercial breaks. On camera, the host and her hunting crew were the picture of teamwork, professionalism, and general, all-round paranormal investigative enthusiasm. Off camera... not so much.

Tensions, it would appear, were running high behind the scenes. Elena Seaton-Downs and co-hunter Richard Mowbry were in a snit with each other over who got more on-camera time (apparently Mr. Mowbry had actual paranormal investigative training, and felt deserving of a greater amount of on-screen recognition; Ms. Seaton-Downs objected for obvious reasons). The director, Greg, was in a snit with BBC Two over a recent budget cut, and was taking it out on the station's on-set representative. And much to the surprise of the entire crew, Camera Man A was in a snit with the show's dedicated historian, Louise Pembroke, because they'd slept together before Louise admitted to Camera Man A that she was married, and refused to leave her husband for him.

It was almost comical to see the team going from squabbling and bickering children one minute, to close-knit, career-minded colleagues as soon as someone called, "Aaaaannnnd... Action!"

A far cry from the professional academics on the Edinburgh dig crew. A testament to the toxic nature of egos when they got too big for one another.

Emmie listened to the goings on from her seated position at the top of the grand staircase. The house was completely dark, save for whatever intermittent moonlight came through the windows when the rolling clouds permitted it. She was given the all-clear by the director to sit there if she wanted. No cameras had been rigged for this angle, but she had been warned that if she were there when one of the investigators walked by, she risked being picked up on a hand-held. If that happened, the producers would blur her face in editing, but the show could not guarantee they would be able to cut her out completely.

In the drawing room, Elena Seaton-Downs was with Richard Mowbry. They'd had the hand-held cameras on for the last half hour, and had been playing nice all that time.

Since filming had started, the petite, Bambi-eyed host of Haunted Britain was as nerve-gratingly on-form as she was in the other episodes Emmie had seen. The woman expressed an expertly rehearsed amount of fear and excitement at every little sound. Emmie was surprised, however, by how many long gaps there were between each gasp and exclamation of "What was that?" Another product of the editing phase of production, she supposed.

So far, Elena's jumping and gasping had been at the normal sounds of the house settling down for the night. At one point she shushed the others and whispered, "Do you hear that? Footsteps." The whole crew fell silent, and listened anxiously to the sound of Lamb climbing the servants' stairs on his way to bed.

"Right," she said now to her co-host. "That's enough of that. Richard, why don't you and I go into the library and meet up with Brent and Louise. I'll take Brent down to the kitchen, see if we can't catch more, and maybe you can take Louise up to the attics."

"Eh, why don't you take Louise up to the attics?" Richard shot back. "There are more cameras downstairs, and you know it."

"You'll go where I tell you, or you can find a new show."

"Cut it out, Elena," sighed Greg from somewhere nearby.

Emmie watched the two investigators stalk out of the parlour—Elena first with chin high—catching Richard's mumbled "Bitch!" as he followed behind.

Soon they were gone, and the house settled back into silence. It was much better that way, she thought. These people didn't belong here. The framed and mounted faces of Tullybrae's lords and ladies agreed. Their painted expressions, slight smiles captured by swirls of cracking oil paint, looked relieved to have been left alone at last.

Fatigue had been creeping over Emmie within the last hour, and was now putting up a valiant fight to overpower her.

"Bedtime," she whispered, knowing that Cael would hear—though she didn't need to say it for his benefit. He would follow her regardless. In fact, she was aware that talking to him was the last thing she should be doing. Encouraging not only him, but herself in this madness. It was only serving to perpetuate the very cause of her distress.

Yet the desire to acknowledge him, to reach out to him as he was reaching out to her was compelling. Like a scab that she knew she should leave alone but just couldn't. No, not a scab. A scab was an annoyance, something ugly and mean and little. This was worse than a scab, more dangerous. It was like an addiction.

Even as this knowledge made her blood run cold, an unbidden thrill ran up her spine. It was a thrill that seemed to have come from Cael—was he pleased to have been acknowledged?

Disturbed by the dichotomy that was warring inside of her, Emmie rose from the top step, and began down the second floor corridor to the servants' stairs.

A sound from behind made her stop.

It was a little girl's giggle. The same giggle that had been plaguing her since she arrived at Tullybrae. Only this time it was close. Very close.

"Hello?" Emmie's voice came out pathetically meek. She winced, and tried again. "Clara? Is that you? Are you trying to get my attention?"

The giggle came again, louder this time. The sound was followed by the creaking of floorboards from further down the hall.

Her synapses were firing on all cylinders. Glancing once behind her to make sure no errant camera had found its way upstairs, Emmie followed the sound down the corridor. A dash of white disappeared in a flutter around the corner at the far end.

"Wait," Emmie called. "Clara, wait."

She jogged down the hall, past to door to the servants' stairs, all the way to the end where the corridor made an L turn into a smaller section of the house.

When she rounded the L, Emmie blinked in surprise. At the end of the smaller hallway, the door to the last room on the right stood open. Light was coming from within.

Her first thought was that Haunted Britain's technicians had rigged a camera in this room, and had forgotten to turn the lights off. They'd opened many rooms that were usually closed, letting out a few decades' worth of dust in the process. But they'd also mapped out the locations of the mounted cameras, and this room hadn't been one of them. Plus, Emmie couldn't conceive that professionals would forget to turn the lights off. With them on, the night-vision cameras would be useless.

"Clara?" she asked again, proceeding warily down the final stretch to the open room. Her voice sounded odd to her own ears. Muted. In fact, everything felt muted, even her own senses.

She came to a halt in the doorway. Inside, there was a table laid out with three cups, three saucers, and a tower of biscuits and sandwiches. Seated in the chair facing the door was a little old lady in a starched black dress.

"Ah, there you are, child."

Emmie started, not believing what she was seeing. She had been in this room once before. Then, it had held nothing but old steamer trunks with vintage, war-era clothing. It was just one of the many rooms still on her to-do list. But here, now, it was neatly arranged with a serviceable brass bed, not unlike her own upstairs. The single, square window was hung with clean lace curtains, and an armoire and a night table stood at attention on either side.

Inside the room, the air was warm and dry, and smelled distinctly of roses. The light, she realized, was daylight. It streamed in through the closed windows. But it was a strange light, sepia almost. Like the colour was being leached out everything it touched.

Time slowed as Emmie took in the scene. The little old woman waited patiently, giving her the space to adjust to her surroundings.

"Why don't you come in and have a seat?" she suggested in a thick Scottish tongue. "The countess and I were just having tea."

"Countess?" Emmie studied the two empty places, confused. Her mind felt like it was stuffed with cotton. Her comprehension, normally so quick, trickled like cold molasses. There was something odd about this, but for the life of her, she couldn't pinpoint what it was.

"Aye, the countess. She's been eager to meet you. We both have."

Unable to identify any sound reason why she should not join in, Emmie moved into the room, feeling oddly disjointed. Tentatively, she took the seat across from the little old lady, keeping the second empty place setting between them.

"Tea?"

Without waiting for her to answer, the woman reached a knotted hand, the skin paper-thin and softly wrinkled, and poured dark, searing hot liquid into the cup in front of her. The steam rose up, unusually fragrant. A splash of milk followed, creating swirls of umber and cream.

"Biscuit?" The woman picked up the tray and offered one of the shortbread cookies on top.

"Lamb," Emmie said, her voice thick. She cleared her throat. "Those look like Lamb's cookies."

"*My* cookies," the woman corrected fondly. "I'd never tell him so, but that lad does shortbread *almost* as well as I do."

Emmie took a tentative bite of her cookie, watching the woman as she did. She was familiar. Reminded her of someone. But her senses were competing with her rational mind, drawing her away from logic and reason towards the more primal sensations of taste and touch. The rich, buttery cookie was like a caress on her tongue; the soft crumble of the texture was deeply satisfying.

"Who are you?" she asked when she was done chewing.

"That's no' important, Emmeline. What's important is you. I think it's high time the three of us had a wee chat, don't you?"

Emmie glanced at the empty chair between them. "Three?"

"The countess, here, is quite worried. And so am I. Her ladyship says to tell you that she can only do so much to look after your well-being. You need to make sure you're looking after yourself. And that means eating well." The woman nudged the tray forward again, urging Emmie to take another cookie.

"The countess is here." Emmie said, half question, half statement.

The old woman let out a throaty sound, almost a laugh. "Oh, she's here. When the roses are here, she's here. More to the point, your Highlander is no'. He's always around you, you know. I tell you, it's bloody hard to look after you when he's always around. But I told him that he's to stay away now. That this is for your own good, because he's causing you a lot of undue stress."

"You told him that?"

The woman nodded, watching Emmie intently. "He's very curious to know what's going on, of course. But he is respecting my request, and he's staying away. To be honest, I don't think he realized the effect he was having on you. He never imagined that his determination to reach you, to influence you, would be interpreted as you've done. You have experienced a very unique set of circumstances that have left you unusually fragile. And who could blame you? We think we're clever as adults, don't we? But really, we have no better grip on the events of our childhood now than we did then."

A warm tear slid down Emmie's cheek. What was this woman saying? How did she know all that? Self-pity, acute and raw, dug into her. She winced from the sudden surge of pain.

"What's this all about?" The woman looked at her with sympathy.

Emmie looked back. She was so *familiar*. Why couldn't she place her?

Resigned, she answered, "I think you already know."

The woman closed her eyes briefly. "I do, love. But why don't you tell me in your own words?"

Emmie looked at her hands, holding the delicate china cup. When she spoke, her words felt stiff and uncoordinated.

"I can't get him out of my head," she said. "Cael. He won't leave, and I don't want him to. He wants me to solve the mystery for him. I think he wants me to find out why he died, and I have to find out..."

She trailed off, afraid to keep going with her thoughts.

"But..." the woman prompted.

"But," she breathed, "it's become an obsession. I can't stop. I know that I'm losing control of myself, of who I am. And I know that I should stop. I should tell Cael to leave me alone and never bother me again. In one part of my head, I know I'm strong enough to do it. But in another... I don't think I am."

"And that frightens you most of all," the woman concluded.

Emmie nodded, defeated. "I led my whole life thinking I wasn't like her. Determined *not* to be like her. I'm terrified that I was wrong all along. That no matter how hard I try to end up different, I'm still like her. In the end, I'll lose my way just like she did."

She stopped then, taken aback by the coherency with which she'd expressed her feelings. Feelings which she'd never before been able to articulate. Just getting her thoughts out like this made her feel a fraction better. She looked at the woman, surprise widening her hazel eyes.

"Your mother. You're talking about your mother's substance abuse."

Emmie closed her eyes, allowing fresh tears to spill freely down her cheeks. "She lost her way. She died because she couldn't keep a hold of herself."

"What was it like?" the woman asked gently. "Why don't you tell me what it was like for you as a child?"

"She was..." Emmie thought briefly. "She was weak. So *weak*. That sounds so horrible of me to say about my own mother, but that's how I feel. Even as a child I thought that. I tried so hard, *so* hard, to make her do better, to make her *want* to do better. I begged her to bring me to school, to take me herself instead of putting me on the bus, because I knew that she'd go right over to those horrible friends of hers as soon as the bus was gone, and do horrible things to herself. I was four then. Four! And even then I thought that if she just saw the other mothers, just remembered what it was like to be outside and... and normal, that maybe she'd want to try.

"And it wasn't like she didn't love me." She wiped the tears from her face with her sleeve. "It would have been easier if she didn't care. As young as I was then, I knew that, too. If she never cared about me, if I was just a total mistake that she regretted, I think that would have been better. But she did love me. She loved me so much. She hated what she was doing to me, but still, she was too weak to escape the drugs. To make herself better."

She fell silent then, feeling surprisingly unburdened. She'd never spoken those thoughts aloud before. Never even thought them from start to finish that way. She'd buried her feelings, convinced herself that they didn't exist. But they'd been there all along, and had not lost one ounce of potency in all these years.

The woman across from her was looking at her with complete understanding. Not pity, which she feared would happen. Compassion.

"She sent me to live with my grandmother when I was five. My grandmother was in no position to take care of a child, but she tried for my mother's sake. Not long after, we found out my mom died."

"An overdose."

"Died while shooting up in her car. I found out years later that she'd probably been with someone. The police found the passenger side door wide open, but nothing was taken, so it probably wasn't a robbery. They think whoever was with her bolted as soon as things started to go wrong."

"That's a heavy burden for a child to have to bear. Especially for such a sensitive and intuitive child. I can see how something like that could colour your perception as an adult. But Emmeline, there's something you're no' taking into account here. Your mother had far greater problems than you know. Her drug addiction was only a symptom of a larger set of issues."

"Like what?" Emmie felt small, child-like. She wasn't sure she wanted to hear what the woman had to say, just as she wasn't sure she could handle not hearing it.

"Your mother, child, suffered from mental illness. Were you aware?"

Dumbfounded, Emmie shook her head. Was it true?

"Of course you weren't. She didn't know herself. She was never diagnosed, you see. And on our side of the line, we don't attach clinical terms to a soul's suffering in life. You might call it depression, perhaps even bipolar disorder. There is no way for us to know now. But she was an unhappy soul for reasons that were beyond her control. And her struggles, love, are something which you will never understand, because you do no' suffer the same afflictions."

"I didn't know that," Emmie repeated, somewhat apologetically. "How do *you* know all this?"

The woman flipped a hand. "How do we know anything over here? We just do. In the end, though, you triumphed from this experience."

"Triumphed." Emmie's brows drew together.

"You did," the woman insisted. "Because you were such an intuitive child, you were able to take what you perceived to be her weakness and make it your strength. In a way, her struggle was a gift, because it forged your character."

"I want to believe that. But I can't. I feel like I'm falling to pieces. Ever since... ever since him. Cael."

The woman eyed her speculatively. "The countess wants her turn with you, and she's quite annoyed with me for having taken so long. But I'll say one last thing: Perhaps the Emmeline that you were trying so hard to construct is no' the Emmeline that you're meant to be. Perhaps becoming who you're meant to be will be a difficult transition for you. You may no' realize it, but this place, and Cael himself, are very much a part of what you're destined for. We're led to places, my dear. No one ever ends up anywhere by accident. You were led here. You're meant to be here."

"Why? What am I destined for?"

"If only I knew," the woman said ruefully. "That's for you to learn. But while you're trying to figure it out, don't fight it. Don't try so hard to be someone you've mapped out in your head. Live your life and the answer will come to you.

141

"And *don't* cancel your plans with that nice young man that wants to take you out," she added. "You'll dash his spirits something terrible."

"Who—Dean?"

"Dean, yes. Go out with him. Have a meal. Have *fun*, for the good Lord's mercy."

Emmie *had* been contemplating cancelling her plans with Dean. She was thinking hard over the woman's words, when the woman pressed her wrinkled hands to the table.

"And now, I'm afraid I cannot withhold the countess any longer. She's determined to have her turn."

"Turn?" Emmie asked, slightly nervous. But the lady just smiled. And faded away to nothing.

"Wait." Emmie shot her hand forth, but the woman was gone.

Then the table began to fade, and was gone. Then the strange, sepia coloured daylight, and then the room itself, until she was left in total darkness.

NINETEEN

"COUNTESS?" EMMIE CALLED into the black void. There was no response.

Wherever she was, it was deathly silent. Her breathing and heartbeat were thunderous in her ears. She was afraid to move, afraid to make any other sound. Her fingers gripped the edge of her chair, nails digging into the painted wood of the seat. Panic crept over her, bringing on the threat of new tears.

Keep calm, Em, she told herself. *You won't do yourself any good by freaking out.* If the countess wanted to show her something, Emmie had to trust that she was in good hands. She had to; she had no choice.

Taking a few deep breaths for courage, she stood. The legs of the chair made a strange scraping sound. Muffled. Shuffling her feet in place, she realized that she was standing on a dirt surface.

To her right, voices sounded. They were faint at first, but grew louder, taking on a tinny quality. They were low and urgent, but she couldn't make out what they were saying. She strained, listening.

"Go," came a whisper from behind her.

Emmie jumped, and whirled around. There was still nothing but blackness in all directions. But the air had become infused with the heady, stifling fragrance of roses.

When the roses are here, she's here, the old woman had said of the countess. The roses were definitely here now. In fact, they were stronger than Emmie had ever smelled before. The countess must be very close.

As if to confirm her suspicion, the whisper came again. This time, it was right next to her ear.

"Go!"

"Go where?" Emmie reached through the dark, fingers groping for anything that might be out there. But there was nothing.

"Countess?"

Still nothing.

"Go where, for frig's sake?" she muttered to herself. "Does anyone ever think that I don't want to see what they have to show me?"

But even as she said it, she knew it wasn't true. If this had anything to do with Cael, then of course she wanted to know. Needed to know.

If the countess wanted her to "go," then her only two choices were to disobey and stay put, or to walk blindly forward. Or backwards. Or, just... walk. Which is what she did. Hands waving back and forth in front of her, Emmie shuffled blindly along the dirt ground towards the distant voices.

She hadn't gone far before the blackness began to shift and transform. Colour danced and blurred, then sharpened into distinct shapes.

Stunned, Emmie took an instinctive step back. She was outside, and it was night. She was standing in front of a primitive dwelling that might have come right off the set of Braveheart or Rob Roy. Two men stood off to the side of the squat stone building, holding the reins to three horses. It was too dark for Emmie to make out their faces well, but they were as rough and dangerous-looking as the men inside the castle of Cael's memory.

She wasn't afraid of them, though. She knew without having to be told that she was not really here. That this had all happened long ago, and she was only a voyeur in this picture. Indeed, when she approached the dwelling's front door, the two men did not see her. The horses did not whicker at her approach. Nobody batted an eyelash when she pulled open the rough plank door and stepped through to the dimly lit, smoky interior.

Inside, in the centre of the room, two men sat together on a split log bench. A rock fire pit contained a low-burning peat fire, and both men were leaning towards it for warmth. They were deep in conversation.

Emmie approached them cautiously.

"He's telling us we must resist them on our own," one man was saying. He was short, but solid, like a boulder with arms and legs. Strands of stringy, greasy hair hung around his face and fell down his back. The man looked like he hadn't bathed in a year. "On our own! We dinna have the men to do it."

"Och, I dinna ken," said the other man, taller, and softer around the middle, with ginger hair that looked like it had seen water and soap far more recently than his friend. "We've no guarantee that they'll even attack again. We drove them off well enough the first time, d'ye no' think?"

"Are ye daft, man? Drive them off once, they'll only come back stronger. The MacIntoshes have the Crown on their side, dinna forget. They'll no' be giving up this land so easily."

Emmie gasped silently. So she had been right! It *was* the conflict between the MacIntoshes and the MacDonalds of Keppoch that was central to Cael's mystery. The conflict that destroyed Clan MacDonald of Keppoch. It had to be. The countess was providing her with a clue, with a direction.

Would she provide Emmie with the answer?

Emmie doubted she would be that lucky, but listened eagerly for more clues she might be able to pick up from these men.

"And why are ye so certain we'll no' be able to withstand them if they do attack again?" asked the second man. "We've a fine force. Young Cael and Master Lawren have seen to that."

"Boys," the first man spat. "Nobbut lads, the pair of them. What do they ken of war?"

The men both looked up at Emmie then. Her entire body froze, every muscle taught and ready to spring and flee. When a shape brushed past her, she nearly cackled with relief. A woman came towards the men from behind where she was standing. She was dressed in a linen shift and holding two cups. They'd been looking at her, not at Emmie.

"Ah, thank ye, *mo cridhe*," said the taller, softer man.

He accepted the cup which the woman held out for him, as did his companion. They both drank deeply as the woman moved back towards Emmie, passed her effortlessly, and crawled into a bed on the other side of the dwelling. As she tucked herself under the covers, two small shapes moved to absorb her into the sleeping tangle of flesh and blankets and warmth.

Children. There must be children in there. Emmie's heart ached for these innocents, who had no idea of the devastation that would (if she'd guessed correctly about the time period) tear their world apart and put an end to their clan.

"Lads, just lads," the smaller man repeated once he'd drained his cup.

"That as may be, but there's half the clan that agrees wi' them. And those are grown men. They believe we've a chance of wi'standing the MacIntoshes. What makes ye think they're wrong?"

"They dinna believe we've a chance," the first man argued. "They're wi' that bastard Cael because he's got the ear of Himself."

"Aye, so what can be done about it? If Himself is behind the lads, we must do as Himself bids."

"That's just the problem. The bastard has the ear of Himself because half the clan is behind him and Master Lawren. And the reason for that is because the bastard and Master Lawren have the ear of Himself."

The second man shook his head, laughing. "I dinna ken what ye expect of me, then. It sounds like a hopeless situation."

The first man glowered, and leaned closer. "We canna withstand a sustained war against the MacIntoshes. I ken ye think so, too." When the taller man looked as though he thought this to be true, the smaller man continued. "Think of yer lads. Think of yer wife. D'ye want to leave them to the mercy of those bloody MacIntoshes? The men listen to ye. They follow what ye say. And if ye tell them they must no' follow the bastard, they'll listen."

"I dinna ken."

"Ye *must* ken! Cael MacDonald must be removed!"

The fair-haired man straightened, and looked at his companion in shock. "What—are we talking about killing him?"

The smaller man did not answer, simply stared at his host.

"This is madness," the taller man objected. "I'll no' be killing young Cael. I'll be having no part in this."

"I'm no' saying *ye* have to kill him. All ye have to do is get the men on our side."

"But ye mean to have someone kill the lad."

The first man nodded slowly. "Aye, I do. We do. All the men. The bastard must no' be given the chance to change back the mind of Himself once we've convinced him no' to stand against the MacIntoshes. The laird must be made to see that to fight is folly, and Cael must no' be there to persuade him again."

This weighed heavily on the mind of the second man. Emmie's heart beat frantically as she listened to the conversation. This man, the taller, fair-haired man who looked like he bathed more regularly, obviously was a respected member of the clan. Was he the one that wronged Cael? Would he agree that Cael needed to be killed?

Emmie was nearly certain he would. So it came as a surprise when his answer suggested otherwise.

"I'll no' go against my laird. I'll no' defy Himself. Convincing the men that we must make the laird change his mind is one thing, but killing Cael is another. I'll *no'* defy my laird!"

They grew still then, and conversation ceased. Emmie waited, her frustration mounting as they continued to sit and watch the fire.

"What does this mean?" she shouted.

That's when she realized that the flames of the fire weren't moving. The men weren't breathing.

The entire scene had frozen.

Emmie spun around, looking frantically about the unearthly still dwelling.

"What does this mean?" she shouted again, this time to the countess.

There was no response. Instead, the images in front of her disappeared as suddenly as if someone had turned out the lights. Emmie was plunged back into the darkness.

No, wait. Come back...

FILMING OF THE ghost hunt had completed. While the cast of Haunted Britain bickered amongst themselves, the crew and technicians dismantled their equipment and shut the house back up. The main wing of Tullybrae had been returned to its usual state (though Lamb would disagree), and only a few stationary cameras and thermal monitors needed to be retrieved from the outlying areas.

Camera Man A was sent by the producer to take down the camera that had been set up in the last room of the upstairs corridor. He fumed as he stalked down the darkened hallway. Louise was threatening to take out a restraining order on him if he didn't back off. How was that fair? He hadn't done anything other than demand an explanation from her. Perhaps he should confront her husband, tell him how she'd used him, broken his heart, then treated him like dirt.

He was so wrapped up in his thoughts that when he walked through the open door of the small bedroom, he jumped at the sight of the girl sitting on a dusty box in the middle of the room with her back to the door.

It was the curator. The cute blonde girl that, for whatever reason, really didn't want to be on camera.

"Dear God, love, you gave me a fright," he declared. "I thought you was a ghost."

Emmie twisted around, and looked at him. Her eyes held the slightly stunned look of someone who had just walked out of a movie theatre.

"You okay?" the camera man asked.

She looked around the room, as if looking for someone. Then her eyes landed on the camera tripod set up in the corner, and she grimaced.

"Ohhhh, God. That wasn't there the whole time, was it?"

The man chuckled and flipped the light switch. Stark yellow light flooded the room from a single uncovered bulb. Emmie squinted at the sudden assault on her eyes.

"You're awright," he said. He crossed the room, stepping over boxes and piles of junk. "This camera went dead about an hour after we flipped the lights. Unless you've been in here all night, we probably missed you."

"I hope so." She stood and stretched the kinks out of her back. "You should remember to make sure the batteries are fully charged."

"We do. This one had a full battery when we got here. It happens a lot in paranormal investigations."

Emmie came up behind him as he began dismantling the tripod.

"Why is that?"

He shrugged. "No one knows for sure. One theory is that ghosts don't have energy of their own, so they draw on energy surrounding them. Did you know that apparitions are most often seen just before a thunderstorm? Parapsychologists believe they're able to draw from the electric charge in the atmosphere."

"Interesting," she said vaguely, staring at the camera in the man's hand.

She wasn't looking at the camera, she was testing out the atmosphere. Cael was here, hovering at the door. She could feel him. It must mean the old woman and the countess were gone, if he was no longer respecting the boundaries they'd set.

She wondered if he knew what the countess had shown her. Somehow, she thought not. In fact, she didn't want him to know. Not yet at least. There was a puzzle she had to tease out. The man with the ginger hair had said he would not defy his laird. It was possible that he had gone back on his word, but Emmie doubted it. The conversation she'd witnessed hadn't been an answer. It had only been another clue.

Half the men of the clan wanted to withstand the MacIntoshes, and half wanted to kill Cael. To what end, though?

That's when she remembered the Campbells. The MacDonalds of Keppoch had appealed to the MacDonalds of Clanranald for help. The Campbells had seen this as a threat and joined with the MacIntoshes to wipe them out and steal their lands.

That must be it. Cael was advocating that the MacDonalds of Keppoch fight the MacIntoshes themselves. If they did that, the Campbells would not have been persuaded by the MacIntoshes to stand against them. Would that mean they would not have been wiped out?

She knew why Cael had been betrayed, but the question was…

Who had betrayed him?

TWENTY

A VICIOUS MIGRAINE was the first thing to greet Emmie on the morning of her date with Dean. The instant her eyes opened to the dishwater-grey light, a wave of nausea-inducing pain dug into the base of her skull. Emmie pitched forward, despite the pain of sudden movement, and groped blindly in the drawer of her bedside table for the half-full bottle of acetaminophen tablets she'd brought with her from Corner Brook. Locating the bottle, her fingers fumbled madly at the red plastic child-proof lid. It popped off with a satisfying *poomph*, and small, blue liqui-gel pills scattered onto the blankets like tiny marbles.

With two of the precious pills squeezed tightly in her fist (the others abandoned on the covers where they'd fallen) Emmie stumbled to the bathroom. Each footstep sent a fresh jolt of torture along her optic nerves, but she made it without being sick. She yanked open the stained brass taps, releasing a geyser-forced blast of ice cold water, from which she drank by snaking her head over the lip of the enameled, cast iron sink. Once she'd managed to slurp in a mouthful, she tossed the liqui-gels in and swallowed heavily.

Zombie-like, she padded back to her bedroom and eased herself under the covers, careful not to cause any more jarring of her brain than necessary. She clenched her eyelids tightly together, as much to block the residual morning light as to contain the rolling anguish that was still attacking her head with relentless triumph. She envisioned an anthropomorphized war between a great, hulking beast and an army of blue, jelly-like infantry taking place on the battlefield of her grey matter.

You're going down, dude! she thought to the imagined beast as she prayed for blessed relief.

Cael was with her. Next to her. Unfailingly loyal, he'd known how much discomfort she would wake up to, and had been there since she opened her eyes. On the one hand, Emmie wished he'd go away. His dogged presence triggered thoughts, and those thoughts triggered pain. On the other hand, one of those thoughts was that she wanted nothing more than to forget everything, forget herself, and dissolve into nothingness with him. To know of nothing but his presence, his comfort…

And then that desire would perpetuate the blasted thoughts, and the thoughts would aggravate her aching head. Damn him!

Damn her.

Come to think of it (since she was doing so much migraine-inducing thinking anyway) damn Dean. Damn his charming, handsome, eager Texan self. She was dreading their impending date worse than a root canal, or some equally distasteful necessity. But the question was: How much of that was because Emmie herself truly dreaded it, and how much was coming from Cael? Was she being affected by his jealousy the way she'd previously been affected by his rage?

Cael didn't want her to go on this date. Didn't want to share her with another man.

"I don't have a reason not to go," she whispered. "He's alive. You're not."

The dread flattened, limped into sorrow. What she'd said made him sad because it was true. It made her sad, too.

Finally, Emmie's migraine began to ease. It chugged laboriously along, losing momentum like a steam engine that had run out of steam. When the last few throbbing whimpers died, she reluctantly sat up. Half the morning was gone already—it was time to shower and dress.

The pounding of the shower head was pleasantly invigorating. She stood beneath the stream, surrounded by the three mismatched shower curtains, and let the hot water loosen her back and neck muscles. As the steam swirled around her, plasticky-smelling from the vinyl curtains and mingled with the fragrance of her watermelon bath gel, she thought back on the events of last night.

When Carol Bowman confirmed Cael's feelings for Emmie, the woman had unwittingly given her a gift. It was the gift of release. Now that she'd slept on it, Emmie no longer felt a need to pretend, to ignore, to stifle. She could acknowledge Cael's feelings, acknowledge that she'd known all along.

More than that, though, now that she'd slept on it, it wasn't so frightening for Emmie anymore to acknowledge her own feelings for Cael. However wrong, however unnatural it may or may not be, there it was. At the very least, it cast her obsession to solve Cael's mystery into a new light, illuminating facets and edges which had previously been obscured by the shadow of her unwillingness to see them. Laid bare, Emmie knew that it was not just Cael's influence that was driving her to seek a resolution. It truly was because *she* wanted to know, too. Had to know. The obsession was as much hers as it was his.

Carol had called Emmie an old soul. *People like to use that expression far too often, but they're rarer than you'd think, those old souls,* she'd said. When asked what that meant, she'd simply responded, *Oh, nothing. Most of the time.*

Most of the time. But not this time. Yet another illuminated facet that Emmie had not allowed herself to see. Whatever was between her and Cael, it went back farther than the span of her short life. Like the hum of an electric current that one didn't hear until someone pointed it out, Emmie was now aware of the vibration of a connection that transcended all known theories of time.

In that context, the little old woman's contribution to last night's monumental revelation held more weight. *We're led to places, my dear,* she'd told Emmie. *No one ever ends up anywhere by accident.*

Emmie hadn't ended up at Tullybrae by accident. She'd been led here. She was meant to find Cael, to learn of his murder and, just maybe, to solve it.

As little as a week ago, she would have thought herself tipped over the edge. Having well and truly gone mad. But Emmie wasn't going mad. The little, grey-haired lady had insisted on that. She was of sound mind. Whatever strain Cael's presence and his demands had put upon her, it had more to do with her perception of her mother's decline and eventual death than anything that might have been a physiological trait, or an inherent shortcoming of personal strength.

And then there was what she'd learned of her mother's shortcomings— which, the woman had revealed, were not shortcomings at all. Emmie's mother had suffered from mental illness. Her drug addiction was not an indicator of a weak character, but instead was symptomatic of an undiagnosed health condition.

Still, Emmie was angry with her mother. She was angry with her grandmother. She knew it was unfair, but that's how she felt. Oddly, though, there was a certain peace that came with allowing herself to admit that she was angry, and had been all this time.

Perhaps what the old woman had told her was true—her mother's weakness had made Emmie strong. She wasn't necessarily convinced of such an explanation, but it made her feel somewhat better to think that it might be true.

This time, when Emmie stood in front of the armoire to dress for the day, she aimed for a look that fell somewhere between the two extremes she'd recently known: The careful, fastidious, professional woman, and the frump who had given up on herself. This morning—though to be fair, it was getting on closer to noon by now—she chose a simple long-sleeve Vneck knit in a crisp white, and her dark, slim-leg jeans. On her feet, she laced up a pair of clean, white Keds she hadn't worn in five years, but which she had brought with her to Scotland for one reason or another.

With Cael close behind, she left the servants' quarters, and joined Lamb in the kitchen for breakfast.

The old man gave a start when he saw her in her clean, simple attire, with her hair twisted into a butterfly clip and face adorned with just a touch of mascara and tinted lip gloss.

"You look very well, my dear," he said in his unshakably formal way. His eyes, though, warmed, betraying his soft heart. "How do you feel?"

"I feel…" Emmie thought, her bottom teeth catching the edge of her upper lip. "Tired. Like bodily tired. You know when you've been sick with the flu, and when it's over you're left weak and drained, but you know that things can only get better from here? I'm not sure that's quite it, but it's as close as I can get."

"Yes? Oh, good. I am pleased. Well, I hope you have an appetite this morning. The butcher had back bacon on special, so I picked up two pounds of it."

As Lamb shuffled to the counter, Emmie stared at his back, brows drawn together. There was something about his demeanour—it was anxious. Like he'd been expecting something, some change in her.

How much did the old man know?

"I'm not sure I'm two-pounds-of-back-bacon hungry, but I could eat," she answered carefully, deciding not to press the matter.

"It's good to see you happy again, love."

"You sweet man, now I feel guilty. I wouldn't say 'happy' is quite the right word. But I'm not unhappy. Let's leave it at that."

After filling her belly to a level that was an inch above comfortable, Emmie retreated to the library to pick up where she left off with her cataloguing. A feeling of optimism stole over her when she closed the door, and heard the firm, metallic click of the latch bolt catching the faceplate. Back to work.

She'd been holed up in her nursery-slash-office so much of late, searching for anything and everything there was to be had in cyberspace and digital archives about the MacDonalds of Keppoch, that she'd completely abandoned the project she'd been hired to do. Her manila tags, her string, her pencils and pad of paper were still there. Haunted Britain's crew had moved them behind the sofa during filming—manila tags, string, pencils and notepads being decidedly out of place in a setting that was supposed to be riddled with spooks and spectres—but otherwise everything was just as she'd left it. Lowering herself to the floor, she sat cross-legged behind the sofa, and took a few minutes to review what she'd already done.

Then she picked up where she'd left off with the late Lord Cranbury's collection of books as if she'd been at it only yesterday.

It felt good to be cataloguing again. To be engrossed in the simple, almost meditative task of recording facts and figures. Her mind was pleasantly blank in some respects, and comfortably aware in others. Cael was still there, of course. She could feel his presence and was glad of it. But in the blank part of her mind, she was content to let the knowledge of his presence be separate from the gut-wrenching thoughts and fears that had plagued her for weeks.

For his part, Cael seemed content to let her relegate him to the background. She worked and he watched, in the same type of companionable silence she and Lamb often found together.

Sometime around mid-afternoon, Lamb came into the library. He was carrying an armload of split logs so large that the poor withered man looked ready to snap in two. Taking advantage of the open door, Clunie scurried in on the old butler's heels, fat orange belly swaying between his hindquarters, and settled himself on top of Emmie's notepad and pen.

"You silly old man, what are you doing?" Emmie accused, hopping up from the floor. "Those are far too heavy for you. Here, let me."

"You'll ruin your nice white shirt," he argued. But he let her take them.

"Why are you doing this? You've got to stop with these useless chores. Old Cranberry's dead."

"It's no' useless. It gets cold in here. I thought you could use a nice wee fire."

Emmie softened, regretting her exasperation. "A fire would be lovely," she relented. "But you could have suggested it, and I would have gotten the logs myself."

"Nonsense. Work keeps my joints limber."

"Limber?" She raised one brow.

"You mock me, but imagine how stiff and slow I'd be if I didn't keep active. The local children might begin calling me the Tinman of Tullybrae."

"Thank you, Lamb. That was very kind of you. You're the grandfather I never had."

The colour that tinged his pale cheeks betrayed his pleasure, despite his awkward nod and wordless departure.

"He's a big old softie under that stoic exterior," she told Clunie. He looked at her expectantly, purring madly. Emmie scratched behind his ears, and he raised his head in sheer bliss.

She added, "That can't be comfortable, sitting on my pen."

She spent the rest of the day enjoying the soft crackle of the flames, the gentle purring of Clunie's warm body against her thigh, and the simple fact of Cael's nearness. At five, the dig crew packed up for the day. Their casual chatter filtered into the library through the glass windowpanes as they trooped out of the field and packed up their van.

Before leaving, Dean stopped by the library. He opened the door, knocking on the frame as he popped his head inside.

"Hey. So I'll pick you up at seven?" The casual tone failed to mask the eagerness that was evident in his countenance.

"I'll be ready," she answered, affecting enthusiasm.

"Great, see you then."

She watched him go. There was a visible bounce in his step, and when he reached the van outside, his jovial banter with Adam and Sophie sounded a little too jovial. It was as she suspected—Dean clearly was hoping for more than the "just friends" outing they'd agreed to.

The awkward feeling he'd dredged up with his quick visit stayed with her the rest of the evening. Her repeated self-reassurances did little to assuage her discomfort.

"You like Dean. He's a good guy. Stop being paranoid."

Nor did her reassurances assuage Cael. The peaceful, quiet intimacy they'd shared in the library vanished. Now, he sulked in the background, reluctantly giving her time and space to enjoy her life.

When Dean returned to the manor, Cael disappeared entirely.

"Looking good," she said playfully when she opened the door.

"I changed my outfit, like, five times," he answered with a comical eye-roll. "You look great, too."

"Thanks."

Outside on the gravel drive was parked a shiny, metallic grey Audi A3 Cabriolet. Emmie balked at the sleek, sophisticated machine.

"Woah! Is that your car?"

"Yeah." He shrugged.

"You sure you didn't go out and rent a set of flashy wheels just to impress me?"

Dean clucked his tongue. "You caught me. Even borrowed my old man's Sunday tie."

"It's funny—I always assumed you guys just drove around in those big white vans all the time."

"Oh, we do. Totally. Stannisfield pays for the gas on those babies, so we'd be stupid not to. But we all have our own cars, too. They're just parked at the hotel most of the time."

He opened the passenger side door for her. Thanking him, Emmie slid into the low, scoop-back seat. Inside, the car was upholstered in butter-soft, charcoal grey leather, and the dash was chrome and black with neon blue gauges.

"So where are we going?" she asked as he climbed into the driver's side and turned on the ignition. The engine purred to life with a seductive sigh.

"How does Aviemore sound? There's this small pub I heard about. It's called the Avie—"

"The Aviemore Arms," she finished. "I've been. It's a great little place."

Dean tipped his head back and grinned ruefully. "You've been. Ah, and here I was hoping to take you someplace new, get you out of that dusty old manor house."

"Even better—you're taking me to one of my favourite places around."

"We both know this is one of the only places around."

Her lips quirked, eyes sparkling with humour. "The sentiment still stands."

The driving, as well as the actual time spent *with* Dean rather than the time spent dreading it, lent a great deal to helping Emmie relax. Her earlier trepidation about his private hopes and expectations for the evening waned. Now that the actual date had arrived, he proved himself to be remarkably easy to be around. She had gotten a sense of it in the time the crew had been at Tullybrae, notably at The Grigg and again at the university when he was introducing her to his skeletal friends. One-on-one, in the close confines of his luxury vehicle, he was even more so. Gone was the cocky lady-killer persona that competed with Adam to flirt with her. That Dean was replaced with a man who was effortlessly charming, with a distinctly Texan flavour. He was witty, self-deprecating and a born conversationalist.

Being with him was natural. Fun. Emmie's earlier burdens, brought on by the slightly oppressive atmosphere of Tullybrae and its ghostly inhabitants, and by her incomprehensible connection to Cael and his mystery, melted away.

"Good to see you again, lass," said the handsome, salt-and-pepper-haired barman when they arrived and found a seat at the Aviemore Arms. "Pint of stout, is it?"

"I'd love one," she answered, somewhere between flirty and friendly.

"And what'll yer young man here have?"

"Tenents. Thanks, bud."

"Sure." The barman winked at Emmie before leaving to fill their orders.

Dean raised an eyebrow at her. "You come here often?"

"No, just the once. He must have a good memory."

"He'd have to be brain dead not to remember a looker like you."

"Come on, now, Deano. Put the Alpha Male act away," she chastised teasingly.

He didn't miss a beat. "No can do. It's a natural male instinct. I'll be peeing on you to mark my territory next." He drew an imaginary square around the perimeter of their table. "Just give me a half hour to get my first pint down."

"Charming."

The evening stretched on, as pleasant as it had promised to be at the start. At times, Dean had Emmie in stitches, and when she wasn't laughing, she was engrossed in the stories he told. He painted a picture of his life in Texas, of the parents that were still there and the high school football friends who had all taken jobs in factories right after graduation. He told her about late-night forays to the old Four Boulders Bridge off Ridley's ranch, and of the test of manhood he and his friends had all taken by jumping into the river below without a scrap of clothing on.

With considerable coaxing, Emmie relayed the details of her childhood in Corner Brook, Newfoundland without delving into any of the particulars. She described for him the smell of saltwater on a rainy morning, and of the sound of the cargo ships when they docked in St. John's. He seemed especially interested in her explanation of the buildings in a seaside town, tall and narrow, clapboard siding painted bright blues, yellows and rust reds.

"I thought Newfoundlanders had accents," he noted when she said as much as she wanted to.

"I can do one."

"Yeah? Let's hear."

Emmie sat back in her chair, eyeing Dean speculatively as she thought of what she would say.

"She's some lop on the pond, buddy what?" she said in a perfect Newfoundlander lilt.

He stared at her, incredulous. "What?"

"I said, 'The water's rough today, isn't it?'"

"That's crazy." He shook his head, in awe of this side of Emmie he'd never seen before. "So why don't you talk that way all the time? Were you born somewhere else, or have you learned how to hide your accent, like me?"

"The former," she evaded.

"Don't know why you don't pull that out to charm the men-folk more often. I find the Texas drawl works wonders on the ladies." He winked.

"I bet you do," she answered dryly, and took a pull of her pint.

It was after midnight by the time the night life at the Aviemore Arms began to wind down. Emmie was surprised by how easily the time and conversation passed—as did three full pints of local stout. She rarely drank that much (her night of copious wine at the one roast beef dinner with Lamb notwithstanding), but was enjoying the slight blur it added to the edges of everything. Dean, who was driving, only had two pints of Tenents, and filled in the gaps with ginger beer and a sizeable selection of appetizers.

"You're going to lose that girlish figure of yours one day if you're not careful," she teased as he shovelled a deep-fried curried spring roll into his mouth.

"Nah, I'm solid. This is what race horses eat just before the Belmont Stakes. Look it up, it's a fact."

He chomped goofily through another spring roll.

"I don't know how you can say something so outrageous with a straight face like that."

"It's a gift. I'm blessed."

When they both agreed they were ready to go home, Dean paid the bill and they left, with the barman's invitation for Emmie—no mention of Dean—to come back soon.

"It's good to see you smile again," Dean noted as he drove them down the winding Highland roads back to Tullybrae.

Emmie watched the stark white beams of the Cabriolet's high-powered headlights part the curtain of night in front of them.

"Lamb said the same thing this morning," she answered eventually.

"Less stressed or something?"

"Something like that."

"Don't take this the wrong way, okay? I don't mean it as an insult, but I wouldn't have thought curating was a particularly stressful job."

She grinned sideways at him. "No insult taken. You're right, it's a pretty low-key job."

"Something else going on, then?"

"Yeah."

Dean gave her a long glance when she did not say any more—as long as he could afford while driving down a winding road in the dark.

"Whatever it was, I'm glad it's done. You had us all really worried."

"Yeah right. I'm sure Adam was practically pacing his hotel room."

Dean raked his fingers through his hair. "Adam's an ass most of the time. But he's a good guy underneath all that. He really cares about people deep down."

Emmie smiled to herself. "I know."

They made the rest of the drive in good time. It was a little after one thirty in the morning when Dean pulled through the gates onto Tullybrae's drive.

Immediately, a sense of extreme agitation prickled the surface of Emmie's skin. She shivered visibly.

"You're not cold, are you?" Dean asked.

"No. Just— No, I'm fine." How could she finish that sentence any other way?

He raised an eyebrow, but didn't comment.

The uncomfortable sensation Emmie felt was coming from Cael—he was not happy. But unlike her usual awareness of him, which translated itself into a localized sensation which allowed her to pinpoint his physical location in proximity to her own, the prickling was everywhere. It was all around her, thickening the air like a dense Highland mist. It was cloying. And Dean was blissfully unaware of it.

He pulled the car up to the front of the house and turned off the ignition. When she moved to open her door, he called, "Stay where you are. I've got it." Hopping deftly out, he trotted around to the passenger side.

"Thank you," she said, outwardly cheerful.

There was a short walk to the front door. Dean hung slightly behind, his hand hovering at the small of her back. It was a possessive gesture, subtle though it was. Another kind of trepidation, one which had nothing to do with Cael, began to sneak into her thoughts. Dean was strangely quiet. Nervous.

Please don't let him be thinking what she thought he was thinking.

She nearly groaned out loud when her suspicions were confirmed. As she unlocked the door and turned the handle, he put a hand out to stop her.

"Em, wait."

Then he hesitated. Then smiled nervously. Then raked his fingers through his hair again.

"Look, I know we said we'd just go out as friends and all—and I respect that. But I think you know by now that I like you."

"Um... yeah," she said slowly.

Despite her wariness, Dean pressed on. "I mean, what guy wouldn't, just to look at you? Wow, that sounded bad—don't get me wrong, it's not just that you're beautiful. You *are* beautiful, but I mean..." He laughed helplessly. "Jeez, I'm making a mess of this. What I mean to say is, you're smart, down to earth, you know? Like, you really seem to have it together."

"I—" The statement took her aback. The notion that she'd been falling apart had been at the centre of her personal crisis for several weeks now. To hear him say she "had it together" sounded odd to her ears. Unnatural. Her unease over what Dean was trying to tell her lessened slightly as she grappled with his assessment of her.

"Oh, Dean. No, I don't. Not really."

"I don't believe that," he insisted, his gaze turning searching. "Have you seen yourself lately? I mean, objectively? A curator at your age, independent and sure of yourself. You know exactly who you are and where you're going. Like no one can faze you. I mean, yeah sure, you wear hoodies and yoga pants once in a while, and you have stress to deal with. But everyone does, right?"

Emmie stared at Dean, interested by the account of herself he was giving. With everything she'd learned over the past two days—about her mother, about herself, about Cael—she wasn't sure of anything at all right now. Did other people see her the way Dean did, she wondered?

"Look," he finished, "the thing is—I was wondering if there might be some point in the near future that we could be... you know... more than friends?"

There was such hope in his eyes that it broke her heart to have to refuse him.

Then again, she didn't *have* to refuse him. Not if she didn't want to. The little old woman had told her to go out with Dean. Well, Emmie had gone. And she'd had fun.

Unfortunately, while she was debating with herself about whether or not she would say no, her mouth had run ahead of her brain and was saying things she wasn't sure she meant.

"Dean. Oh my gosh. I'm flattered, really. And you're really cute. Believe me, I'm not oblivious to the fact that you're a hottie. It's just... I'm really not in the right headspace to think about dating just now."

His face fell a fraction, but he kept his hopeful smile in place.

"It's not you, it's me, huh? Universal code for 'I'm not into you, I'm into someone else.'"

"That's not it. I'm not seeing anyone else." It wasn't a lie, per se. "And I swear, at any other time of my life, I'd totally be into you. I'm serious," she insisted when he made a playfully dismissive gesture. "If I were on the market, I would jump at the chance to go out with you in a heartbeat."

He looked at her for a moment, considering her sincerity.

"All right," he allowed. "I'll believe you. You're not trying to soothe my ego, and you don't really think I'm a gargoyle."

Emmie released a surprised laugh. "Gargoyle?"

Her stomach flipped nervously when his expression grew serious.

"So I won't ever bring up the subject again, I promise," he said, his voice low and sensuous. "Just... please don't be mad at me."

"For what?" Her own voice was a whisper.

"For this," he whispered back.

Dean leaned forward, slowly, hovering a moment.

Emmie knew he was giving her the opportunity to back away. To say no.

She didn't. She remained still, and let Dean kiss her.

There were so many reasons why. Guilt, pity, curiosity. Even annoyance with herself. After all, there was no logical reason why she should turn him down. His lips, when they touched hers, were warm and soft. Real. His kiss was gentle, respectful.

Amid the turmoil her mind was in, one thought surfaced above all the others:

This is nice.

Or it was almost nice, *could* be nice if she would just let herself enjoy it. But she couldn't. Emmie was already starting to think of what she'd say or do when the kiss ended. And it angered her that she couldn't just enjoy what was right in front of her, when it wasn't Cael.

If it were Cael…

Suddenly, Dean pulled away from her. A sharp hiss escaped through his teeth.

"Ah! What the—"

He reached his right hand over his left shoulder and rubbed at it. Then he turned a circle to look behind him.

"What?" Emmie asked, somewhere between alarmed and dazed.

"Something just… Jeez, that frickin' hurt." He turned another circle. "Something just scratched me."

"Scratched you? What, like an animal?"

"Bat, maybe?"

They looked at each other, neither of them convinced by the possibility.

Emmie inclined her head towards the house. "Here, come inside so I can look at it in the light."

She pushed opened the heavy front door and led Dean into the foyer, where she flipped the light switch on the wall.

"Turn around." She put her hands lightly on his shoulders, and when his back was to her, she pulled aside the neck of his shirt. The start of three distinct scratches marked his skin at the base of his neck, and there was a smudge of blood on his shirt.

"You're bleeding. Come on. We'll get some Polysporin on that."

"Nah, don't worry about it. I'm sure it's nothing," he said half-heartedly. Predictably, he made no objection when she led him up the stairs.

"Sorry for the climb, but my first aid stuff is all on the third floor," she apologized as they entered the servants' staircase.

"So this is where you live," Dean observed. As they headed to the bathroom, he took in the surroundings with interest. "Man, it's like stepping back through time, isn't it?"

"This whole house is like stepping back through time."

"Lamb up here too?"

"He's on the men's side."

"Why doesn't that surprise me?" he said wryly. "A proper British butler. That man belongs in another time, too."

When they reached the bathroom, Dean took a seat on the closed lid of the toilet, and turned away from Emmie so she could attend to his injury.

Delicately, she pulled at the hem of his shirt, lifting it up. He followed her lead, pulling the garment the rest of the way over his head. She made an appreciative note of the fact that he kept his arms in his sleeves, instead of eagerly shedding the whole thing as some amorous would-be suitors might do.

She also couldn't help but note his back. It was smooth and muscled. An elaborate tattoo of a fierce-looking American bald eagle covered his right shoulder, and spread down to the bottom of his ribs.

"Nice ink," she offered. "Very Americana."

"When in Texas," he quipped. "What would be the Canadiana version, I wonder?"

"A ninja beaver."

Dean laughed, and so did Emmie. She was glad of it. The moment of joviality helped to dissolve some of the tension that had flared up at that kiss.

She examined the scratches closely. They were long and harsh, and like his tattoo, they extended from his left shoulder down to the base of his ribs. The blood that had smudged his shirt was superficial, but it could still use a disinfecting. One never knew—it might have been a bat after all. Though Emmie didn't believe that for one minute.

She took out the plastic Rubbermaid container with her first aid supplies that she kept under the sink, and fished out a box of gauze pads. Running one pad under the tap, she dabbed away the blood, following the scratches from top to bottom.

"What does it look like?"

"Like... claw marks," she answered begrudgingly.

Dean was silent for a moment.

"I think there's definitely something to the theory that this place is haunted," he said uneasily.

"I said there was. I wasn't making it up when I told you about what I'd experienced. Remember, at The Grigg?"

"Yeah, I remember. But didn't you say you thought it was, like, a benevolent spirit? A comforting one?"

"I did."

"Well?"

She huffed. "I'm not a ghost expert, am I? No one's ever scratched *me* before. Maybe they're anti-American."

He twisted back to look at her, humour quirking the edge of his lips. "Wouldn't they have tried to scratch *through* Hubert then?"

"You named your bald eagle tattoo Hubert?"

"It was either that or Agamemnon."

Emmie snorted. "I'm not even going to ask."

She finished dabbing Dean's back, and attached the gauze pads with surgical tape. When she was done, she stepped back and let him put his shirt back on. Clothed, he stood up, smiled warily, and shoved his hands in his pockets.

"I should probably go."

"Yeah. Thanks for tonight. I had fun."

"Me too. Thanks for letting me take you out."

He leaned in again, but this time he kissed her on the cheek.

"I'll walk you out," she offered.

He nodded, smiling wryly. "I'd say no need, but hell, I'm not sure I want to be walking through this house alone right now. I'm not sure I like the idea of leaving you alone here, either."

"I'm not alone. I've got Lamb."

"Yeah, right." He rolled his eyes. "If you scream, it would take him a year just to make it to you from the other side of the floor."

"Aw, leave the poor man alone. He's spry enough... for his age."

They left the third floor in silence, and made their way through the darkened house to the front door. Dean got into his car, and with a final wave, drove back out to the main road. When she could no longer see his tail lights, Emmie shut and locked the door.

It was two in the morning, but she had no intention of going to sleep. She had a Highlander to find. Cael had crossed a line, and whether he liked it or not, she was going to have it out with him.

TWENTY-ONE

"CAEL? CAEL, WHERE are you?"

Emmie climbed the grand staircase, feet hammering into each carpeted step.

"Cael. Stop hiding, we need to talk." She stopped, shook her head, and muttered to herself, "Well, not 'talk,' per se—you know what I mean. *Cael!*"

There was no sign of him. No tingle, no inkling, nothing. Still, she charged through the darkened corridor on the second floor, hoping to pick up on where he was hiding, and knowing it was probably a futile exercise. After all, how did one uncover a ghost if that ghost did not want to be found? It wasn't hide-and-seek. She couldn't just look in a closet or under a bed and, *Aha!—There you are!* Nope, in that respect, Cael definitely had the upper hand.

After much stomping, Emmie was fairly certain the second floor was empty. So was the third floor. There was still the ground level and below stairs, but she had little hope those areas of the house would prove any more successful.

Frustrated, she wandered back to the grand staircase, her ire markedly deflated. She paused in front of the enameled Rococo mirror mounted above the upper landing.

"C'mon Cael," she implored in a whisper. "I don't know what you want from me, but you've got to help me figure it out here."

A small, almost imperceptible movement to her right caught her attention. Emmie stared ahead, eyes wide, tracking the movement in her peripheral vision. She did not want to turn her head, to look on the source directly.

Because, on her right... there was nothing but the mirror.

Someone was in the corridor behind her. Coming towards her. Inch by inch, Emmie turned around, breath suspended, to confront whomever was there.

The corridor was empty.

Yet, when she turned back to the mirror, there most definitely was someone there. Cael. He was standing about ten feet behind her, directly beneath the plaster arch that separated the corridor from the landing.

The sight of him took Emmie's breath away, and she forgot all about being upset with him. She stared, in awe of the figure before her, reflected in the mirror.

He looked apologetic. He knew he'd done wrong to Dean, and he was sorry for having displeased her. Funny thing was, Emmie couldn't recall the reason *why* she was displeased with him. She was like an animal caught in headlights, blinded, and powerless to turn away even though the consequences might prove disastrous.

She dared not breathe as he walked forward. His eyes were trained on her, watching her through the glass. And at some point, though she couldn't quite determine when, the glass was no longer there. It had sort of melted away along with her reflection, and Emmie hadn't even noticed until Cael stopped directly in front of her. He held out his hand, solid and three-dimensional, inviting her to take it.

He was inviting her to step through the mirror—or, through where the mirror had been. He was asking her to come with him into that other world, the one of memory, illusions and half-truths. Incomplete truths which prevented a man from understanding his own death.

This wasn't like last time. It wasn't a dream, nor was it being forced upon her. She was being given a choice. She could take his hand and follow him, or she could turn around and walk away and remain at Tullybrae. Instinctively, Emmie sensed that her choice, whichever one she made, would be significant. It was the answer to an ultimatum he'd given her the first time he'd brought her into his world. Either she belonged to him, or she did not.

There was no deciding for Emmie. She already knew that she would let him take her wherever he wanted. She knew even before her arm lifted and her hand slipped comfortably into his.

When his fingers tightened over hers, the hope, the expectation and the fear that had written themselves on his rather expressive face blossomed into an aura of joy.

She stepped forward, her own heart joyful, and as she passed through the invisible boundary that separated her reality from his, the world as she knew it fell away. In its place, the walls of a castle took shape. The close, creaking interior of Tullybrae morphed into the drafty passageways and flagstone floors that she'd seen before. Around them, echoes of the past rippled on the currents of air that made the lit torches dance and undulate.

Cael led them. Though Emmie did not know where he was taking her, or what he meant for her to see, she trusted him. Through the narrow passageways, down steep stone steps and along smoke-filled corridors she let herself be led. Farther and farther down they went until she thought they must be descending into the bowels of the earth, and then back up again, into a large, cave-like space. It had high, wide, uncovered windows, and it was very clearly the kitchens.

If only she knew what castle this was. Did it still exist, or was Cael's memory all that was left of this place?

The chambers—several open spaces that were linked together by thick stone columns like honeycomb—bustled with life. The kitchen staff, mostly men, were engaged in preparing all manner of food. They darted between tables and countertops, punching pastry dough, preparing meats, chopping root vegetables and greens, onions and herbs. A spit boy sat by the large open hearth, looking thoroughly miserable as he cranked an iron handle slowly and mechanically.

Though the chatter of the inhabitants was exclusively Gaelic, Emmie understood it, just as she had before. This was Cael's memory, after all, and her command of a language she didn't speak was due to him. It was an odd kind of understanding, the harsh, garbled syllables blending with a grasp of meaning that was as melodious as if she spoke it fluently.

Through the honeycomb kitchens Cael brought her, not bothering to step aside for moving bodies. Emmie and he were the ghosts here, not these busy people. Faces passed, but the eyes did not see, the senses did not detect. She looked at these people, each one, and saw the contentment of every-day monotony in their countenances. They were as blissful as she when cataloguing. Emmie smiled, feeling somewhat of a kinship with these long-dead beings.

They stopped when Cael decided they'd reached their destination. In a remote corner, a bread oven was being tended by a stout, grey-haired woman and a dark-haired boy about seven or eight years of age. Daylight from a nearby window, a vent for the oven, projected a shaft of light onto the boy's dirty, gamin face.

"That's it," she instructed him in a grandmotherly way. "There ye go. Put the faggots in through the door. Aye, just like that."

The boy struggled to lift a lit bundle of twigs, as wide around as he was and almost as long. He held the bundle at an awkward angle, careful to keep the burning ends away from flesh, clothing and hair. His small face was scrunched with effort, but not a sound escaped his lips. This was a boy who was bent on proving his manhood.

Once the bundle had been shoved into the oven, the woman picked up a door of fired clay that had been leaning against the base, and covered the opening with exaggerated finality.

"Grand. Just grand, wee Cael. And that's that. We'll let the oven heat for an hour or so, and then it shall be time to bake our bread."

"Cael, that's you," Emmie whispered. Her heart melted as the sweet little urchin looked up at his teacher with pride.

Cael, who was still holding her hand, straightened with his own pride at the boy he'd once been. He gave her arm a gentle pull, moving her so that she was standing in front of him. When his arms encircled her middle and his chin rested on her shoulder, she tilted her head slightly to accommodate him. Her hands grasped the smooth sinew of his bare forearms, fingers pressing into the warm flesh.

"We'll make sure to tell yer father, aye?" the woman was telling Cael the child indulgently. "Himself will be so pleased wi' how well ye're learning the running of his castle."

The boy nodded solemnly, the weight of the responsibility taken in earnest. It reminded Emmie of that earlier memory of Cael and his father, the one where the clan chieftain publicly recognized him as his son, and bestowed upon him the gift of the ornate kilt pin to mark the occasion. Emmie knew now, thanks to Paul Rotenfeld at the University of Glasgow, that the clan chieftain was Angus MacDonald, second of Keppoch. There was no way this little boy could know it yet, but he would grow into a man that would please his father greatly. The future of Cael the child was mapped out already.

In the midst of misty-eyed affection, the vision changed. The images of the kitchens, of the woman and of Cael as a child ran together like watercolour paint under a running tap. The light brightened, and when her vision sharpened again, Emmie blinked at the sudden materialization of a new memory.

They were outside. The air was crisp, the sky bestowed with a gentle sun. Fresh dew dappled the blades of grass and dense scrub, making the hills look like a carpet of emeralds. Birdsong, high and tittering, indicated that it was morning, and judging by the fresh scent of delicate new growth, it was likely spring.

From somewhere further out, the clang of metal on metal interrupted the birds. A chorus of cheering, rowdy voices rose up into the air.

Cael released Emmie and straightened. She was disappointed at losing the intimacy, but was mollified when he took back her hand. Inclining his head towards the noise, he gave her a heart-stopping grin, and led her onward.

Her first thought was that there was a duel, or a skirmish. She hoped he was not about to show her bloodshed. Injury and death did not belong to such a glorious morning as this. As they drew closer, the voices became clearer. They were male, and the telltale cracking of newly-deepening vocal chords suggested that they were boys on the cusp of their teen years. They, too, were speaking Gaelic.

Cael halted when they reached the crest of a shallow ridge. Below, the land opened up into a flat plain where a number of boys, perhaps twelve or thirteen of them, were playing at swords. Beyond was the castle that was their home, and the outbuildings and dwellings that surrounded it.

In the centre of the group were two boys. One was large and powerful, destined to be a fighter. He had long, messy hair which was braided, and which stuck out in odd spots. It made him look markedly frightening, though he couldn't have been more than fourteen. He moved with the confidence born of his sheer size, all force and no strategy.

The dark haired boy, his opponent, was everything this large young man was not. He was smaller by a head, and fine-featured, the gamin face of the kitchens developed into something that promised a quiet handsomeness. Lithe and graceful, he was outmaneuvering his opponent with every lunge and thrust of his blunt practice sword.

He was winning, and he knew it.

Cael's hand tightened on hers, and his grin grew wider.

"I see you." Emmie nodded, smiling herself. "I've got it, you're a superstar."

When a particularly brilliant feint, and then a swift upward thrust brought his larger, and very surprised opponent down, she nearly cheered.

Cael the twelve-year-old laughed, and turned to another boy standing in the crowd that circled them. The other boy, short and solid, and with sandy-coloured hair, stepped into the ring. The pair hugged and clapped each other on the back, sharing the victory.

The boy who had just lost sprang up from where he'd fallen unceremoniously on his backside. Thrusting a thick arm between the two boys, he shoved young Cael in the shoulder.

"Ye bloody cheated, ye *toll-toine*."

"I did no'," insisted young Cael. "Ye're just sore ye lost, ye *luinnseach mhor*."

"Ye tricked me. Ye didna fight fair."

"Ballocks. Ye mind what Master MacBevan says: Chivalry is for the English. When ye're fighting for yer life, there is only winning and dying."

"Aye, Tom. Ye're no' *English*, are ye?" Cael's sandy-haired friend jeered.

The boy called Tom looked like he wanted to hit one of them, but by the way the boys in the circle were starting to form groups around whichever opponent they were backing, he thought better about his odds. Instead, he picked up his practice sword and spat at Cael's feet.

"Tcha. It doesna matter ye won anyway, Cael. It doesna count when ye're fighting a bastard."

Cael's youthful face grew dark, and he took a single, menacing step forward.

"What did ye call me?"

"Ye're nobbut a bastard," the boy repeated. "No' worth an old whore's pap."

Of the two of them, it was the sandy-haired boy that took the most offense to this.

"Ye'll look no better than an old whore's pap by the time I'm done wi' ye," he shouted, and then lunged forward, teeth bared like a wild animal.

Anticipating his friend's attack, Cael darted around behind Tom, jumped on his back and threw a slender arm around his neck. The effect was to wrench an unsuspecting Tom's head back, giving Cael's friend a split second of surprise to land a punch square to the jaw.

Tom staggered and fell, landing on Cael. But Cael held on, wrestling the larger boy until he was on top of him. From there, Cael's friend jumped in, and it was soon a brawling, wrestling tangle of arms and legs. The boys who had been watching broke their respective ranks, forming a circle again, and cheering and egging the three boys on as they punched, kicked, bit and generally slugged it out.

A shout from the near distance worked its way into the screams and cursing. "Lawren! Cael!"

From the direction of the castle, an older boy approached the circle at a run. He was perhaps not yet twenty, but was already showing the signs of heavy work. Or training, if that work was with a Highland broadsword. He was lithe and graceful in his strength, much the way Cael was, but with the sandy-coloured hair of the other boy.

Reaching the mass of flailing limbs, the young man began tearing the boys apart.

"What is the meaning of this?" he demanded, the collar of a homespun tunic in each hand with Cael dangling from one and Lawren from the other. "Lawren, ye wee grouse, ye ken better than to be fighting. Is this how we treat our kinsmen?"

"He called Cael a name, Ennis," Lawren jutted his chin out and pointed accusingly.

"Aye, and I just called ye a grouse, but ye're no' having a go at me."

"But he called Cael a *bastard*."

This insult, apparently, was unacceptable. Ennis's head turned ominously towards Tom, who stood defiantly with his hands on his sturdy hips. His eyes narrowed to slits and raked Tom from head to toe.

"Ye'll mind yer tongue when ye speak to my brother."

"Yer *bastard* brother," Tom taunted.

Unwise. No sooner were the words out of his mouth than Ennis dropped the shirt collars he was holding, and slugged Tom in the gut. Tom doubled over like a sack of grain, and all the boys who had been watching, whether they'd been cheering on Tom or Cael, began to laugh and point as Tom curled into the fetal position.

Ennis glared at Cael and Lawren in turn, and pointed a finger at them.

"Dinna ye dare tell Father."

Then he put an arm around each boy, and with one backwards glance of distaste, he led them away.

Emmie understood what Cael was trying to show her, remembered the names from his earlier memory. These young men, Lawren and Ennis, were his brothers, and Cael was trying to impress upon her that they were close. The circumstances of their births—Lawren and Ennis legitimate, and Cael not—had not in any way damaged or stunted their bond of kinship.

Cael was telling her that he believed neither Lawren nor Ennis had anything to do with his death. But then, Emmie already knew Ennis couldn't have. He died before Cael had been recognized officially as the son of Angus MacDonald. Her earlier, fleeting suspicion that Lawren had betrayed his half-brother out of jealousy did not fit with what she was seeing here. These boys loved each other.

She looked at Cael. There was sadness in his eyes as he surveyed the remembered scene. She squeezed his hand reassuringly. He squeezed back.

"I don't think it was your brothers either," she told him.

The vision once again changed, shapes and images running together like water. The light dimmed, and when the vision cleared, it was night. The dark, starless sky was visible through the narrow slits of windows, and the stone walls of the great hall flickered orange with firelight. Unlike the last time Cael showed her this place, there was not the gaiety of a meal. This time, the hall was empty, cleared of trestle tables, mangy, unkempt dogs, and even mangier clansmen and women.

In all, this memory had a much more sombre feel to it. Something was going on—a meeting or discussion. In the middle of the room, in front of the blazing central fire pit, was a group of perhaps twenty men or so, and in the centre of those men was Cael. He was the age he was now, the only age he would ever reach, and he spoke animatedly to the men around him. At his side was the chieftain of the MacDonalds of Keppoch, Angus MacDonald. He listened to his son, now a confirmed member of the clan, beaming with immense pride.

And why should he not be proud? Cael was a handsome man, a born leader. He held his audience captive with every word, every gesture, every inflection of voice.

"We must strengthen our defenses," he was arguing. "Fortify our weak spots around the perimeter of the castle. The eastern gate sustained damage in the attack, did it no'?"

"Aye, Cael," confirmed a wiry, older man. "The trellis was battered in. 'Twill take a day or two to fix."

"Put MacCrioch on it," ordered Angus. "If Cael says it must be repaired, then that is my decree."

"And the watch," Cael continued. "We must double our numbers."

"Consider it done, Cael," declared a tall, muscular man. An obvious fighter.

"And we'll patrol heavier, too," Cael added. "I promise ye this, lads: When those bloody MacIntoshes come back, we'll be ready for them. They'll no' be taking our land from us. We can resist. We *will* resist."

The men around him cheered and whooped, and fawned Cael with praise, which he was happy to accept.

But not everyone in the group was happy. There were two who stood on the fringe who were not as enthusiastic as the rest. Emmie glanced behind where she and Cael stood, surveying the larger hall. That's when she noticed the other three men standing outside the main doors. Their arms were crossed over their chests, and they watched the oration with obvious hostility.

She tried to alert Cael to what she was observing. She tugged on his hand.

"There are men over there," she said, pointing.

He stared at her, and shook his head, perplexed. This baffled Emmie. Was Cael unable to hear her? Was she unable to tell him things, to help him put the pieces of his murder together? He seemed to understand that she was trying to tell him something, he just couldn't figure out what it was. He didn't even seem interested, come to think of it. He turned back to the image of himself, reliving that moment that had played itself out hundreds of years into the past.

"Not everyone agrees with you," she said anyway.

The thought occurred to her that he might not be able to see them, even if he could hear. If this was his memory, then it was likely he would only be able to see what *he* remembered. And if he hadn't seen those in the crowd and on the fringes who were displeased with his plan when he was alive, then he probably wouldn't see them now.

If that was true, then it would be up to her to see what Cael could not. If she was going to solve his mystery for him, Emmie would need to observe and remember small clues like this. She committed to memory the faces of the men who were against Cael's plan. Next time, when the colours would shift again, the light would change, and another memory would come into focus, Emmie was determined that she would not allow herself to be distracted. She would be the watcher of forgotten details.

But this time, the light didn't change. The colours didn't blend. Instead, they were walking. Cael led her out of the great hall, through the castle corridors, and out a small door into the night beyond. The cold, sharp air filled Emmie's lungs as she took a deep breath. The scents of the Highlands were invigorating, no matter what the time or century. The surety of Cael's hand, and his strong, confident presence, made her feel secure. Safe and at peace.

The direction in which they went took them past the cluster of dwellings skirting the perimeter of the castle. Occasionally, hushed voices drifted through the crudely covered windows, hinting at various degrees of domesticity within. Cael brought Emmie to a small hut with a thatched roof at the very edge of this little development. Despite its small and unassuming size, it was neatly constructed, and had and air of quiet pride about it.

The wooden shutters on this hut were open despite the chill in the air. Cael let go of Emmie's hand. Resting his palms on her shoulders, he moved her so that she was standing at the window. His cheek was close to hers, smooth and soft at her temple. His dark hair tickled her neck, and she had a sudden desire to turn her face into it and breathe in the scent of him. Woodsy, smoky. Alive.

This desire made her heart ache. Being near him, it was so... *wonderful*. Too wonderful. Once this memory ended and she was transported back to Tullybrae, there only to have the intangible sensation of his presence, it would hurt terribly. To know he was there but to have nothing of him to touch, to hold. Nothing of him even to see.

But at least she had now. For however short a time, she could put the inevitable hurt in the back of her mind, and just let everything be wonderful. She leaned against him, felt him lean his cheek into her, and together they watched the memory Cael wanted Emmie to see.

This memory was of himself and a woman. His mother. She had the same strong, clear brow, the same dark hair and dark eyes. She was a beautiful woman, fine boned and fine featured. A delicate, feminine version of her son. There wasn't much to this vision other than a sense of familial tranquility, but this was what he wanted her to know. Mother and son were engaged in a companionable silence, comfortable with their lot in life and with each other. The Cael inside the hut whittled a piece of wood while his mother mended a shirt. The pop and hiss of the peat fire in the pit between them was the only sound.

Emmie envied it. Envied them. They may not have much, but they were happy. They were a family. It had never been like that for her with the Tunstalls. Grace and Ron had wanted it to be, and so did Emmie. But that feeling of family had never solidified for her.

Once, a long time ago, when Emmie was maybe ten years old, she and Grace tried to make raspberry Jell-O together. They'd followed all the instructions and left it in the fridge for the required time. For one reason or another, though, it had never set quite right. It was mostly wobbly, but still a little runny. They'd eaten it, and they'd laughed, and their lips had turned unnaturally red, and they'd acted as though it was as good as proper Jell-O. But they had both known there was a measure of pretending in there. That's what it felt like for Emmie, living with the Tunstalls.

"Your Jell-O's set just fine," she said, more to herself than to Cael.

In response, he pressed his lips to her temple. Emmie closed her eyes—heaven help her, she could lose herself in this memory happily if given the choice, and never find her way back.

Around them, the sky was lightening to the surreal, colourless blue of early dawn. She'd been with him for a while now, but when Cael led her to another place, she did not at all mind. He was in control of this memory, and whatever he wanted to show her, she would willingly witness. As long as she got to stay with him a little longer. Here, like this.

They walked beyond the hut, hand in hand, into the open ground. They walked a long way, on and on until the castle was no longer visible. In the distance was a dense stand of alder and crab apple trees, whose fresh spring leaves were beginning to show their brilliant green hues. Cael helped her to enter its enchanting shade, guiding her over fallen branches and around low-reaching twigs. In the centre of the stand was a small stream. It wandered through the trees with a life of its own, gently bubbling on its way to other places.

Cael turned to face her. He looked into her eyes, telling her of the peace he found in this place.

"This was your spot, wasn't it?"

It did seem like a place that would belong to him. Quiet but strong, and utterly beautiful in its simplicity. A deep longing for this place and time filled Emmie. She looked at Cael, was touched by his obvious love for this place. It was his land, he belonged here. It was home. That was something Emmie had always wanted for herself—a true home. To know that she belonged to a place as he did.

Cael gazed back, searching her face. Looking for something in its depths. When he touched her cheek with the back of his fingers, Emmie's breath caught. She closed her eyes, letting him trace the line of her jaw with a fingertip, then follow the line over her lips. He was as entranced by her as she was by him. This touch, this moment—he'd wanted it for so long. So had she.

His hand slid beneath her hair and cupped the back of her neck. Emmie held perfectly still as he leaned closer. She waited, feeling as though she were standing on the edge of a precipice...

Then his lips touched hers, and she fell. Cael was kissing her. Kissing her with a need that surmounted the centuries between them. It was a rough-tender kiss, both poignant and desperate.

Emmie kissed him back. She was freefalling headlong without any safety net or any idea of where the ground was. And she didn't care. Let her fall, let the ground come and swallow her up. As long as they were falling together.

The last vestiges of awareness, of remembering that none of this was real, were forgotten. It was of no consequence that Cael was dead, that he had died a long time ago. He was real now. She was being pulled into his world, her mind and her soul willingly given to a force that was larger than either of them. It was like an ancient magic, a prophecy. Something she couldn't fight and didn't want to.

She was kissing him.

She was home.

TWENTY-TWO

L AMB HAD JUST made the climb up the rear staircase from the kitchen when Famke and Ewan came tearing headlong towards him. He staggered backwards a step, startled by their sudden appearance, and his wrinkled fingers tightened on the door handle to keep himself from tumbling back down the stairs.

"Lamb," Famke exclaimed, beaming from ear to ear. "Oh jeez, don't fall. Lamb, we found them. Come see."

The old butler looked from one eager face to the other. "Wha—What's this, now?"

"You won't believe it—we found them," Ewan repeated. "We found the mass burial site. Three individual skeletons so far."

"It's unbelievable!" Famke was bouncing in her steel-toed work boots. "A major archaeological find. The legends are true."

"Don't get ahead of yourself," Ewan warned. "We found bodies. We don't know for sure when they died or who they were."

Famke puffed her lips dismissively. "Oh, please. We know exactly who they were. Don't take this from me, Ewan. I have never been part of a team before that has unearthed *Skeletresten*. I've always come in afterwards, *wanneer al het werk wordt gedaan.*"

Ewan snapped his fingers in front of Famke's face. "English, woman. You're getting all flustered. Lamb here doesn't speak Dutch."

"You don't know that," Famke countered teasingly. "Lamb, where's Emmie? She will want to see this."

The lines in the old man's forehead deepened. "Well now, she didn't come down for breakfast this morning. I'm sure she's fine, though. She did have a night out with that young man Dean. She's probably having a lie-in."

175

"Of course she's fine," Famke assured him. "I'll find her. You will want to see this, too. Ewan, you can take Lamb out, can't you?" She skipped off towards the rear staircase before either of them could answer.

Ewan chuckled, and held out an elbow for Lamb to take. "Shall we?"

Lamb nodded once. "I think I would like that. You know, I've lived at Tullybrae most of my life, and have always known of the graves. But until you folks came along, it was never anything but a story."

Arm in arm, the two men made their way outside. Ewan walked at a pace that was comfortable for Lamb, though he was as eager as Famke, and could hardly keep from bouncing himself. He was entirely unaware that the stoic silence of his elderly companion hid a mountain of worry. Nor was he aware of the ghost of the little old woman in the black dress who followed behind, wringing her hands.

By the time Ewan and Lamb reached the front door, Famke had already made it up to the servants' quarters.

"Emmie?" she called into the empty space.

There was no answer except for the slow drip of a leaky tap from the bathroom.

Figuring she might be in the nursery and already at work, Famke came back down and headed towards the front of the house. But when she popped her head into Emmie's office, Emmie wasn't there, either.

By now, she was becoming a little concerned. Traversing the rest of the second floor hall at a trot, she meant to go downstairs and check the kitchen. Perhaps Emmie and Lamb had missed each other in passing.

Rounding the corner of the upper landing at the top of the grand staircase, Famke came face to face with a figure standing in front of the full-length mirror.

"My God, Emmie, you scared me." She placed a slender hand to her breast.

Emmie didn't move.

"Em?" The Dutch woman approached cautiously. "Em, *liebchen*—Earth to Emmie."

In a daze, Emmie turned slowly and looked blankly at Famke.

She tried again. "Em, wake up." She gave Emmie's shoulder a gentle shake.

The shake was what brought Emmie back to the present, what tore her away from Cael's embrace. One minute she was lost in the bliss of kissing him, and the next, she was staring into Famke Bomgaars' concerned face. The shock of the sudden shift of place was like being thrown into a pool of frigid water. She blinked rapidly as Famke's image came into stark focus. Her eyes darted left, then right.

Light. It was daylight.

Oh, God, had she been standing here all night? That couldn't be possible, she wasn't the slightest bit tired. Quite the opposite, in fact—she was hyper awake, her senses crackling with electricity.

Those hyper aware senses picked up Cael immediately, homing in on him without conscious effort. He was still here, but his presence was faint. Like a flashlight struggling to shine on a dying battery.

Once she'd determined Cael's whereabouts, she became embarrassingly aware that Famke was still watching her.

"I... um... I zoned out there, didn't I?"

Famke's graceful brows drew together.

"That was frightening, Emmie. Are you sure you're all right."

"Really, everyone's got to stop worrying about me all the time. I'm *fine.*" She brought herself up short, cheeks turning pink. "You didn't deserve that. Forgive me."

"There is nothing to forgive," Famke assured her. Then, gently, she said, "Hey, we found something out there. You'll never guess what."

Emmie smiled, trying for enthusiasm—unsuccessfully. "Yeah? What did you find?"

"We found," Famke paused for dramatic effect, "the murder victims. Three so far. Isn't it amazing?"

The smile froze on Emmie's face. The murder victims. Cael. They'd found him.

"That is amazing," she said, her voice unsteady.

Famke didn't seem to notice. "Well, come on then. You're about to be a part of history."

She snatched Emmie's hand and pulled her down the stairs. Emmie let herself be taken.

Panic had begun to build in her chest. Cael—where was he? Why was he not by her side? He was always by her side. At first, she wondered if he'd somehow tired himself out by pulling her into his world. But the closer they got to the dig site, she began to fear that, instead, he was upset about the excavators' discovery.

His earthly remains had been buried and forgotten for hundreds of years. What if he didn't want to be found? What if he didn't want *Emmie* to find him?

Outside, Sophie and Adam were hunched over Dean's trench. The top of Dean's head was visible. Clad in a dirty orange Texas Longhorns baseball cap, it bobbed gently as he worked. When Sophie glanced over her shoulder and saw Emmie and Famke emerging from the house, she straightened and waved her arms over her head.

"*Eeemmm*, come quick." To Lamb and Ewan, who by then had only covered half the distance from house to field, she added, "Get a move-on, Lamb. You're holding up the show."

Emmie, who was still being pulled along by Famke, felt as though her own legs were as stiff as Lamb's. It was only by conscious effort that she kept moving, that her knees didn't buckle from beneath her.

When Dean looked up from the trench, his eyes were sparkling with the same reverence he showed for the skeletons at the college. With one hand at the edge of his ball cap bill, he shielded his brow from the sun which struggled to shine behind a translucent wash of cloud.

"We found them, Em. Can you believe it? We *found* them!"

That reverence was something she recognized. It was the same awe, the same respect for lives long past that all history lovers had. It was as though the object being discovered, or examined, or even simply admired, was a link to a person who had lived and loved, laughed and cried. She didn't resent Dean for his reverence. Under any other circumstance, she would have shared it.

Right now, though, she just felt sick.

"This will be the fourth," he was telling her and Lamb, the latter of whom had finally reached the trench.

Emmie barely heard him. She was unwillingly absorbed in the methodical strokes of the stiff-bristled paint brush he was using to dust away the loose dirt. She watched, her chest tight, as he switched to a trowel and carefully carved away the impacted dirt around a smooth, round object. It was the same colour as the earth in which it was buried, and zipper-like cranial sutures were highlighted by the soil crusted into them.

It was a skull. Cael's skull. She felt it like a punch in the gut when Dean finally cleared enough dirt away to gently pry it from the ground. He held the skull up to examine the face. Then, equally as gently, he removed the freed jaw from the earth. In the excitement of the moment, he fitted the jaw to the skull and held the completed piece like a prize.

"Wow," he murmured, shaking his head. "Just... wow."

His finger worked back and forth over the rough bone of the jaw, an absent-minded caress. Then he stopped, and frowned. Unhinging the jaw from the cranial socket, Dean turned it over and examined it.

Two slices marked the remains, one on each side, just below where the ears would have been. They were deep, angry cuts, each about a quarter-inch long.

"Holy crap. You guys, look." He tipped the jaw bone upwards so that his colleagues could better see the evidence. An amazed grin spread across his face, and his eyes gleamed with academic glee. "This one's throat was slit."

As soon as his gaze landed on Emmie, his face fell—she was as white as a sheet and trembling.

"Em, oh my God. Em?"

Emmie couldn't hear him over the roaring in her ears. Her body wouldn't stop shaking, and a strange, strangled gasping was coming from her throat.

There was no indication that this was, in fact, Cael. It was nothing more than a centuries-old skull. Yet she knew it was him. The empty eye sockets crusted with dirt, the ghastly, fleshless grin...

It was him.

His throat had been cut—that's how he'd died. The windpipe beneath the tender flesh had been severed. The breath which had been warm on her cheek only minutes ago, and the strong, graceful neck which she'd admired... more than admired... had been violated, mutilated. Destroyed.

His life had been taken from him, and those marks on his jaw confirmed it.

She knew she was hyperventilating. If she didn't stop, she was going to faint. But she couldn't stop. Couldn't command her mind to take control of her body's visceral reactions.

"Someone grab her," Dean shouted. With the skull and jaw still clasped together in his hands, he leapt out of the trench. The sight of Cael's remains were more than she could stand. She staggered back, palms outstretched, blubbering incoherently.

"Emmie, please, let me take you inside," he implored at the same time that Sophie and Ewan rushed to steady her.

"Naw, mate. Let me do it," Adam said.

Ewan shook his head. "Adam, I don't think that's a good idea."

"I got this." He fixed Ewan with a look that said he would take no arguments.

Ewan studied him for a moment. Assured that Adam was taking this seriously, he relented. "Awright, mate. You've got her."

"Soph, why don't you take our man Lamb here inside," Adam suggested. "We'll need a strong cuppa, milk, and a shot of whiskey."

Bending slightly, he swooped Emmie up into his arms and carried her across the field. The others watched them go, each of them at a loss to account for her reaction. In their minds, that skull was nothing more than a historical artefact, no different than any other they'd encountered before.

"Christ, you're lighter than I thought," Adam muttered when he reached the house and fumbled with the door knob.

If Emmie hadn't been so consumed by shock, she might have laughed. But the sight of that skull had been too much.

Cael was dead. Inarguably, factually dead. He had been betrayed and horribly murdered.

And his ghost... His ghost had fooled her, had made her believe that he was with her. But he was not. No matter how much he showed her, or how convincingly he reconstructed his world for her, it wasn't real. It was all an illusion.

This was her world. The only world. And it was one in which Cael's true existence was in a collection of bones excavated for archaeological record.

Keeping up a running commentary for her benefit, Adam brought Emmie up to the third floor, to her room, and laid her on the bed which was still made from the night before.

"Stay there, love," he ordered, not unkind.

He left her briefly to find the bathroom, where he soaked a hand towel in cold water from the tap. When he came back, he laid the towel over her forehead and eyes.

"Deep breaths," he instructed.

From under the damp, cool cloth, Emmie became aware of the sound of chair legs scraping across the wooden floor.

"Careful, that's an antique."

Adam gave a low chuckle. "There she is. Thought we'd lost her for a minute."

"I don't know what's wrong with me."

"Nothing's wrong with you. It was just a shock, that's all."

"Shock." Emmie frowned. "You guys weren't shocked. You saw Dean—he was practically drooling."

Adam sat back in the chair. He looked at Emmie, chewing on his lip. "Hey—you want to hear something?"

Emmie breathed once. The shaking was starting to ebb, and the roar in her ears had subsided almost to nothing.

"You tell me. Do I?"

"Dunno, love. But I'm gonna tell it whether you want to hear it or not."

A wry smile tweaked the corner of her mouth. "All right. I'm listening."

"You know, when I was in my mid-teens, maybe fifteen or sixteen, I was a complete tosser," Adam began. "Like, a total minger. I cut class more often than I went. Me and me bezzie mates were blatted every weekend. It was bad. If you were to tell my tenth-form teachers that I would one day be where I am now, they would have carted you off as barmy."

Emmie lifted the cloth off one eye and looked at Adam. He was hamming up his East-Ender slang for what was an obvious attempt to lighten her mood, and they both knew it. She appreciated the attempt.

"So what happened to make you turn around?"

Adam's face grew sad, his gaze turning inward. "What happened was that this one night—we were being our usual wanker selves, hanging out in the pubs, wandering around, making a racket, that kind of thing. This night, though, we got into it with another group of lads. We started arguing, then it turned into a right good punch-up. We thought it were all for fun, you know? That's what lads do. They get blatted and then they brawl. But these lads—we should never have started anything with them. One of them pulls a knife and stabs me mate, Stuart, in the belly. The one who did it and his mates, they all legged it, of course."

He paused, recalling the scene as he was telling it. "I remember throwing myself to the ground and pulling Stuart to me. He was shaking, and his face was turning white. It was dark—I remember that much. But I could still see how white his face was going."

"I'm sorry," Emmie said after a time.

Adam's gaze returned to the present, and his eyes landed on her. "It's funny the things that go through your mind at times like that. Did you know? When I fell, I hit my knees on the pavement so hard that the pain shot up my legs. It was bloody unbearable. And I remember hating myself for thinking about how bad it hurt when Stuart was there in me arms, dying. For weeks, my knees hurt so bad. Like, I probably chipped the bone or summut. All me mates, and me mum and dad, they were telling me to go to the hospital and get x-rays in case I had broken something. But I wouldn't. I was so angry. That's one thing I've never really forgiven myself for, thinking of how much pain I was in then."

"Stuart died?"

Adam nodded. "Died in my arms. Died before the medics arrived."

He leaned forward on the chair, and reached across Emmie to pull the cloth off her eyes entirely. Balling the cloth in his fists, and resting his elbows on his thighs, he said, "The reason I'm telling you all this is because the look on your face out there reminded me of how I felt when Stuart was in my arms dying. I don't have any—" he made air quotes with his fingers, "*life lessons* for you here, and I don't think I'm making you feel any better. But... I dunno. I guess I'm trying to say that I know how you feel. The others, see—when they're handling bones and such, I always get the sense that it's more clinical. More removed, you know? But when I'm in the presence of those old bones, I can't help thinking about the mortality of it all. About Stuart, and how he must be no more than bones by now. None of the others felt a life leave a body. They don't understand death the way I do—and the way you do, I suspect."

Emmie studied Adam. Committed to memory his earnest expression and the concern that creased his brow.

"You put up a good front. Nobody would know that underneath that cocky, chauvinist exterior there's a serious side with a soft heart."

He smiled his goofy smile at her. "Yeah, well, we all put up fronts, don't we? Don't go telling anyone about mine, though. I've got a reputation to keep up."

That conversation stayed with Emmie long after the crew had gone home for the night. Without hitting on it directly, Adam had gotten to the heart of her startling reaction out there in the field. She hadn't fully comprehended it herself at the time. But Adam had.

The events of the past twenty-four hours were starting to fall into place like a giant rubric. Maybe Cael had known that morning that he was going to be found. Maybe he pulled her into his world, showed her the intimate details of his life which had nothing to do with his murder because he knew she was going to see his body. He wanted her to remember him as he was then, not as the grizzly collection of skeletal remains he was now, marked by the evidence of a brutal death.

Maybe he knew that when Emmie saw those bones, it would be a stark reality check for her.

And that's exactly what it had been. Those bones proved to Emmie that Cael was dead, that she was destined to lose him, just like she'd lost her mother. She'd loved her mother terribly, and her mother had died. She loved Cael terribly, and Cael was dead.

She had to solve Cael's mystery. *That* task was something she would not abandon. She was too far in to simply give it up. But for the rest of it...

The rest of it was that she had to find a way to let Cael go. It was time for her to realize that he was already gone. Her heart would break, but better now than later. Cael's ghost could cause her nothing but heartache either way.

By the time she fell asleep that night, she'd made a decision. She would solve Cael's mystery. She would put in the man hours with gusto to find out whatever she could, and then once she'd solved it, she was done. Her obligation to him would be fulfilled.

Then she would let him go.

TWENTY-THREE

PROFESSOR PAUL ROTENFELD climbed out of his car at the University of Glasgow, and walked around the History building from the staff parking lot in the rear. He was in a chipper mood today, but that was a typical state of being for Paul most days. This morning, he was wearing his favourite hand-knit sweater vest, he had his wife's hot-packed chicken curry lunch in hand, and the sleep-scented warmth of his daughter's cheek was still on his lips from the goodbye kiss he'd planted there while she was dreaming.

He had a moderate day planned: a final undergrad lecture in Ancient Civilizations at ten, and then an afternoon of planning the fall semester outline for the new Media and Society course he'd recently been approved to teach.

With his thoughts thus engaged, he was not at all prepared to encounter the young woman outside his office door. She was seated on the carpeted floor in the hall, with her back against the wall and her knees drawn up to her chest. It was not unusual to find students seated on the ground in any number of locations, folded compactly into cross-legged obstacles, heads bent over open textbooks. But it caught Paul off guard when this obstacle bolted upright at the sight of him.

"Emmie?" he said, when his eyes fixed on her. "This certainly is a surprise. To what do I owe this pleasure?"

The young lady was doing her best to affect an air of composure, but her wild-eyed gaze and the slight wobble in her voice when she spoke betrayed her.

"I'm so sorry to burst in on you like this, Dr. Rotenfeld—"

"Paul."

"Paul," she corrected. "But, um… do you remember you said I could review the donated records that came from Moy Hall? You know, the ones you said might include documents from Keppoch Castle?"

Paul raised an eyebrow. "Of course."

"I need to. I want to… I—I mean, review them, that is."

"Why yes, that's not a problem. But you look a little wound up. More than a little—no offense. Have you eaten today?"

"Er… no," she admitted. "I got into town at about eleven last night, and spent until midnight trying to find a place to stay. Then I woke up early to come here."

"How early?"

She eyed him sheepishly. "Six-thirty."

Paul took a breath, measuring her with a look of gentle consternation. "Emmie, sweetheart. I know how historians' minds work—hell, I'm friends with Iain Northcott for God's sake, and you can't cart that man away from a dig site in a strait jacket when he's getting close to a discovery. But even *he* knows that no discovery is worth starving yourself over." He paused, allowing his words to have an effect—to no avail. Sighing, he said, "Come on, let's get you to the cafeteria and get something into you. I have a class soon, but after that, I'll get you set up so you can spend the day in the archives."

An hour and a half later, Emmie had been given a visitor's pass, a digital access key, and space in a small research room with cinderblock walls and a single tall window that overlooked the staff parking lot.

The volume of records from Moy Hall exceeded what she was expecting. There were at least twenty cardboard packing boxes, more than a few of them in a moldering state, along with three heavy-duty Rubbermaid totes full to the top, each aged plastic lid caved in and cracked from decades of bearing the weight of the tote stacked on top of it. Another dozen bundles of file folders tied with twine completed the collection.

Because Paul was unable to commit himself to helping her, it fell to Emmie to lug each box up to her research room one by one. He apologized when he had to leave, but procured for her a dolly cart, and pointed out the location of a small elevator in the basement where the records were kept.

It had been no exaggeration, Emmie discovered, when Paul told her these documents hadn't been catalogued yet, and going through them would be a lot of work. They had been poorly packed. It was likely that the lot had been shipped from Moy Hall by a distant family member, or a junior clerk from the local governing council, who had no idea how important these documents might prove to be. She could hardly blame the university for not having done a better job once they arrived. The archives were full of uncatalogued documents, items and artefacts. It was Scotland, after all—

history here was far richer and longer than it was in Corner Brook, Newfoundland.

Document by fragile document, Emmie reviewed what had come from Moy Hall. Most of it was inconsequential to her cause—financial transactions, larder inventories, wills, post cards and photographs. And also, most of it was too recent for what she was looking for, having been amassed within the last two centuries or so.

Still, she persisted. She needed to solve Cael's death, and that meant doing everything she could to track down evidence of his existence.

At five that evening, Paul popped his head into her little hideaway to check on her.

"I'm heading out for the night," he told her.

Emmie looked at the time on her phone. "Oh—oh yes. I'm sorry."

She rose and began to pack up her belongings.

"No. I didn't mean you have to leave now, too," he interjected. "You've got your own access, you can come and go as you please. Just thought I'd stop in, see how you're doing."

She looked at her pile helplessly. Five hours and she'd only gotten through about half the moldy packing boxes.

"I think I may be here for a few days."

"That's no trouble. This room and the access pass are yours for as long as you want them."

"Thank you," she said. She met his gaze with sincerity. He smiled knowingly, and bid her good night.

Emmie stayed for another two hours before returning to the budget hostel she'd found last night, on a side street called Shelley Road which was close to the university. In her hands was a take-out portion of fish and chips wrapped in newsprint and saturated with malt vinegar.

The first thing she did once she'd demolished her dinner was call Lady Rotherham to let her know of her plans.

"Of course," the lady exclaimed. "You take the time you need. I'm curious, though. This side project—it doesn't have anything to do with Tullybrae, does it? Not that I need it to. You're entitled to pursue your own interests. I'm more than happy with the work you've done so far."

Emmie felt guilty—she knew she could have done so much more, if it hadn't been for Cael. She decided to be at least somewhat truthful with Lady Rotherham. Emmie owed her that.

"Not with the job I'm doing specifically, but it does have to do with the land surrounding Tullybrae, and the mass grave."

"Really? Do tell."

"That kilt pin the excavators found, it was from the MacDonalds of Keppoch, you remember?" Emmie asked, making up her excuse as she went along. "Well, I'm researching records that came from Moy Hall where documents from Keppoch Castle were also found. I know it's a long shot, but I thought it would be interesting if we had some kind of identity for those men that were buried on Tullybrae land."

Yes, that would work. That sounded reasonable.

Evidently, Lady Rotherham thought so, too.

"Fabulous," she breathed into the phone. "Oh, can you imagine? Emmie, you have a nose for this kind of thing. Next time I talk to Boomer, I'll tell him all about it."

Now Emmie felt even guiltier. Lady Rotherham had no idea she was being hoodwinked.

Emmeline Tunstall, you should be ashamed of yourself, she thought dully.

After saying good bye to her employer, Emmie next made a call to Lamb to assure him that she'd made it to Glasgow and gotten settled. Then she made a short call to Grace and Ron, using the astronomical overseas toll rates as an excuse to end the conversation early—which did not please Grace, who responded with an Oscar-worthy guilt trip. Nevertheless, Emmie was soon free.

She spent two more days at the University of Glasgow, pouring over the documents from Moy Hall. Disappointingly, they yielded no results. They did, however, yield a clue that *might* keep the trail warm. In a land transfer document that came after the time the MacDonalds of Keppoch were said to have been destroyed, Emmie found mention of the name Lawren MacDonald.

Lawren, as in Cael's half-brother? The timing was right. And why else would a person's name be on a land transfer document unless that person was in possession of some kind of status and wealth?

Like Angus MacDonald's son and heir, perhaps?

The document transferred the land and estate of Stowe Castle to the aforementioned Lawren MacDonald. A quick Google search revealed an image of Stowe.

The excitement that had flared in Emmie's breast plummeted. Stowe Castle was a ruin. Barely more than a hollow shell. Less than that—*half* a hollow shell. There was no surviving brickwork above the ground-floor window holes.

But Emmie was a professional historian. She knew better than to admit defeat. It was still a lead, however improbable a one, and she was still intent on following it.

Returning the Moy Hall documents to the archives, she thanked Paul profusely for his generosity and left the university. It took a little over fifteen minutes to pack up her hostel room, and soon she was on the road, heading to the village of Kippen, outside of which Stowe Castle was situated.

She arrived late in the afternoon, as the sun was starting to disappear over the hills. The ruin, she discovered when she got there, was now a tourist feature. It was also part of a great manor house, Stowe Manor, which had been turned into a hotel. Half of the estate's front lawn had been eaten up by a paved parking lot, with the rest of the lawn extensively landscaped to compensate. Flower beds had been turned for the winter, but were peppered with colourful pots of fall mums. The parking lot was edged with meticulously sculpted hedges which were beginning to brown from the cold.

The manor itself reminded Emmie of Tullybrae in its size and quiet grandeur. It was Jacobean in style, with a red brick, irregular façade that was dominated by a series of large windows which changed randomly in size along its length. Looking up at it, Emmie took a deep breath for luck, and walked from her parked car, up the front walk, and inside.

She was met by a slender, attractive young woman at the reception desk. Her glossy brown hair shone softly in the glow of a desk lamp, and she looked at Emmie like she couldn't care less about her arrival.

"Can I help you?"

Emmie had a bad feeling about this. She put on her brightest smile, hoping to disarm the young lady.

"Hi there. I'm Emmie Tunstall. I'm curator at an estate called Tullybrae. Not sure if you've heard of it—it's east of Aviemore."

She was met with a blank stare.

"In the Grampians."

Still nothing.

"Okay... well, I suppose there's no way to ease into this. I'm on the trail of a historical figure. He's more or less unknown, and relatively unimportant. But I found a mention of Stowe Castle, and I was hoping I could pick up the trail by coming here."

"If this historical figure isn't important, then why are you looking for him?"

Emmie's spine stiffened. "I have reasons."

"I don't know if you've noticed, but the castle's a ruin," the young woman said flippantly. "Been that way for nearly a century. You're not going to find anything out there."

"I realized that," Emmie answered, her smile growing tight. "I thought that perhaps any pertinent documents which may have existed might have been moved to the main house."

The young woman's blank expression morphed into a cold, condescending smile of her own.

"I'm sorry, but we cannot simply allow people off the street to come in and rummage around in our vault."

"I'm not 'someone off the street.' I told you, I'm curator at Tullybrae House."

"Yes, you said. But you could be the queen herself, and you wouldn't be getting down there. You've not been authorized to access Stowe's confidential documents. There's nothing I can do for you."

Emmie stared at this young woman, incredulous. Seriously? She wasn't going to help her? Never before had she been denied a scholarly browse through historical records at the castles and grand houses on her year abroad. It was sort of an unspoken rule. A universally accepted perk of the trade. Who did this person think she was?

That... that... bitch!

Emmie ground her fists into her thighs. She was tired. She was dirty. And she was strained to the breaking point. An acute urge to yank a fistful of glossy brown hair by the roots tickled her brain.

"Thank you," she said instead, matching the young woman's cold stare. "This was obviously a waste of both of our time."

She turned on her heel and left.

By this time, it was too late to drive back to Tullybrae, and Emmie was too exhausted to try it. In the village, she found a quiet inn called The Cross Keys, took a room, and fell into a fitful sleep. Images of the receptionist from Stowe Manor plagued her. The young lady with her smug smile towered over her, large and mountainous, while Emmy herself was the size of an ant. Stowe stood in the background, documents and records bursting from its windows and chimneys, and that wretched girl would not let Emmie pass. Her great, designer shoe-clad foot threatened to stomp on Emmie every time she tried. And all the while, Cael was begging. *Save me*, he whispered.

"I can't, she won't let me pass," Emmie shouted to the sky.

This only made the horrible receptionist cackle with glee.

It was a thoroughly unpleasant dream, and she woke to a rainy morning in a tangle of blankets and a sheen of sweat.

But the night had also brought her to a resolution: She was going back to Stowe Manor and she was going to confront that self-important young woman. Perhaps the receptionist hadn't cared about the name of Tullybrae, but she might care if Emmie dropped the names of Lord and Lady Rotherham. Nobility in the United Kingdom was still a big thing, wasn't it? And if she didn't, then Emmie would barge in and find the woman's supervisor and drop her names there.

By St. Christopher, and St. Patrick, and St. Michael and whatever other saints she could dredge up from her shady knowledge of Catholicism, she was ready to do battle.

As it turned out, when she arrived back at Stowe and marched through the front door, a battle was not required. Instead of the smug, beautiful, glossy-haired receptionist, it was another woman—older, grey-haired and as pleasant as a receptionist should be.

"Welcome to Stowe Manor," the woman said. "What can I do for you this morning?"

The wind knocked out of her sails, Emmie forgot what she'd planned to say. She was too tired. In place of the tirade she'd rehearsed on the way over, she launched into a decidedly embarrassing monologue.

"My name is Emmie. Emmie Tunstall. I'm curator at Tullybrae House. I was here yesterday because I wanted to see any historical records you might have that came from Stowe Castle—if they still exist. But I was told unequivocally by that horrible girl that I wasn't allowed, so I had to leave and take a room at an inn. But I'm back now because I really need to see them. I need something, anything that might help solve a problem I'm having at Tullybrae. And I've really got to try."

By the end of her monologue, her voice had raised substantially in pitch, and her cheeks had grown pink.

The woman nodded knowingly. "Oh, yes. That would be Annette. Well, I don't know what you're hoping to find, and I'm sorry that Annette has misled you, but we have no records here that are not contemporary and confidential. Everything that was taken from the castle before it fell into ruin was moved to the parish kirk. But that was over a century ago."

"So some records have survived, but I can't see them."

Oh, God. Her lip was wobbling. She was going to cry.

Don't cry, don't cry, don't *cry!*

The woman gazed at her for a moment, sympathy creasing her brow.

"Look, love," she said. "Here's what you do. Go up to the kirk. Tell Father White that you'd like to see the boxes from Stowe, and tell him that Betsy Druce said you can. He can call me if he'd like to make sure. But I warn you, whatever is there is likely in rough shape, and I'm not at all convinced you'll find anything of use."

A spark of hope, doused by the high-and-mighty Annette, sizzled to life. "Oh, thank you!" Emmie exhaled, beaming. "Thank you, thank you, *thank* you!"

She was in her car and on her way to the kirk in no time. As it was just up the road from the manor, she arrived a total of three minutes later.

The priest accepted her story at the mention of Betsy Druce's name, and he decided that no call was required. A small, gentle man with gray hair and fashionable spectacles, Father White brought her down to a dusty cellar room and set her up with a chair, a lamp, and a small folding table.

"I'm sorry for the damp and filth," he apologized. "But these boxes are rather heavy, and I don't think we two could easily lift them if we were to try and bring them into the sanctuary for you."

"This is fine," Emmie assured him. "After the last few days, I'm just happy to be able to see them."

"Would you like a cup of tea?"

"That would be wonderful."

Father White smiled benevolently, and turned to go. At the foot of the stairs he paused and turned back. "Do watch for rats and mice. These cellars are full of them, I'm afraid. They normally stay away when a light is on, but you never know. Those wee beasties grow bold of a time."

Emmie glanced uncomfortably over her shoulders and around the room as the father's footsteps thumped up the stairs to the safety of ground level.

Within minutes, however, any unseen rodents were forgotten as she immersed herself in the contents of the boxes.

Unfortunately, Betsy Druce was right. There did not seem to be much here that was relevant. Many of the documents were recorded on paper, instead of the more durable parchment used for official communication, and these were crumbling to nothing. Record after record she examined. Of those that were whole and still legible, each one was meaningless to her search. By minute degrees, the spark of hope that had rekindled upon meeting Mrs. Betsy Druce dimmed.

She was about to give up, when her fingers brushed against the next document in the box. It was a folded piece of parchment, not unlike many she'd already uncovered and subsequently discarded. A wax seal had once been on it, but all that was left of its existence was a discoloured stain about the size of a silver dollar. The parchment was severely yellowed, and thickened to rawhide at the creases where it had likely been exposed to water at some point. But the second her fingertips came into contact with the document, a shiver skittered up her spine.

Her hands shaking, she unfolded the piece of parchment. The warped and thickened edges cracked as she opened it, but the document remained intact. It was a letter, and miraculously, the script was legible—the blotchy patches, typical of quill and ink, had not run and smeared with time.

The letter—damn it all!—was written in French. In that respect, it was no different than most of its contemporaries, since French was the commonly accepted language of communication among nobility. To Emmie's misfortune, her grade school French was murky at best. She'd quit after the ninth grade, as soon as the education system lifted the mandate to continue.

Thank Google she lived in the age of the smartphone!

Digging in her purse for a notepad and pen, she copied the ancient script. Then, taking the notepad, pen and her phone, she left everything else behind and went up to the sanctuary where there was a signal and daylight, there to begin the painstaking process of transcription.

The letter, when she had deciphered it, proved to be astonishing...

My dearest Margaret,

To begin, I must beg your forgiveness for not having contacted you these many years, though such actions are, I am sure, unforgivable. You were as a mother to me, more so than my own mother, I regret to say. I therefore have no reasonable explanation for why I have not written to you sooner.

I have but one purpose in seeking you out now, when I am in the winter of my life, and you so many years older than I. But I feel I must do this, while there is still time. I am writing to you because I must assuage my guilt over the death of your son, my brother, Cael.

I write the name now, having not spoken it aloud for longer than I can recall. Yet I remember him as if we were still young and he were still by my side, laughing and lively in his way. Indeed, he will always remain a young man, while I have grown old. But such rosy sentiment does not account for why death came for him at so young an age.

It is a death for which I know you have never stopped trying to find a reason, and until more recently, it was a death for which I, myself, did not have an answer. But upon the passing of my father, I learned the reason for certain.

I am sorry to say that, what you and I both suspected all along was, in fact, correct. Cael's murder was to silence him. The men who were with him that night on the raid, and who died with him, were sacrificed so that Cael could be killed without the intent being obvious. There were some of the clan who did not want to stand against the MacIntoshes alone, some who favoured seeking assistance from the MacDonalds of Clanranald. But my father was the ultimate authority, and he was with Cael. However, as you know my father all too well, he knew no loyalty to anything but the clan. Neither friendship nor kinship, nor the bonds of fatherhood went before the good of the clan. Such was the nature of the man we both knew.

Though my brother had the support of most of our kinsmen, my father was persuaded in whispers and behind closed doors that seeking help from Clanranald was the surest way for Keppoch to remain safe. He was persuaded also that to deny Cael was to cause strife, for those who were with him would surely be unhappy with the decision. In the end, he was persuaded that Cael's death was the only solution. So while he smiled to my brother's face and praised him for his bravery and leadership, my father plotted to kill him.

It is some small mercy that Cael never suspected his own father was the one who betrayed him.

These lordly actions, as you know, my father always saw as his divine duty. He never regretted anything, though he should have regretted much, and I can only trust that God has judged him justly, whatever He in His all-powerful wisdom determines to be just. However, it was with immense surprise that I received my father's confession only days before he took his last breath. He admitted also that he regretted his involvement in Cael's death. I do believe him to have been genuine, at least in part—although, I do not know how much of that was because Cael's death made no difference. The MacDonalds of Keppoch were destroyed anyway.

It may sound as though I am defending him, but I promise you, my dear Margaret, that this is not so. In truth, I do not think I can ever forgive him for taking my brother from me. To Ennis and me, the bonds of blood were not weakened where Cael was concerned; we three were as full brothers, and loved each other as full brothers. The pain of Cael's loss has not lessened in all this time, and I only pray that he and Ennis have found each other in His Holy Kingdom.

I tell you this now because I can no longer bear the thought that you will one day go to your grave never knowing what happened to your only son, and I will go to mine having kept my father's secret from you. I sincerely hope that I have done God's will in enlightening you, and that this knowledge may bring you a small measure of peace in understanding the reason for our beloved Cael's death.

I hope that you may one day forgive me, if not in this life, then perhaps in Heaven.

Yours,
Lawren MacDonald.

TWENTY-FOUR

THE DARK HIGHLAND roads, treacherously narrow and poorly paved for long stretches, sailed past the car windows as Emmie sped towards Tullybrae. Literally sped—she was driving too fast. Dangerously, foolishly fast. One stray sheep, one pot hole, and she would lose control, possibly to plummet down an unguarded incline. She was acutely aware of this, yet she couldn't seem to wrench her lead foot off the gas pedal.

She had to get to Cael. She had to make him understand what she'd learned.

And how the hell was she going to do that when she wasn't able to talk to him?

Her foot nudged the pedal down another notch.

It had been his father. His own father had betrayed him. The vileness of it all, the heartless cruelty.

"His own goddamned *father*," she expostulated at the windshield, smacking her palms on the steering wheel for emphasis.

So much of what she'd seen made sense now. In Cael's memories, his father had been nothing but proud of his son, illegitimate though he was. In the countess's vision, where the two men were conspiring against Cael, the one had resolutely stated that he would not go against Angus MacDonald. *I'll no' go against my laird. I'll no' defy Himself. Convincing the men that we must make the laird change his mind is one thing, but killing Cael is another. I'll no' defy my laird!*

She remembered the words so well that the man might as well have been there in the car with her, speaking them all over again.

Well, he hadn't gone against his laird, had he? By the admission of Lawren MacDonald, Angus MacDonald, second of Keppoch would do whatever it took to protect his clan, even if it included deceiving and

193

sacrificing his own son. Angus MacDonald had given his blessing for his men to remove his illegitimate son in secret, so that none of Cael's supporters would know why.

Cael had been deceived. He'd been wronged, just as Lamb said.

There had been a reason why Emmie found out what she knew. A reason for why Professor McCall had recommended her for the Tullybrae position, for why the dig crew had befriended her, and invited her to Dr. Iain Northcott's party. A reason why she'd been connected with Paul Rotenfeld. Who just happened to have in his possession (or near enough) the one document that would give her the answer she was looking for. A document which, if the relatively scant size of the general historical record was any kind of benchmark, should not have survived. But it had, and it was all leading back to this. She had the answer to Cael's mystery.

The little old lady had told her on the night of the ghost hunt: *We're led to places, my dear. No one ever ends up anywhere by accident. You were led here. You're meant to be here.*

Emmie *was* meant to be here. She was more certain of this than she'd ever been of anything in her life.

The blue Fiat Panda—structure and driver and innocent sheep miraculously unharmed—screeched to a halt in front of Tullybrae, sending a spray of pebbles against the masonry.

"Cael," she called, shrill and breathless as she burst through the door. "Cael, where are you? This is important. Cael?"

There was nothing. No sign of him.

She ran up the stairs to her bedroom. "Cael?"

Still nothing.

Now what was she supposed to do? She'd solved the mystery, so didn't she need to tell Cael? Put his soul to rest?

Or (the thought occurred to her as she searched the house) was it possible that *because* she'd solved the mystery, she'd already put his soul to rest?

He wasn't gone, was he?

But wasn't what she wanted? And what Cael needed?

Then why did she feel like she could hardly breathe at the thought that she'd never see him again?

No. No! Emmie shook her head furiously, refusing to believe it. That wasn't how it was supposed to be. She was supposed to have at least a small amount of time with him. If only to say goodbye. Determined to find him, Emmie took her search outside, into the cold night, where a mist had begun to gather. It was a thick mist, and high. It distorted the luminous moon which, until now, had shone without a wisp of cloud to block it out.

She ran around the house, from the front to the rear. She ran over the gravel walkways among the hedges and flower beds of the gardens, and out to the silent, empty land beyond.

"Cael!" She was crying now.

There was not a trace of him. Nothing to suggest that he'd ever been here. She looked back over her shoulder at the dig site where her friends had been working for the past few months. The bones of the murder victims—ten in total, including Cael—had been removed. The excavation complete, those old bones had been taken to Edinburgh University for examination, recording and storage.

Oh God—was this really it, then?

Emmie's chin dropped to her chest. Her shoulders sagged, and she sobbed helplessly.

Cael. He was gone. And she was well and truly alone.

What kind of cruel joke was this? What had all this been for? She'd done everything she could for Cael, had given up so much and driven herself half-mad in the process, and for what? So that she could learn some heartless life lesson—that in the end, she had no one?

Well if that was it, then Emmie hated God. She hadn't ever been convinced that a god existed before, but now she was. He did exist, and she hated Him.

She was just about to tell Him this, to raise her head and declare it to the heavens, when a flicker through the mist halted the scream in her throat.

Something was moving out there. The fog moved in eddies and swirls around a shape that was advancing on her.

Cael.

She cried out in relief. A wide, uninhibited smile broke across her face. Any minute, she would see his smiling face, too. But as Cael came close enough that she could see him in detail, she realized that he was not smiling. There was nothing of relief, or of happiness or of anything positive in his demeanour.

"Cael," she said, growing serious. "I know who betrayed you."

He said nothing. Either he couldn't hear her, or he wasn't listening. She tried again anyway.

"It was your father, Cael. Your father betrayed you. He sacrificed you for what he thought was the good of the clan."

Still Cael made no response. By now, Emmie was becoming angry. She was here. Cael was here. She had the answer to his mystery, and she was supposed to tell him.

So why didn't he seem particularly concerned with the answer?

Around them, the fog began to thin. Emmie scanned their immediate surroundings—the fog was only thinning around *them*. It was like an inverse halo, like being inside a bubble.

195

"What's going on?"

The only answer Cael made was to raise his hand to her, holding it palm up.

Save me, she heard, but not from his lips. It was a breath on the breeze, desperate and pleading. *Save me.*

Cael's eyes burned into hers, urging her to take his hand. Emmie looked at it, following the lines on his palm, the veins in his wrist. The mist that formed the convex walls of their bubble vibrated, alive with a life of its own.

It was then that she realized what he wanted her to do. Without having to be told, without needing to have anyone lay it out for her, she instinctively knew. It was like the mist was telling her, infusing her with a higher understanding: To save him, Emmie had to go with him. Armed with her knowledge of the past, she needed to cross the divide between Cael's world and hers. And this time, it would be the last time.

If she took his hand now, she would not be coming back.

Her mind warred with itself. Emotions, fears, questions and thrills crashed into each other, rendering her incapable of sorting through the tangle and focusing on any one thing. Emmie looked at Cael. The faces of Grace and Ron danced in her brain. Of Chase. Of Lamb and Dean, Adam and Sophie, Famke and Ewan. Camille. Professor McCall. Her friends back home in Corner Brook. They were the only life she knew. She couldn't leave them, could she?

Emmie's mind froze. She panicked. She shook her head before giving herself the time to think through what she was doing.

"I can't," were the words that came out of her mouth.

These words he did hear. His brows drew together, refusing to accept what she was saying. He shoved his hand an inch closer, his eyes begging her to take it.

"Cael, I can't," she repeated frantically. "This... this is all too much. I mean, I went from feeling like I had my life together to feeling like it was falling apart, to finally feeling like it might have a purpose after all. I... Cael, please. Be reasonable."

She heard herself speak, heard herself saying those words. Inside, her mind was screaming, *What are you doing, you fool? What are you saying?*

Two voices, two Emmies, neither one in control of the body that needed only to reach out and take Cael's hand. And as the voices warred with each other, as her heart was finally beginning to win out over the protestations of her brain, Cael's expression changed. His face turned from resolute and urgent... to horrified.

Betrayed.

Oh, no. Dear God, no. Wait. I want to change my mind.

The words would not come.

Cael took a step back. Then another. The look he gave her was one of complete and irreparable anguish, and Emmie knew she'd made the wrong choice.

She'd made the wrong choice! She *did* want to go with him. She *could* turn her back on her friends and her family. If it all meant that she would be with him, she could do it.

But it was too late. With a final lingering gaze, Cael turned away from her. Then he disappeared.

"Cael?" Emmie called, a new kind of panic spreading through her.

Her legs started to move. With halting, stumbling steps, she began to run into the mist without any idea of where she was going.

"Cael."

The halting steps moved faster, sped up, and then she was running. Running as fast as she could, and as far as she could, until she felt like her lungs were going to burst. She stumbled and fell several times, scraping her palms and ripping a hole in her jeans. He Uggs grew soaked with dew, and the cold autumn air stung at her cheeks, nose and neck.

She ran until her legs ached. Until she thought she was going to die of exhaustion.

She ran until... she saw a light.

In the distance. Was it a light? Yes, it was. Firelight. A campfire.

Cael! A burst of adrenaline fuelled by hope propelled her those last few metres.

It *was* Cael, she saw as she drew near. Splendid and alive, he sat on the ground, holding his hands to the low, orange flames of a fire pit. Around him were more men—Emmie counted nine. Some were sitting like he was, some had settled down for the night, with their plaids wrapped tightly around their shoulders and heads. Two were finishing a meal of some sort.

She gave these men only a cursory glance. It was Cael she wanted, Cael who made her chest swell with joy. He stared blankly into the fire, which cast dancing shadows over his face and hair. His fingers, which not so long ago had tightened over hers and threaded into her hair and cupped her neck so gently, now idly folded and unfolded a long blade of grass.

Emmie approached, certain that now everything would be all right. She would tell him she made a mistake. And he would listen, and he would hold out his hand to her once more. This time, she would take it. She would not let the voice of her cursed, rational brain win this time.

"I've changed my mind," she told him. "I'll come with you. Tell me how to save you and I'll do it."

The brief surge of relief died. He wasn't listening; he didn't see her. Looking at him, she saw that this was not even her Cael. It was just another memory, a replaying of the past, of which she was not a part.

Still, she had to try. She had to find a way to tell him what she knew. She got down on the ground, on her knees, and pressed her hands into her thighs. Looking into his eyes, she prepared to speak.

A shadow moved behind him. Emmie had only a second to look up before there was another shadow, then another. A group of men, larger than the group around the campfire, slipped silently from the background, swords raised.

"No," Emmie screamed. "Cael, behind you!"

It did no good. She was not a part of this memory, her voice had no place in it.

Reacting on instinct, Emmie pitched forward, and threw herself in front of Cael to protect him. But he was not solid—or she was not. She fell through the remembered images and hit the ground with a painful thud, striking her head on the ground. Her vision jarred, and her head exploded with pain. Wincing, she rolled over in time to see the hilt of a knife—a *sgian dubh* or a dirk of some sort—crash into Cael's temple.

Cael tumbled to the ground, landing beside where Emmie had fallen. A stream of blood trickled down from his temples, and his eyelids fluttered. The man who had hit him stood over him, spat grotesquely, and smirked.

It was the man she had seen from the countess's vision, the small mean one with the dark, greasy hair. The one who had argued for Cael's death. His smirk spoke of victory, of evil.

You bastard. Emmie thought the words, unable to speak them because she was crying—open mouthed, gasping and heaving.

She reached for Cael. Her hand found nothing but air.

The horrible little man grabbed a handful of Cael's hair and wrenched him so that Cael was spun onto his stomach. Cael fought uselessly, stunned by the blow to his temple. Under the brute force of his foe, he was rendered helpless.

Around them, the invaders had swarmed in, double the number of the poor wretches whom they were intent on killing. They overwhelmed Cael's companions. Steel on steel rang out into the night, unsettlingly like the sounds she heard from the practice swords of Cael's boyhood memory. These men had been caught unaware. The clashing metal did not last long.

By the time Emmie was able to gain control of her frozen limbs, they were all dead.

Still dizzy from her fall, Emmie scrambled in the dirt to put herself in front of Cael, who was now facing the other way. She needed him to hear her. She needed *someone* to hear her.

"Cael, you have to listen to me," she sobbed. "I know who did it. I know who betrayed you. Please, let me fix this."

Her plea went unheard. In a last ditch effort, she raised her eyes to the sky, begging the God whom, only minutes ago, she had sworn to hate forever.

"Please. I'm sorry. I made a mistake. Please, let me fix this."

God, it seemed, wasn't listening either. The evil little man who had conspired against Cael ran his tongue over his teeth, revelling in his victory. Then he grabbed Cael beneath the chin and wrenched his head backwards. The soft, vulnerable flesh of Cael's neck was exposed.

The cold steel of the man's knife glinted in the firelight. It moved in front of Cael to his left ear. Emmie knew that the blade would slice to the right, and she was powerless to stop it.

In the instant before the inevitable happened, Cael's eyes slid in her direction.

At her.

Cael *looked* at her.

Across time, their eyes met and he saw her. It lasted for only a fraction of a second, but to Emmie it was an eternity. In that time, the enormity of her mistake engulfed her, knocking her down and carrying her away like a tsunami. She could have changed the outcome of this massacre, could have stopped it from happening. Cael was about to be murdered, and it had suddenly, agonizingly become her fault.

As they looked at one another, they both knew she'd failed him.

A flick of the wrist, a flash of the knife, and the blade dragged left to right. Its razor sharp edge sliced Cael's windpipe, scraping the bones of the jaw just below the ears—marks that, hundreds of years later, would retell this horrifying moment to archaeologists in a manner that was far too academic to do it justice.

Cael's eyes closed. His mouth fought to drag air into his lungs. Blood, hot and red and thick, streamed from the neat, straight gash in his neck.

Cael's head lowered to the dirt. He died.

Cael died, and Emmie felt like she was dying with him.

She sobbed so hard that no sound escaped her lips. Her chest threatened to implode with the force of her grief. She reached out, reached for Cael's hand.

Her fingers slid over his warm, solid flesh. Blindly, she pulled his body to her and cradled him, rocking him and weeping.

Around them, the campfire died. The dead men faded, and the night turned to twilight. It was only she and Cael, his body. They were alone.

Emmie was alone.

WHEN LAMB WOKE up the next morning, he found Emmie's powder blue Fiat Panda parked in front of the house, with the driver's side door thrown wide open.

"Mother, is she here?" he demanded. "Where is she?"

Mrs. Lamb only shook her head.

He wasted no time in calling the police, who determined the occasion to be serious enough that both the Scottish Mountain Rescue and the Search and Rescue Dog Association of Scotland were brought in. Within an hour of the search having gotten underway, a three-year-old border collie named Jessie scented her path and discovered her.

Emmeline Tunstall was a mile away from the estate, wandering and incoherent.

She was raced to the Ian Charles Community Hospital in Grantown-on-Spey, slightly northwest of Aviemore, where she was admitted and treated for hypothermia, dehydration and exhaustion. A small piece appeared in the local paper about the incident, but it was not enough to make the headline news. Hikers went missing all the time in the Highlands. Most were found.

Within forty-eight hours, the lost curator from Tullybrae House recovered from her ordeal.

Physically, at least.

Mentally, though, the hospital staff couldn't account for why the young lady wouldn't eat. Why she wouldn't talk, and why she would do nothing but stare out the window and, on occasion, weep silently.

Lady Rotherham visited Emmie often, as did her friends from the dig crew. Lamb, who had refused to leave her hospital bedside since she was admitted, had called her parents in Corner Brook, Newfoundland. Beside themselves with worry, Ron and Grace Tunstall were on the next flight out, arriving at the hospital two days, two layovers and very little sleep later.

Emmie remained oblivious to it all. She did not seem to care that her friends, family and loved ones had been driven mad with terror over nearly losing her.

She did not even seem to care that her life had been saved out there in those hills.

TWENTY-FIVE

"HERE'S THE LAST of it, sweetheart."

Grace pressed the scarred wooden door of the armoire closed, a pile of Emmie's clothes draped over her left forearm. They were pants, slacks and blouses that Emmie had chosen with such care and attention in what seemed like a lifetime ago. They'd meant so much to her then, represented a life she'd wanted to live and a person she'd wanted to be. Now, they were just clothes. Fabric and thread and buttons and zippers. Nothing more.

Emmie sat on the antique brass bed, back in her room at Tullybrae House. She'd been released from the hospital the day before, medically recovered from her ordeal. Grace had wasted no time booking a return flight to Canada for the three of them.

Emmie was going home. It hadn't taken much persuasion from her adoptive mother to convince her, though Grace had considered it a personal victory. Anyone could see just by looking at the once optimistic, bubbly young curator that something inside of her had died, had left her the sallow, quiet girl she was now, who looked as though her very will to live had been drained away.

For Emmie, the choice to go home had been simple. She could not bear to be in a house where the very essence of the place was so thoroughly tied to Cael. To know that he wasn't here anymore, that she failed him. To know that she, too, had betrayed him—it was more than she could bear.

Everything that had happened since she arrived, things which, now that she looked back on them, were downright miraculous—their connection to one another, the countess's intervention, the visions, the mystery, the final document that revealed Cael's death—it had all been for nothing. It was not

201

enough to say she'd fallen in love. That was too weak a word. Her soul had become inextricably entwined with his, her very life force linked with his.

In the end, it hadn't made one bit of difference.

Grace sat down on the bed, in between Emmie at the foot and the open suitcase at the head. She began to fold the clothes over her arm, placing them on top of one another in the trunk with exaggerated care. Emmie watched Grace's hands move, watched her fingers smooth and her dainty arms flit back and forth. Then she looked at Grace, gazed at her face. It was probably the first time that she'd ever really *looked* at the woman who had been a mother to her since she was that frightened, six-year-old child who had just lost her mother and her grandmother and everything she'd known.

She was a beautiful woman, Grace Everett Tunstall. Still trim and attractive in her late fifties, she had soft blonde hair that she wore in stylish, shaggy layers to her shoulders. Large blue eyes with dark, full lashes dominated a face that was remarkably smooth of wrinkles for her age. People who didn't know the family often connected those eyes with the crystalline blue eyes of her brother, Chase. Grace always smiled and thanked people when this happened, despite the fundamentally incorrect assumption.

If Grace Everett had been able to have children of her own, surely they would have been blessed with those eyes. They were too beautiful not to pass on genetically. But such was fate—from her late teens, Grace Everett had known she could never have children of her own. She was cursed with weak kidneys. A pregnancy would put too much strain on her organs, a potentially fatal strain to herself, and certainly to any baby that she would be unlikely to carry to term.

Yet another disappointment in a long line of things that were never to be.

"I always liked this on you," Grace said, holding up the gauzy white blouse Emmie had worn the first day she came to Tullybrae. "It makes you look like that Greek statue. You know, the lady with the arms. Miles something."

"Venus de Milo."

"Yeah, that one."

"She was naked from the waist up."

"Oh. Well, you know what I mean."

When Emmie let the banter die, Grace gave her daughter a pitying smile. Her hand raised to Emmie's cheek, cupping it in a mothering way. Emmie let Grace have this moment, even though it was uncomfortable for her. Whatever she might say about her, Grace was a natural mother. Far be it for Emmie to deny her that.

"Camille called again while you were asleep."

Emmie's gaze drifted back to the corner of the room, to the spot where the antique plaster was peeling away from the wall.

"I should call her back."

"No need, sweetheart. She and I had a lovely conversation, and she understands that you need to go for your own reasons. I made her see that. She wants you to call when we get back to Corner Brook, to make sure you got home and settled okay. She understands that you have your reasons for leaving." Her look turned even more pitying. "Oh, baby, I wish you would tell me what's wrong."

Emmie continued to stare at the crumbling wall.

"Well, in your own time, then. How about I go see if I can get Lamb to show me around the kitchen? There's no problem too big that can't be solved by a hot cup of tea and some homemade chocolate chip cookies."

Patting Emmie's sweatpants-clad thigh, Grace rose and left the room. Emmie listened to her light footsteps as they descended the staircase, counted each step and heard her reach the landing. The landing where Emmie and Cael had first encountered one another.

She did love Grace in her own way, truly she did. But the woman had an uncanny knack for making things worse when she was trying to make things better. The simplistic assertion that tea and cookies could make anything better only deepened Emmie's despondency

Time did not cure her of the feeling. The later the hour, the stronger was her urge to close her eyes and sleep through eternity like Snow White. If only there was a witch's poisoned apple she could eat to bring on eternal oblivion.

It occurred to her to wonder—if she were given such an apple, would she accept it? Had her mother's descent into drug addiction not been the same thing, a self-imposed exile into oblivion to escape the burden of her mental illness?

The irony was not lost on Emmie. After all that happened, she really was like her mother deep down. Because right now, Emmie had no doubt that she would take that apple, take a huge bite, and fall asleep forever.

As night wore on and the house grew quiet, Emmie remained awake. Across the hall, Grace and Ron were in one of the empty rooms, tucked into their hastily assembled bed. It was another of the serviceable brass servants' beds, mass-manufactured in a Victorian factory. Neither of her adoptive parents had admired it with the same reverent fascination she had upon first discovering it. Such things were beyond them. Ron had complained of the creak when he sat on the mattress, and Grace had noted in her passive-aggressive way that "Folks back then were just smaller people than we are now. It's fascinating, really."

Emmie could hear Ron's soft snoring even now, long after the lights had gone out. What the time was, she didn't know. She'd already unplugged her digital alarm clock and packed it away with the rest of her belongings. But it must have been hours that she'd lain awake, staring up at the ceiling. Sleep this night was as elusive as the Highland mist—no matter how far one walked into it, it was always ahead still. And behind. Never something one could grab hold of, command and control.

A sharp tug on the blankets at the edge of the bed brought Emmie back from the mire of her thoughts. Her head jerked up, and she peered into the dark room.

"Grace?" was the name she called out. Immediately, she felt silly. Why would Grace be pulling on the edge of her blankets?

As if to confirm Emmie's silliness, Grace coughed in her sleep from across the hall. A dainty and very Grace-like cough.

Emmie propped herself up on her elbows. She hadn't been imagining that tug, hadn't been half asleep.

A giggle broke the silence. Light and cheerful, a child's laugh. It was not the laughter she'd heard in her dreams, or muffled on the Highland air. This laugh was close.

"Clara?"

For several long, tense seconds, there was no movement in the room, the only light source coming from the moon that shone through the antique skylight. Then, slowly, the top of a head rose from the edge of the mattress, visible through the brass rails of the footboard. Wispy, child-like tangles of satiny hair, light in colour though not quite blonde, shimmered in the moonlight.

Next were a pair of dark, round eyes. Intelligent and intent, they beheld Emmie with the curiosity and fearlessness of youth.

Another giggle, and the figure at the end of the bed stood abruptly. She was small. Her stature might put her at five or six years old, but the wisdom in her eyes made her look nine or ten. A plain brown dress hugged her slight frame, tied with a sash high on the waist. The hair which, at the crown, was tangled, tumbled over small shoulders in stringy waves.

She was an urchin—utterly adorable in her unkempt way. The little girl smiled shyly. Emmie sat up fully, marvelling at the sight of her.

"Clara," she said again. This time, it was not a question.

The girl held out a petite, dirt-smudged hand. She wanted Emmie to come with her. Without a second thought, Emmie rose from the bed, obliging the little girl. When she moved to stand in front of her, Clara slipped her hand into Emmie's, looked up into her face, and gave her arm a gentle pull.

Emmie followed Clara as she took them out of the bedroom and down the servants' hallway. She glanced into the darkened bedroom across from her own as they passed Grace and Ron. Without any natural source of light, this room was ink black inside. She could only make out the risen lump of blanket under which the two bodies of her parents were sleeping. Ron was still snoring, the gentle cadence masking the creak of the floorboards beneath Emmie's feet.

Dressed only in a pink spaghetti string camisole and the sweats she was wearing that evening, Emmie continued to let Clara pull her along through the house, down the stairs, and out onto the gravel drive. Barefoot, she walked over the pebbles to the dewed grass, around the side of the house and through the rear gardens. When they reached the edge of the estate where it met the Highlands beyond, they slowed to a halt.

Standing amid the rolling mist was the little old woman in the starched black dress. Next to her was another woman. She was startling to behold in her finery. Her dress was Baroque in style, of a deep gold silk with a broad lace collar, pointed waist and voluminous sleeves. A luxurious pile of auburn hair was crafted into an elaborate style, accentuating her handsome face. She was statuesque and striking. It was the countess. The sixth Countess of Cranbury.

She and the little old lady watched her with visible pride. Clara dropped Emmie's hand, and skipped over to the countess, whose rose perfume mingled with the earthy scent of the natural flora around them. The countess wrapped her arms around the child lovingly, allowing her to lean back against her gown as though she were Clara's own mother. And she was, in a way. These three women were a family; they held for each other a love and a bond which had been forged of shared place and death.

Emmie looked down at her feet. The mist was rolling around her ankles, pulling her out to the trio of women. She breathed once, deeply, then took a step into the hills and joined them.

"Emmeline, love. Why so sad?" the old woman said.

"I lost my chance," she answered, her voice thick with tears that threatened to fall. "I lost my chance to save him."

The lady smiled, her lined face strangely youthful in the moon's glow.

"You're an intelligent young woman, my girl. What on earth made you think you only get one chance?"

Emmie stared at the woman, her brow furrowing. "But... but I betrayed him. I failed him."

"No, sweet child. His *father* betrayed him. You did not."

"I— But— He was killed. He died because I wouldn't go back with him." Emmie looked from the old lady to the countess.

The little woman sighed. Tilting her head, she took both of Emmie's hands into hers. "This is asking a lot of you, I know. To leave everything behind to follow the path you were meant to walk—it's a lot to take in. You wavered. Who wouldn't? But our futures are never set out and us only one chance to take them. There are many chances in life for us to find our way to the lives we are meant to live."

"Is that true?" Emmie looked to the countess. Both she and Clara nodded, the countess benevolently, Clara an encouraging bob of her small head.

"But when am I going to get another chance? He's gone, I've lost him."

"You haven't lost him," the old woman insisted. "He is no' gone, and you will go back. You've already made the choice to go. You made it even as you were telling him no."

Confused, Emmie shook her head. "Then how do I find him? Will you take me to him?"

"Actually," the woman paused, and glanced meaningfully to the countess, "we came to bid you farewell."

"Farewell? Where are you going?"

"It's no' where we're going, my love. It's where you're going. You crossed the boundary of time when you stepped through the garden and into the mist. You're half-way there."

Emmie's eyes flew to her feet, watched the thick mist lapping at her ankles. The boundary—she'd crossed it? Was she really on her way to Cael? Her heart sang at the prospect. But another part of her, the pragmatic, cautious part, could not overlook the gravity of the situation.

"Grace," she said. "And Ron and Chase. My friends. I won't get to say goodbye. They'll wake up and... and what? I'll be gone? Just like that?"

"Aye," the woman answered gravely. "And it will hurt them tremendously. But one day they'll understand. Maybe no' in this lifetime. But after it."

"Lamb." His name was the hardest of all for Emmie to say, the thought of leaving him behind the most painful.

"My son understands better than anyone that your destiny is no' here."

It was a lot to absorb, too much in too short a period of time. Emmie looked back at the house, the outline of which was blurred by the fog.

"Did any of it have meaning?" she asked Mrs. Lamb. "My life? My mother's life? Was any of it for a purpose?"

"Such things are no' for us to know—" Mrs. Lamb paused, as if listening to something in the distance.

"We've had our turn it seems," she told the countess. To Emmie, she said, "Now there is someone here for you."

Cael! He was coming for her. Coming to take her with him. This time she would go without question, without hesitation. Emmie looked out to the hills, in the direction the three women were watching. Her heart could have burst with the anticipation of waiting, and when she finally spotted the figure walking towards them, her feet itched to run to the tall, broad form of Cael.

Only, as the figure drew closer, Emmie realized that it was neither tall, nor broad. The face was not the face that haunted her dreams and caused her to ache from longing.

Instead, the smile on the face, when it became clear, was a smile which she'd only ever seen through the glass of a picture frame. At times, it had been an enigmatic smile, a reassuring one. It had been sympathetic and proud and indifferent, all depending on Emmie's mood.

And now, the smile was real. The face was real.

"Mom." Emmie's voice cracked. Tears flooded her eyes and spilled down her cheeks.

Her mother stopped directly in front of her, eyes full of life and love. She was radiant—a little taller than Emmie, with the thick brown hair that Emmie only half remembered from very early childhood. The hazel eyes, a hue which she'd passed on to her only daughter, studied Emmie, taking in every line of her face.

Emmie had often thought about what she would say if ever she were to stand before her mother like this. She'd thought about the questions she would ask, the accusations she would make, the things she would tell her. Was her mother proud of her? Was she sorry for her choices? Did she love Emmie?

Now, with the opportunity standing so close, Emmie saw that none of it mattered. She knew the answers already. Pride, love, regret, hope—they were all spoken without a single word.

Emmie's mother stroked a forefinger along her daughter's brow, clearing a wisp of golden hair from her forehead. Then she embraced Emmie, pulling her close and holding her tightly. Emmie breathed in her mother's indefinable scent, committing it to memory, holding onto the moment for as long as she was fortunate enough to have it.

When the embrace ended, Emmie's mother stepped back, winked knowingly, and gave a small backwards nod.

Go to him, she was saying.

Emmie glanced to Mrs. Lamb, the countess and Clara. They looked back expectantly, saying nothing in words but everything with a gaze, a smile, a tilt of the head.

Farther in the distance, the fog cleared. Beneath the gentle glow of the moon, Cael was waiting for her.

This time, Emmie was sure. The voices in her head which had before made her doubt, question, fear—were silenced. She belonged with Cael. He was her home. Eagerly, she traversed the short distance between them. It was bittersweet, knowing that she would be leaving loved ones behind. But above all, it was right. That's what she held onto, what kept her feet moving.

Cael waited patiently for her to join him, as peaceful and beautiful and strong as she'd ever seen him. She stepped up to him, and looked into his eyes. This was not a dream, not a vision. It was real. *He* was real.

When she placed her hands in his, the warmth ran through her palms, up her arms, and straight to her heart.

"Save me," he said. He spoke the words aloud. They were not a whisper on the breeze, or an echo in a dream. It was Cael's voice.

"Save me," he said for the first time. And for the last.

"Yes," was her answer.

When Emmie said this, Cael's eyes closed. He savoured the word, the one word which all along had been the key to his salvation. Then he took her in his arms, bent his head, and kissed her.

As the mist closed around them, the two figures disappeared, vanishing into the folds of time.

TWENTY-SIX

TULLYBRAE HOUSE – ONE YEAR LATER

HAROLD LAMB STOOD behind the gleaming, custom-built cherry stained reception desk in the brand-new foyer-turned-lobby of the Tullybrae House Museum. His dry, wrinkled hands wandered restlessly over the piles of paper, the binders and the keyboard that were hidden from sight by the foot-tall ledge at the edge of the unit.

Oh, how he wanted to grab for his Swiffer duster and retire to the study to commence with his cleaning ritual, the same one he'd carried on with despite the death of his former employer, the late Lord Cranbury. But he had been expressly forbidden to clean and putter by his current employer, the Countess of Rotherham, while visitors were touring the house.

He observed the main staircase, watching surreptitiously for the reappearance of the seven visiting tourists and the manor's tour guide, who were currently on the second floor, judging by the footsteps and hushed chatter that reached his ears.

For the third time in as many minutes, he straightened the framed photograph tucked away under the ledge where curious visitors wouldn't see it. It was a graduation picture. The subject's sunny curls tumbled elegantly over her left shoulder, and her smile was bright and hopeful beneath her blue and gold cap and gown. Her mother, Grace Tunstall, had sent it to Lamb when he called and asked for something he could have to remember her by.

Of course, everyone who came to visit the newly opened Tullybrae House Museum knew the story of the young curator who had disappeared, gone missing one night, never to be heard from again. They asked questions, cruel questions that certainly they thought were innocuous. Was she a flighty girl? Not very responsible? Was there something wrong with her, perhaps—not quite right in the head?

One tactless woman had even dared to suggest that Emmie might have been kidnapped and murdered. "You see it all the time," she'd said gravely. "Young girls taken in the dead of night, raped and killed. For all we know, her body could be out there in the wild right now. Maybe eaten by wolves or buried under the soil. If that's the case, she'll never be found. Poor thing. Did you know her, Mr. Lamb?"

For his part, Lamb deflected their questions, feigning indifference. But each one cut him a little bit, keeping fresh the wound that refused to heal.

It was not just Lamb who was hurting. Emmie's disappearance had cut a lot of people very deeply. Her parents were devastated. Her brother had flown to Scotland from his job in Toronto to help with the search. Lady Rotherham, the excavators from Edinburgh University, even Dr. Iain Northcott and his friend Dr. Paul Rotenfeld had come out to help.

But days turned into weeks, and there was no sign of her. She was gone. Missing, presumed dead, given the state in which she'd been found only a few days before that. Foul play was not suspected.

Everyone was left shaken, but it seemed to have particularly devastated the little one on the excavation team, Sophie Miner. Long after the others had lost interest, she was still calling Lamb, writing him at the newly-created Tullybrae House Museum email account (which he was still learning to use).

Eventually, though, she too had given up.

At length, the visitors completed their tour of the second floor, and reached the landing where they were visible from the lobby. Lamb pretended to be busy with the papers in front of him.

"Yes, they're now in the archives at the University of Edinburgh."

That was Brigitte speaking, Tullybrae's resident tour guide. She was a pleasant girl, bright and attractive, but nowhere near as captivating and warm-hearted as her predecessor had been.

Of course, she was talking about the bodies. Everybody wanted to know about the murder victims that had been unearthed last autumn. There had been twenty-two of them in all. Inevitably someone always asked about either the Digging Scotland episode or the Haunted Britain episode, both of which had aired the past winter.

"And can you tell me what's known about them?" This was an elderly gentleman with a full head of white hair and a pot belly.

"Well, now, I'm not too sure about that. This is Lamb's specialty. Lamb?"

He looked up as the group descended the grand staircase, unaware of the oil-painted eyes of Tullybrae's lords and ladies watching them.

These people didn't care about those eyes. Emmie had. Emmie knew their significance.

"I'm sorry?" Lamb said.

"What's the story about the massacre again?"

He waited until the group reached the bottom of the stairs to begin his tale. It was not the first time he and Brigitte had acted out this routine. The first time they'd done it, it was because Lamb knew the story better. Now, it had become habit that Brigitte would ask him to tell it when someone should inquire. Someone always did.

"Well now, as the story goes, the murders date back to fourteen ninety-two. It was the time of conflict between the MacDonalds of Keppoch and the MacIntoshes, and there was a dispute over whether the former or the latter legally held the land. You see, Highland clans being what they were, it was physically held by the MacDonalds, but only by force. On the other hand, it legally belonged to the MacIntoshes—the Crown, as I understand it, had officially granted the land to them—and they were intent on retaking it."

As they always were, the visitors were fascinated by the tale. Lamb continued, bolder now, as was the routine.

"The MacDonald clan was divided. Many wanted to resist the MacIntoshes themselves, while a small but determined number of them wanted to appeal to the larger branch of the clan, the MacDonalds of Clanranald, for protection."

"I'm a MacDonald of Clanranald," declared the white-haired man.

"Someone always is," Lamb jested dryly, which wrought a laugh from his audience.

"*Dh'aindeoin có theireadh e*," the man continued, oblivious to the fact that the butler's joke had been at his expense. "That's the war cry, you know."

"Back to the story," interrupted a slender, middle-aged woman, casting an annoyed glance at the man. Giving a short nod to Lamb, she said, "Go on."

"Very well," Lamb replied. "So these determined men managed to turn the ear of the chief, and were granted permission to set an ambush to wipe out the most ardent of those who wanted to resist the MacIntoshes alone. As it turned out, this latter group were warned ahead of time. Prepared for the ambush, they set one of their own. Ten men slaughtered their would-be twenty-two assassins and escaped death. The dead were buried where they were killed, and the failed attack caused quite a rift in the clan—after all, the ten realized they'd been betrayed and set up for execution by their own laird, Angus MacDonald, for none in the clan would carry out such a bold act without the Keppoch's blessing. In any case, the MacDonalds of Keppoch did manage to resist the MacIntoshes on their own, without the aid of their Clanranald counterparts, and the land remained in Keppoch control."

"What's remarkable about this story is how much we know about it," Brigitte jumped in as she typically did at this point. "The account of this event comes from the diaries of a Mrs. Emmeline MacDonald. The reason it's remarkable is the fact that a woman of her station, better than a peasant but unimportant within the clan hierarchy, was educated enough and had the presence of mind to record as much as she did, and in as much detail. There are volumes and volumes filled with the most minute of descriptions about this conflict—names, dates, occurrences—and also about everyday life at the time." Enigmatically, Brigitte concluded, "It was almost as if she knew somehow that her works would survive and be of interest to future generations."

"That is interesting," the white-haired man agreed. "Where are those works now?"

"They're on display at the British Museum of Natural History. They're quite an achievement within the historical record, yet Mrs. MacDonald remains relatively obscure when next to the more important figures of history."

After a few more random questions from the visitors about the house, the television episodes, and about the missing curator, Brigitte led them all to the gift shop, which had previously been the library. Lamb remained behind the desk, glad to be alone again. His eyes drifted to the picture of Emmie, and the longing for the girl who had been like a granddaughter to him for that short time resumed its hollow ache in his frail chest.

A cool hand patted his shoulder from behind.

"I know, son," Mrs. Lamb said soothingly. "It hurts. But you know it was what she was meant to do. And you know it turned out well for her in the end."

It was unusual for the tiny old woman to comfort her son. She certainly had done little of it in life. But ever since Emmie's disappearance, she'd offered more comfort to Lamb than she had even when he was a boy.

Lamb blinked back an errant tear, and said the only thing he knew to say. It was the same thing he always said. But this time, there was no exasperation, no annoyance. There was only an acknowledgement of the hurt he felt, and the truth in what Mrs. Lamb said.

"Yes, Mother."

ABOUT THE AUTHOR

Veronica Bale is a freelance writer, copy editor and author of women's fiction and Highland historical romance. She holds an Honours Bachelor Degree in environmental writing from York University in Toronto, Ontario.

When Veronica is not writing, she is an avid hockey mom and a voracious reader. She lives in Durham, Ontario.

Visit Veronica online at www.veronicabale.com. She loves to hear from her readers.

Made in the USA
Middletown, DE
04 May 2023

29951034R00130